Praise for
Rapunzel Untangled

"Rapunzel, Rapunzel, let down your hair, so that I may climb the golden stair." Forget the ancient nursery rhyme your mother read to you! This Rapunzel is a twenty-first century damsel, complete with computers, Facebook, and Skype. Locked in a tower by a wacky mother who insists Rapunzel will die if she comes in contact with others, this modern day Rapunzel lives a sleepy, boring, little life . . . until she friends Fane on Facebook and the truth is unraveled as he shows her the world outside the tower. *Rapunzel Untangled* is the fun, exciting, and sometimes frightening adventure of 17-year-old Rapunzel as the sleeping beauty awakens and discovers the truth about her life.

—SHERRY GAMMON, author of *Unlovable*

A fun, quirky romance taking an old fairy tale and setting it in the modern world with a fabulously creepy house and swoon-worthy love interest. A very cool twist on a favorite fairy tale, set in the modern world, and combining an interesting mix of original story and fun new ideas. Rapunzel is an incredibly unique love story that kept me second-guessing until the very end.

—JOLENE PERRY, author of *Insight*

Cindy takes one of my favorite fairy tales and reimagines it in the best possible way. *Rapunzel Untangled* is filled with romance, villains, heroes, magic, and Facebook. Loved it!

—KAREY WHITE, author of *For What It's Worth*

This book had me from the beginning! I couldn't put it down. . . . It turns out that Rapunzel doesn't just sit in her tower all day. She learns about life in her own interesting way, using modern tools like Facebook to educate herself. She takes risks. She's not just some airhead waiting to be saved. Rapunzel is delightful, Fane is absolutely hilarious, and the story will keep you guessing until the end.

—SHANNEN CRANE Camp, author of *The Breakup Artist*

What I thought was going to be a sweet and innocent fairy tale turned out to be a "tangled" web spun with lies and deceit. Cindy C Bennett's *Rapunzel Untangled* is a new kind of paranormal novel fraught with intrigue, danger, and believable romance. Every reader who loves original YA will be absorbed by this compelling read.

—RACHEL MCCLELLAN, author of the Fractured Light series

Take everything you think you know about Rapunzel and throw it out the turret window! Cindy C Bennett brilliantly modernizes the classic tale of the girl with golden locks. Not just another fairy tale, *Rapunzel Untangled* is a riveting, edge-of-your-seat, contemporary romantic thriller. Bennett captivates your senses and holds onto them from start to finish. This is a definitely a book that belongs in your personal library.

—STEPHANIE CONNELLEY WORLTON, author of *Hope's Journey*

Rapunzel Untangled is everything you'd want from a modern fairy tale retelling: smart, funny, romantic, and true to the spirit of the original story. Ms. Bennett has created a strong heroine that you'll fall in love with right from the first page, and her dashing hero is absolutely charming. The plot is intriguing, suspenseful, and sometimes dark, but interspersed with humor and heartwarming moments that make this a great read for anyone who loves a good fairy tale. You won't want to stop reading until you reach the last paragraph—and then you'll slow down, because you won't want the story to end.

—HEATHER FROST, author of the Seers trilogy

Rapunzel

untangled

Rapunzel Untangled

Cindy C Bennett

Sweetwater Books
An Imprint of Cedar Fort, Inc.
Springville, Utah

The views expressed within this work are the sole responsibility of the author and do not necessarily reflect the position of Cedar Fort, Inc., or any other entity. This is a work of fiction. The characters, names, incidents, places, and dialogue are products of the author's imagination, and are not to be construed as real.

ISBN 13: 978-1-4621-1156-5

Published by Sweetwater Books, an imprint of Cedar Fort, Inc., 2373 W. 700 S., Springville, UT 84663
Distributed by Cedar Fort, Inc. www.cedarfort.com

Library of Congress Control Number: 2012953785

Cover design by Angela D. Olsen
Cover design © 2013 by Lyle Mortimer
Typeset and edited by Melissa J. Caldwell

Printed in the United States of America

10 9 8 7 6 5 4 3 2 1

*To my dear friends and critique partners known as the Wigz
(you know who you are Sherry, Cami, and Jeff). Without you,
my writing wouldn't be anything more than a fun hobby.*

*And to all of my fellow romantics in the world who share my
fantasy of—and hope for—happily ever after,
whatever that might be.*

Also by Cindy C Bennett

Geek Girl

Author's Note

✳ ⋅ ✳ · ✳ · ✳ ✳

As a young girl, I was endlessly fascinated by fairy tales. From Cinderella to Red Riding Hood to Snow White, I loved them all. I particularly loved Rapunzel. The Rapunzel story I knew was the traditional story where Rapunzel is given away by her father in exchange for some rampion (a type of plant) for his wife. When Rapunzel grows, a prince hears her singing and falls in love, eventually climbing up to be with her. The witch Gothel blinds him when she finds out, cuts off Rapunzel's hair, and sends her to wander in the forest. The prince finds her when he hears her singing. She then cries over his blindness, her tears being the magic needed to restore his sight. That always fascinated me, the idea of true love being able to find one another no matter the odds (have I told you I'm a romantic?).

When Cedar Fort offered me the chance to write a Rapunzel retelling for Sweetwater Books, I jumped. As I sat down to write it, and began thinking about it, I realized it really is a dark story. No matter the version, the basic premise is always a young girl kidnapped or given away, locked in a tower by a crazy witch, and forced into solitude. I began writing my contemporary retelling and without warning my story became very dark. How could it be anything but, right?

Not to worry, it isn't a complete downer. There's humor and romance for my Rapunzel along with the insanity of being locked in a tower for nefarious purposes.

I've had a few early readers wonder why no one remarks on her strange name or the coincidental similarities between her life and the Rapunzel fairy tale. Simple, dear reader. The story of Rapunzel doesn't exist—at least in my Rapunzel's world. The fairy tale has never been told. *Rapunzel Untangled* is a *retelling* of the original tale. So sit back (or lie in a bubble bath as I do when I'm about to dig into a new book) and let go of all of your preconceived notions of what the story of Rapunzel is, and take a new ride with me. I hope you enjoy. As always, happy reading!

Prologue

* . * ' *. * *

The woman stiffened, captivated by the child on the opposite side of the apple-filled bin. Still an infant, arms and legs flailed as she happily batted at a stuffed giraffe hanging from her car seat's handle. The seat was firmly attached to the front of the shopping cart. The woman felt a shift inside of her: *here* was the child, the one she'd waited for. She admitted that somewhere deep inside she doubted the prophecy and believed what others claimed, that Vedmak was nothing more than a false warlock who only wanted to avail himself of the vast wealth that could be provided by the woman. But now, here was the proof, here was the child that had been foreseen . . . no, *promised* her by Vedmak.

The baby glanced her way and she drew in a quick breath. The bright green eyes that looked at her reflected intelligence above a happy smile. But that wasn't the thing that had drawn the woman in the first place, though it reinforced the prophecy. Instead it was the thick, long blonde hair that sprouted from the baby's head. It was pulled up into a bow just above her forehead, with some strands trailing down on the sides, long enough to brush her ears.

She sidled a little closer on the pretense of examining the many red apples spread out before her. From this position, she could hear the conversation between the baby's mother and another woman wearing a large, floppy hat who appeared to be an acquaintance.

"How old is the sweet baby now?" the acquaintance asked as she took the baby's tiny hand into her own. The baby cooed and grasped the offered finger. The woman felt a burning in her chest at the audacity of the floppy-hatted woman so freely touching the magical child.

"She turned six months three days ago," the mother said with a grin that bespoke of both love and exhaustion at the same time. "She's getting to be such a busybody. She can already scoot, and I suspect it won't be long before she's crawling."

The woman felt a tingle of alarm. Her time was shorter than she thought.

"Her hair is amazing," the intrusive floppy hat said. "I don't believe I've ever seen hair so long on someone her age."

"Yes," the mother agreed. "She was born with a shock of blonde hair, and it doesn't look like it plans to stop growing anytime soon. I'll have to cut it before long if she's going to be crawling around. I already have to tie it back for her to scoot."

The woman's tingle turned into a full-body screaming alarm. She'd have to act very, very soon or all would be lost. The chatting women turned her way, and she realized she'd made a small squeaking noise. She forced a calmness on her face and smiled politely at them. As if sensing something about her, they moved away as one. The woman grabbed a sack and threw a few apples in. She must appear composed if she were to pull this off. Excitement and dread mingled in her chest until she felt she might explode with it.

She walked to the front of the store and paid for her bag of apples, noticing the young mother a few lines over with her own basket of groceries. As the woman spied the items the young mother had—diapers, baby food, formula—along with the other groceries, she realized she was woefully under-prepared. If only she'd listened to the warlock, believed fully in what he had said, she would not be in the predicament she now found herself and could act immediately.

Outside, she slid into the driver's seat of her car and slid down to make herself inconspicuous. A few minutes later, the young mother exited the store and walked to her own vehicle parked a short distance away. The woman watched as the mother first placed the baby in the car, securing her, before returning to her cart to place her purchased groceries into the trunk. The woman cursed herself once again—such a missed opportunity at this moment with the mother distracted.

She supposed she could force herself to be patient for this moment. She'd waited this long, hadn't she? She would have to move quickly to prepare, but she could do it . . . she *had* to do it. The fate of her daughter rested upon her shoulders. Not just her shoulders, but also that of the young child with the magic hair. She put the car into gear and followed the unsuspecting pair from the parking lot.

chapter

1

Rapunzel stood in the rounded alcove separating her rooms from the outside world. Her window served a single purpose—an escape for her in case of fire. Her mother was a bit . . . overprotective. She supposed it was with good reason.

She leaned out the open window and breathed in the fresh air, letting the early morning sun warm her cheeks. It was early enough that the workers hadn't shown up so she felt safe in doing so. Her mother would be in soon with breakfast, at exactly six o'clock, the same as every morning for Rapunzel's life. Her mother was the only clock Rapunzel would ever need.

She gazed across the expanse of green lawn dotted with several large trees of different varieties and surrounded by lush flower beds. From her window she could see the long, gabled line of the back of the house—places she had never been because of her diagnosis—and several of the outbuildings. Once in a while she glimpsed the gardeners going in and out of the greenhouse or shed, but she always ducked low so they wouldn't see her watching.

A bluebird flew near and landed on the sill. She smiled. "Good morning, Angel," she said softly so as not to startle her little friend. She slowly reached a hand out and opened it, palm up, sunflower seeds exposed. Angel flittered up with a chatter of alarm, but only a few feet before landing again. Rapunzel waited patiently. Angel hopped twice, moving closer to the treat. She stopped, chattering again as she looked around in short, quick head turns. Two more hops put her even closer. She continued the pattern while Rapunzel waited, barely breathing. Finally Angel hopped into her hand and grabbed a seed, then flew to a nearby tree branch, crunching her treat while she watched Rapunzel. This was usual. She'd been doing this for a few weeks now. Still, Rapunzel waited.

Angel returned, landing directly on Rapunzel's palm. Rapunzel gasped lightly, but Angel stayed. This time she continued to eat the seeds, all the while tickling the palm of Rapunzel's hand with her tiny pinprick feet. A grin spread across Rapunzel's face. Angel had never come back before, let alone stayed to eat from her palm. Suddenly Angel lifted her head in alarm and flittered away, crying out as she did so.

"Rapunzel!" Her mother's voice, full of recrimination startled her away from the window. She turned guiltily, scattering the seeds on the ground below.

"Mother, I—"

"Do you know what could happen to you?" her mother cried out, hurrying forward to push past Rapunzel, slamming the window closed. She swung toward Rapunzel and pulled her into a painful embrace. "You could be taken from me."

"*Taken* from you?" Rapunzel questioned. That seemed an odd way to put it.

Her mother released her and stroked her hair, almost frantically. "You know what I mean. Your *disease*," she whispered the word as she always did, afraid that speaking it aloud would somehow cause it to take fatal hold. "You must be always careful, Rapunzel. Always vigilant."

Rapunzel nodded. She'd been opening the window for years, and nothing bad had happened. She wondered, not for the first time, whether her mother was wrong about the severity of her disease. She would never tell her mother she often opened the window, afraid she would take away her one small freedom. Not only that, she couldn't be absolutely certain that her mother was wrong. She could have just been lucky so far.

"Yes, Mother," she said. "I promise to be more careful."

"Good," her mother purred. "Now, let's have our breakfast and then begin your lessons."

They left the stone alcove, which was much like a turret, through the open entry into the main room. A sitting area was to their right, with a kitchenette to the left. Rapunzel made use of the kitchen area as much as possible even though many of her meals were made downstairs by their cook, with the exception of her lunches, which she made herself most days. But she did have a fully stocked fridge and pantry from which she could bake if she really wanted to fix herself something to eat.

While they ate, Rapunzel examined her mother

unobtrusively. They looked nothing alike. Her mother's dark hair and eyes were the opposite of Rapunzel's blonde hair and green eyes. Even their statures were different, Gothel being three inches taller than Rapunzel's five-foot-five. Gothel was stout where Rapunzel was slender.

Once they finished their meal, with her mother sneaking constant looks at Rapunzel as if to see whether she was still all right, they moved into a second alcove slightly larger than the first, this one bearing no window. Within were her desk, computer, printer, and a large number of books. They were all books that had been required reading at some point in her schoolwork. Her mother felt that reading for pleasure was a sin. Still, Rapunzel had managed to find a way to do so without her mother's knowledge.

They sat down together, and Rapunzel opened the book that gave her the outline of her schoolwork for the day. She placed her finger on the page and scrolled down as she read. "Today is pages 293 and 294 from the math book; read the history of the Hundred Years War; study European geography for the test next week; chapter twenty, 'Plants and Their Structure,' for biology—"

"Yes, yes," her mother said, flipping her hand impatiently. Rapunzel knew that her mother hated this, the schoolwork. She remembered clearly the day when she was six and her mother had brought home her computer. She'd also brought home all of the homeschooling information she'd been able to get her hands on. She'd taught Rapunzel how to read but felt Rapunzel needed more. Her mother had tried to help her learn the computer but gave up quickly in frustration, leaving Rapunzel to figure it out on her own with the strict admonishment to use it for nothing other than schoolwork. And she had—until recently. "It seems you have it under control. Do you need my help?"

"No." Rapunzel's answer was expected. It had been the same since she first learned how to find answers herself. Her mother never touched the computer; she felt it was an item that brought evil into their home but had been forced to allow it when she became too busy to spend the time needed teaching Rapunzel. It had been drilled into Rapunzel how important it was to expand her education.

"Well, then, I'll leave you to it." She stood, running a hand down Rapunzel's hair and moved toward the alcove entrance, stopping there to turn back. "I have errands to run that will take me all day. Shall I have a tray sent up for dinner?"

"No, I'll make my own today."

"Fine. I'll be back later tonight, then."

Rapunzel waved at her, waiting until she heard the outer door close and lock before she pushed her workbook aside and turned excitedly to her computer. She bounced eagerly in her chair while waiting for it to boot up. Finally it came on and she clicked the little icon that brought the world into her little room.

She had accidentally discovered this new site called Facebook when searching for information on facial structure for biology and had hit enter after typing in *face*. Well, probably not a *new* site, but definitely new to her. On it, millions of people who existed in the real world connected in ways she could only dream of. She could click on any number of names and read small amounts of information about people who lived a normal life and were not confined to a two-thousand-square-foot world in fear of death by being exposed to any foreign germs. She'd had to create an account, which terrified her. What if her mother found out?

She began her usual clicking, hungrily reading about all their lives. Then she had an idea. She went to the search bar and typed in the name of the local high school. Immediately a long list of names came up beneath. She caught her breath. Here were other kids her age that lived nearby. Kids that she'd be going to school with, be *friends* with, if it weren't for her stupid disease.

She slowly scrolled down the list, tears pricking the corners of her eyes as she scanned their names and faces and imagined knowing them. One name in particular caught her attention and she stopped, staring at the face that grinned back at her. The name read *Fab Fane Flannigan*.

She clicked on his name. His page opened up to reveal a bigger photo grinning at her. His hair was dark, brushing his collar at the back, two loose strands framing golden eyes that laughed, a patch of hair on his chin. Next to that picture lined up a few other photos: Fab Fane Flannigan with various groups of kids, laughing in all of them. Her eyes moved to the *Add Friend* link. She moved her cursor over, hovering above the button, her mind swirling with the potential consequences of clicking on it. Her gaze was drawn back to the laughing face of Fab Fane Flannigan and, with breath held, she clicked the button.

chapter

2

Rapunzel paced back and forth in the small kitchen area as she ate her macaroni and cheese. It wasn't exactly a healthy dinner, but it was quick, hot, and she could carry the bowl while fidgeting. She walked to the alcove entrance and stared at the computer.

Still no answer.

She felt foolish. She shouldn't have done it. If she knew how to retract the friend request, she would. What would he think? She looked down at the bowl of mac and cheese. It had congealed into a lumpy orange glob. She dropped it into the sink, her appetite gone. Grabbing the edge of the sink, she took deep breaths, trying to calm her frantic pulse. Then she heard it—the small noise telling her she had a message in her email.

She ran to the alcove, dropping into her chair as she read the words. *Fab Fane Flannigan has accepted your friend request.* She grinned, then shuddered. What now? Almost immediately a second message popped up. *You have a message from Fab Fane Flannigan.* She stared at it in consternation. What did that mean? She clicked on it and her

Facebook page opened to the messages page.

> Hi, mysterious friend. There isn't much info on your page. Who are you, RG?

Rapunzel stilled. Of course he would want to know who she was. She was surprised he'd even said yes to the request, not knowing who she was. She didn't have any information on her own page that would give away her identity. She was careful of that. Finally, she lifted her fingers to the keyboard.

> *Hi, Fab Fane Flannigan.* She took a breath then continued. *I don't mean to be mysterious. You wouldn't know who I am, but I live in the same city as you. I don't go to your school.*

As she hit the enter button, the message popped up in a small window at the bottom right of her computer, startling her. When he answered, it came up in the same window.

> Ahh, the mystery deepens. You say you don't go to my school, indicating that you are my age, anyway. Are you? Or are you one of those creepy stalkers who hunts down innocent children on the Internet and invites them into the back of your van for some candy?

Rapunzel's mouth dropped open.

> *I assure you I am not a stalker!*

> Just what a stalker would say.

> *I am NOT a stalker. I am a seventeen-year-old girl.*

Well, that makes sense then. All the girls want me.

Rapunzel was offended. What an arrogant—

Just kidding!

Oh. I thought you were serious.

Sorry, I forget sometimes that my sarcasm doesn't translate well through the written word.

Rapunzel smiled, enjoying the first conversation she'd had outside her mother in . . . ever—if this could be called a conversation.

I'll keep that in mind for future reference when you say something ridiculous.

So, you're saying we have a future together?

She laughed.

Like that. Good example, Fab Fane Flannigan.

You're learning. And you can just call me Fane. Or Fab. I answer to either one. What shall I call you, besides RG? That's very . . . androgynous.

Her stomach tightened. If there was one thing she was certain of, it was that she couldn't give away her identity. She decided to try a different tactic and see if he would drop the question.

Big word, Fane (Please note the lack of Fab). Did you have to look that one up?

Har-har. Is that sarcasm from the mysterious RG who is avoiding the question and refusing to tell me her name?

I can't tell you my name.

Rapunzel held her fingers over the keyboard, debating. Finally she decided she could be honest. She felt protected by the anonymity of the Internet.

My mother doesn't know I am on this site. I'm trying to stay incognito (do you need to look that up as well?).

Incognito: having one's identity concealed, as under an assumed name, especially to avoid notice or formal attention.

Very good.

Thanks. If I guess your name, will you confirm (ala Rumplestiltskin)?

She had to give him points for persistence.

Maybe.

I love a firm answer. Let's see . . . is it Roman Goddess?

Haha.

No? How about Raging Giant?

Closer than the last one.

Regina Gregory?

No.

Rebecca Guillotine?

No.

You wait. I'll figure it out. Answer me one question, though. Are you hot?

Rapunzel was surprised by the question. Why would he care whether she was hot or cold? Did he think the temperature of her room would give away her location?

> *No, I'm quite comfortable, thank you. What an odd question.*

> I don't know if I should laugh or not. Are you kidding around with me?

Why would he think she was joking about this?

> *No. Why?*

> Okay then. *shrugs* Well, G2G. The parental unit is yelling for me to get off the computer.

> *What is G2G? And what is a parental unit?*

> Look it up, RG. Same time tomorrow?

She felt a happy warmth spread through her belly at the invitation. She couldn't remember the last time she'd had so much fun. In fact, she didn't think she'd *ever* had this kind of fun.

> Yes.

> TTYL (look that one up also).

Rapunzel laughed, signing off Facebook. She Googled the terms, hoping that her mother wouldn't discover that she'd used the computer for something other than home-work. She smiled when she discovered what the terms meant. With a happy sigh, she put the computer to sleep and leaned back in her chair.

"Rapunzel?" She jerked at her name. She hadn't

realized how much time had passed. She was relieved she'd signed off before the arrival of her mother. She'd have to be more vigilant next time.

"In here, Mother!" she called, going out into the main room.

"Still doing homework?" her mother questioned suspiciously.

"Yes, I was studying for . . . the test. The one I told you about." She hated lying to her mother but didn't want to lose the chance to have another conversation with Fab Fane Flannigan.

She looked at Rapunzel for a few long seconds, but she should have no reason to disbelieve her. Finally she said, "Come," and led the way into Rapunzel's spacious bedroom. The room was dominated by a large, four-poster bed, a heavy mahogany wardrobe, and matching vanity. Rapunzel sat in the chair at the vanity as her mother picked up the brush. She pulled the brush through Rapunzel's long tresses, beginning at the crown of her head until she reached the end of the heavy fifteen-foot length. She continued the ritual until Rapunzel's hair softly gleamed, exactly seventy-two strokes.

"You know how important it is to keep your hair in perfect condition, Rapunzel."

"Yes, Mother." Rapunzel barely listened to the words, knowing the expected answers she had learned by rote.

"There are many people depending on it, Rapunzel."

"I know, Mother."

"Your own future depends on it. Don't ever forget that."

"I won't, Mother." She turned to look at her mother, a thought coming to her on the heel of her conversation with Fane. "Mother, what is your name?"

"Why, Rapunzel, what a strange question." Rapunzel didn't think the question as strange as the thought that she didn't know her own mother's name. "You know my name."

"No, I don't. I know you go by Gothel, which is our last name, but I don't know your first name."

"Everyone calls me Gothel."

"Why?"

"Well, Rapunzel, is that important?" Something in her mother's voice caught her attention and she sat up straighter. The warning tone brooked no argument. Rapunzel had learned that at an early age.

"I suppose not," she answered slowly.

"Of course it's not. I'm your mother. What else should you need to know?" She soothed her hands down Rapunzel's hair as she always did before standing. "I'll see you in the morning."

"Good night . . . Mother," Rapunzel answered. *Why won't she tell me her name?* she wondered, disquieted.

After her mother left, Rapunzel plaited her long tresses into a thick braid. Once she was finished, she lifted the heavy mass and pulled it over her shoulder, looking down at the blonde strands. Her hair held magic. That was something she'd always known and had been drilled into her since her birth. Her mother had told her of the prophecy: that Gothel would give birth to a child with golden hair that would grow at an accelerated rate and that the fate of the world's future rested in her mane of gold. Gothel had been told the story, seen the proof, and couldn't deny the truth in what had been foretold. The disease, the one that prevented Rapunzel from leaving the tower, was more proof. She was only grateful that her mother could visit her. Rapunzel was impervious to her mother's germs.

She moved to her bed and lay down in the luxurious softness. As she closed her eyes, her thoughts returned to the golden-eyed boy who made her laugh. Only twenty more hours until she could converse with him again.

chapter

3

Rafael Grenada? Rambo Greenleaf? Did you look up those terms from last time?

No, no, and yes. Do you have your dictionary at the ready to use more big words?

Ha-ha. I use a thesaurus. Let's see, maybe it's not your name. Maybe it's an acronym (no thesaurus needed for that one). Really Great?

I am really great, but no, that's not what it stands for. JK (see, I learn too). What classes do you take at school?

Boring ones. Are there any other kind? Romance Greeter?

LOL, what is a romance greeter? What kind of boring ones?

Ugh, please, no LOLs allowed. I HATE that particular slang! With a passion! It makes me want to hurt someone (not really). I don't know what a romance greeter is. I thought it was you. I take calculus, language arts, history—all the usuals. I'm on the basketball team and wrestling team. Really Gregarious?

Okay, no more LOLs. Any other acronyms I took time to study and learn that I should avoid so as to not offend your acronym-sensibilities? I certainly don't want to be responsible for someone being hurt. I don't really know what all the usuals are as I don't attend school. I also know nothing about basketball and wrestling. Sorry. :o((is the frown emoticon acceptable?) Not really gregarious, either.

Raggedly Gabled? Emoticons are fine, and I can live with most acronyms without danger of violence, especially as you took the time to learn them. Do you live under a rock? Just curious since you HAD to study all the annoying acronyms, you don't attend school (how do you get away with that? It seems to support my creepy older stalker theory, BTW), and you don't know anything about basketball. Wrestling I can understand, I guess—but basketball? Who doesn't know anything about basketball? Maybe someone named Rushing Gorgonzola?

Haha on the names, and no as well. I don't live under a rock. I live high above them, in fact. I said I don't ATTEND school. I didn't say I am not of school age. I get my schooling at my home. Is it unusual to not know about basketball? I suppose I better do more studying.

Actually, if there were an argument for you really being a teenage girl named Rough Gollum, it's the fact that you don't know about them. You are home schooled? Why? Too smart for public school, or . . .

I'm not too smart, no. I can't

Rapunzel hesitated, taking a bite out of the crisp apple sitting on her desk. How much did she dare tell him?

leave my house. What is a Gollum?

WHAT???? You don't know who Gollum is? You MUST live under a rock. Haven't you ever read The Hobbit? Or Lord of the Rings? Or seen the LOTR movies??? Wait... what do you mean you can't leave your house? Grounded for life?

She quickly went to a new window and Googled "grounded." It took her a few minutes of reading through the various links that came up to finally decide he must be referring to the punishment definition of the word.

Hello?

I'm here. No, I'm not grounded. It's a long story, and one I'm not ready to share yet. No, I haven't read those books or seen the movies. Should I?

Asking if you should is like asking if you should breathe. The answer is a resounding yes! Okay, I won't push for an answer to this new mystery, but I'm begging, PLEASE, for some kind of hint on your name.

How about this: my first name begins with an R and my last name begins with G.

You're killing me, Smalls.

Smalls. Another character I should know about?

Yes, but I'm not going to tell you where. You'll have to discover that on your own.

Rapunzel closed her eyes tightly, thinking, debating. Then, before she could change her mind, she quickly typed:

Rapunzel

There was nothing but her flashing cursor, then

Rapunzel? That's your name?

Yes.

You're not kidding around?

No.

Unusual. Rapunzel. Never heard of it. I like it.

Please don't try to guess my last name.

Okay, you win. For now. Rapunzel. I'll give you an answer as well. When you're seeking out the LOTR movies to watch (as I know you will based on my awesome recommendation), then also look for The Sandlot. One of the best movies ever.

It's now on my list of Awesome Recommendations by Fab Fane Flannigan. Thank you.

You'll be thanking me even more after you read/watch them all. Rapunzel. We shall then discuss. Rapunzel.

Are you going to keep repeating my name like that?

Yes. Rapunzel. I like your name very much. I like the way it looks. Rapunzel.

Rapunzel cringed. What if he started telling people about her, and word got back to her mother?

But you won't... I mean, remember what I told you about my mother?

I remember. Your secret is safe with me. I haven't told anyone about my mysterious FB friend. Who would believe me that I have some hot, enigmatic, strange correspondence with you?

Rapunzel blushed. She had since looked up other uses for the word "hot" and suspected she knew which usage he meant each time he said it.

Been hitting the thesaurus again? Just curious: what makes you think I'm hot? I may look like a gargoyle. And . . . thank you for keeping my secret.

Even if you look like a gargoyle (which would mean you're about 3 feet tall and made of stone) I think your MIND is hot. Even if you find mine so lacking, you think every conversation requires a thesaurus.

I don't think . . . okay, DID you use a thesaurus?

Maybe. And that's the only answer you're getting.

I don't think your mind is lacking, for the record.

You're welcome (for keeping your secret).

Rapunzel smiled, then glanced at the little digital clock at the bottom of her computer. She could talk to Fane forever, but unfortunately it was almost six, which meant her mother would soon be coming for dinner.

G2G.

TTYT.

You misspelled that. It's TTYL.

No I didn't. It means talk to you tomorrow. I WILL talk to you tomorrow, right?

Right.

Good.

Rapunzel signed off the computer, writing down the names of the books he had told her about. She didn't know how she could talk her mother into movies to watch, but she could easily convince her of the books. She hoped.

chapter

4

I need a few books for my language arts course," Rapunzel told her mother. She took a breath and in a rush said, "And I'll need a couple movies because they go with the books and I have to write a paper on the differences."

"Movies?" her mother asked. "You need to purchase movies as well as books?"

Rapunzel chewed her lip as she nodded, thankful that in this one area, her mother preferred to not get involved. She wished Rapunzel's education to be just that: *Rapunzel's* education. "But there's a place on the Internet where you can watch as many movies as you'd like if you pay a monthly fee. Sort of like renting them instead of buying them." Fane had told her of the site, of course.

"Oh. Well then why don't you just do that, Rapunzel, if you need it for your education?"

Rapunzel cringed at her deception. Her mother had given Rapunzel a credit card to use when ordering necessities for school, though she gave Rapunzel the address of her office to have the items sent. She said she didn't want delivery men bringing their germs to their door, which didn't make sense since Rapunzel knew there were construction workers around most days.

"Now, I need to talk to you about something important," her mother continued, the conversation about movies forgotten. Rapunzel sat in the chair and turned for her mother to begin her ritualistic brushing, always done in counts of six. It was Rapunzel's responsibility to keep track on the little clickers used for just such a purpose. One clicker kept the individual tally up to six, which was then reset. The second clicker kept track of how many times they'd cycled through the first. When it reached twelve, they were done.

"Coming up is a trip I must take."

Rapunzel jerked around at the announcement. Her mother had never been gone for more than a day, always returning for their nightly ritual. She felt panicked at the thought of being alone.

"A trip? What do you mean? What kind of trip? For how long?"

Her mother smiled, and Rapunzel couldn't help comparing it to the open smile that reflected in Fane's photos. His smiles seemed to radiate from his eyes. Her mother's smile, in contrast, was flat and didn't move past her lips. How had she not noticed this before?

"Calm yourself. I won't be gone long. Six days isn't such a long time, is it?"

"*Six days?*" Rapunzel yelped.

"Please, Rapunzel, enough of the dramatics. Cook has agreed to stay in the house while I'm away so you won't be alone."

"But what if there's a problem?" Rapunzel asked. She had never met Cook and wouldn't recognize her if she saw her. "She can't come in here. I can't go out." Her chest tightened and her breathing escalated.

"I've thought of that, Rapunzel," her mother said, jerking her hair to turn Rapunzel back around, and continued brushing. Rapunzel systematically began clicking, even though her mind raced. "Give me some credit, please. What count are we up to?"

Rapunzel glanced down, did the math. "Sixty-eight."

Her mother gave four more long strokes with the brush. "There." She sat the brush down and placed her hands heavily on Rapunzel's shoulders, looking at Rapunzel in the mirror. "I have a surprise for you." She stood, stroking the blonde hair. "Come with me."

Rapunzel did as she was told, though she felt like screaming. She clamped her lips tightly shut and followed her mother. When they reached the sitting area, her mother reached into her bag, then turned and handed Rapunzel a strange, plain white rectangle with elastic loops on each end. Rapunzel simply stared at it and with an exasperated grunt her mother took it from her.

"It's a medical mask." She lifted it to Rapunzel's face, placing it over her nose and mouth and fastening the two loops around her ears. Rapunzel immediately felt claustrophobic. "Should there be an emergency, you can put this on and it will protect you from the germs."

Rapunzel stared at her over the mask, then as her words sunk past the panic, she felt something new. Hope.

"You mean," she began excitedly, "that with this on, I'm protected? I can go outside my rooms? Maybe even outside the house?" Her mind filled with visions of being able to meet Fane in the gardens below.

"Of course not!" her mother snapped, startling her. "Don't think it for one second, Rapunzel. The danger is very real, very present. Put that thought immediately out of your small mind." The blaze in her eyes calmed as she seemed to realize Rapunzel's alarm. She soothed a hand down Rapunzel's arm then reached up to remove the mask. "It's a temporary barrier, my dear child," she said soothingly. "It will help if absolutely needed, but it can't keep the threat completely away. Do you understand?"

Rapunzel nodded, mute with her disappointment. She hoped that this mask was a new way for her to have something akin to a normal life. It crushed her to realize it wasn't so. Finally, she found her voice, smaller now. "When will you go?"

"Not for a few weeks, Rapunzel. I want to give you plenty of warning so that we can both prepare." She pulled Rapunzel into her tight embrace that was more painful than comforting. "I don't relish the thought of going. I wouldn't leave you if I could avoid it. I promise the time will fly as if on the wings of a bird. I'll be back before you know it."

Rapunzel shuddered in her mother's arms. The speech sounded practiced, unnatural to her ears. She hadn't had any conversations outside of her mother. She supposed she couldn't really judge.

"Where are you going?"

Her mother pushed her abruptly away. "I told you. On a business trip. You really must learn to listen better."

"I mean, where, as in, where will you be? Maybe I can look it up on the computer so I can picture you there."

Gothel's face hardened. "Why would you look it up, Rapunzel? The computer is a device for your schoolwork. Nothing more. Have you been using it for other things?"

"No," Rapunzel quickly assured her, even as her heartbeat increased in tempo at the falsehood. "Of course not. It was just an idea."

Her mother studied her for long moments. Apparently satisfied, she turned away. Rapunzel walked toward her bedroom after her mother left. Just before stepping through the high wooden doorway, she turned toward the stone alcove that held her computer. Without allowing herself to weigh the consequences, she entered and woke the computer.

Immediately her Facebook message box popped up.

> Well, look who's being a night owl.

Rapunzel smiled when his message came.

> *Isn't that redundant? Aren't all owls night owls?*

> And a bit testy so late.

Rapunzel sighed.

> *Sorry. Just got some bad news.*

> Now I'M sorry for being such an insensitive jerk. Care to share?

> *In a few weeks my mother is going away.*

Like, forever?

Of course not. But she'll be gone six days.

Oh, I'm sorry. I thought you said you had some BAD news.

Rapunzel stared at his message. How could it be anything *but* bad news?

It IS bad news. She's never been gone before.

Afraid of being left home with the old man? Is he that bad?

Rapunzel's brows scrunched at the words.

There is no old man living here that I know of.

Oh, sorry. Insensitive again. I suppose I've never asked about the familial situation there. Just you and your mom? No siblings?

No siblings.

Wait, are you saying that you will be home alone?

No, Cook will be here with me.

Ah, well, I guess we can't all have the perfect dream come true. But seriously, how vigilant is this Cook guy? Is sneaking out an option?

Rapunzel shook her head at this odd sentence.

Cook is a woman. Why would I want to sneak out?

Oh, my friend, you haven't lived until you've snuck out at least once. I can't believe you've made it to 17 without having done so.

Do YOU sneak out often?

Well . . . no. But then, I don't really need to. The parental units are pretty cool about giving me rein as long as I toe the line.

Should any of that make sense to me?

Uh . . . *pauses awkwardly*. You don't get out much, do you?

She wondered if she had said something that sounded ignorant of the world. Of course, she *was* ignorant of the world, so it would make sense that she sounded so.

No, I suppose I don't.

Would you like to? Sometime? With me, I mean.

Rapunzel stared at his words. They reflected the momentary fantasy of Fane and the garden she'd had such a short time ago as she stood with the mask covering her face. Yet she'd been assured by her mother that the fantasy was still just that.

Maybe. Sometime. But I can't yet.

Can't. That's different than WON'T, right? Wait, don't answer that. My mom always tells me never to ask anything I don't want to hear the answer to. So let me change that to: Awesome. I look forward to "sometime."

Thank you, Fab Fane.

What did I do to elicit you using my TRUE name?

Haha (I'm saying that sarcastically, FYI). No, really, thank you. I was feeling kind of depressed. Now I'm smiling after talking to you. If this can be called talking.

Sounds better than "keyboarding at you." Glad I could make you smile. My day is now complete.

Rapunzel knew he teased, but she couldn't stop the warm tingle at his words. She signed off and went to bed with the smile still on her face, thinking of Fane rather than her mother's impending trip.

chapter

5

Rapunzel's next two weeks seemed to speed past as she rushed through her homework each day in order to either spend time talking to Fane or reading the books he'd suggested. She was quite taken with *The Hobbit*, but wasn't so crazy about *The Lord of the Rings* series. However, she did enjoy the movies.

> *Gollum is a horrible little creature. I can't believe you compared me to him.*

> I DIDN'T compare you to him, if you recall. I simply borrowed his name to fill in for the G of your name.

> *Oh. Well. Still, I can assure you I look nothing like him.*

> Intrigued, definitely. And now wondering as well. What DO you look like?

Rapunzel thought about his question. She hadn't ever really considered what she looked like. She hurried into her room and picked up her small hand mirror, then returned to the computer to look into it as she answered him.

> *I have long, blonde hair. It's heavy. Gives me a headache*

sometimes. Green eyes that, if you ask me, are too large for my face. Straight nose. I've read my shape of upper lip described as a bow, though I can't fathom how it looks like a bow. Lower lip slightly . . . chubbier, I suppose, than the upper. Chin is neither too large nor too small. I'm sixty-five inches tall, and I weigh 115 pounds. Hands and feet seem appropriately sized, as does head. Does that help?

Okay, I'm using one of my hated acronyms: ROFL. The only thing you left out was your actual shoe size. You only get more and more interesting the more I talk to you. And yes, you sound hot.

Rapunzel flushed at his words. How else was she to describe herself? She decided to put the question to him.

Well, how would you describe yourself if asked?

Handsome. Debonair. Striking. Sensitive yet daunting. In a word: perfect.

Okay, now I'm ROFLing—and slightly nauseated. Have you ever been accused of humility? Come on, I'm serious.

Fine, fine. *holds hands up in surrender* Brown hair in need of a haircut if my mom is to be believed. Eyes that are neither dark enough to be called brown or green enough to be called hazel. Really light brown, I guess. Have a small goatee that said mom is after me to shave, but I like it. Makes me look older. Great cheekbones and strong jaw . . . oh, sorry, slipped into non-humility again. Um, yeah, I guess that's it. Besides, you can see my pics on FB, right?

Yes, I can. I just wondered how you would describe yourself if I couldn't see them. How tall?

Six-six, which is great for the basketball career, not

so great for fitting into my small car, or through most doorways. And people literally hate me if I'm in front of them at a concert or movie.

Rapunzel tried to imagine standing next to him, a full foot taller than her. She had nothing to reference it with though because her mother was the only one she ever stood next to, and she was only three inches taller than Rapunzel.

Shoe size?

Haha.

Rapunzel smiled and shifted in her chair. Then Fab's next words appeared:

Do you have a camera on your computer? You could take a picture of yourself and send it to me. I promise not to show anyone.

Her stomach tightened at his words. She did have a camera, but she didn't think she was ready to reveal herself quite that much. What if he thought she *did* look like Gollum? Besides, if he didn't keep his promise, she would definitely have her computer taken from her. Or worse, if one of his friends were to see it and send it, she might be stalked and kidnapped, her death sealed. She'd been told the horror stories by her mother when she first got the computer and so had never utilized the camera in any way.

Hello? I'm guessing the dead silence means no.

Oh, sorry, it's just that

She couldn't tell him the truth. So she typed

the camera is broken.

Bummer. For me, I mean. Just wondering: do you think I might ever get to meet you? I mean, we live in the same city. You can't be all that far from me. Where do you live?

She didn't honestly know where she lived. She knew the name of her house, but not her address. Having never been outside, she didn't even know where it was located within the city. Afraid that would sound odd, she instead wrote,

Now who sounds like a stalker?

Touché. Fine, keep your mysteries. But would you at least consider meeting me somewhere? I would really, really like to meet the enigmatic Rapunzel G.

G2G. TTYL.

She quickly signed off, knowing she was being an utter coward. Hopefully, he would think her mother had shown up, since it had happened before. His words panicked her nearly as much as her mother's announce-ment that she would be leaving on a trip. He wanted to meet her; the idea made her heart soar. But the reality of her situation was as cold and stark as her stone walls. She couldn't be exposed to anyone, or she would die. No matter how much her heart was breaking at the thought that her first and only friend wanted to meet her, she had to say no. She was sure in the knowledge of the fate of any other decision. She wiped the tears away as she heard her mother enter her room and call her name.

"I'm here, Mother," she said as she walked with heavy heart to her bedroom to have her magic hair brushed by her only possible companion.

chapter 6

"Mother, do you think they will ever find a cure for my disease?"

Her mother flinched, as always, at her casual use of the word *disease*. "Please, we must concentrate on this."

Rapunzel obediently turned her eyes back to the task before them. Her mother required that she write out a step-by-step daily plan, including everything she planned to eat, what she would study or read, and what she would do with her free time during her absence. Rapunzel had a pretty good idea of what she would be doing in her free time and struggled with what to write, so she added in several books that she'd be able to read quickly. Hopefully, that would free up much of her time.

"I'll make myself dinner every night," Rapunzel said, pointing to the blank spots on the schedule.

"Why ever would you do that? Cook will be here. She can bring your dinner each night."

"I *like* to cook," she said, standing and moving to the bookcase that rested against the gray stone wall next to the door. She turned to her mother. "Who is Cook anyway? Is she a maid or something?" She'd never seen or met her, only eaten food cooked by her and either left at her door or brought up by her mother.

Her mother looked at her oddly. "She's the cook."

Rapunzel laughed. "Our cook's name is Cook? How ironic is that?"

"Of course it's not her name," her mother scoffed.

"Her name isn't Cook?" Rapunzel was confused. "But then, what is her name? Why do we call her Cook?"

"*We* don't call her anything." She stood and closed the folder that held the schedule. "She is the cook, therefore I call her Cook. Her name is unimportant."

Rapunzel's eyes widened. She opened her mouth to voice her surprise at such an attitude when her mother froze. Rapunzel followed her gaze and saw what had caught her mother's attention. Earlier she had dropped a glass of orange juice that shattered. She thought she'd cleaned it up, but now saw the sticky spot under the cabinet's edge. Dread tightened her stomach.

"Rapunzel," her mother said, voice quivering, face suddenly pale and clammy.

"I'm sorry," Rapunzel quickly apologized, rushing over to the sink to wet a cloth. She dropped to her knees and frantically scrubbed at the spot.

Once she was certain the sticky area was more than clean and had been sterilized with the bleach solution, she turned back to her mother who stared blankly at the spot where it had been. "It's gone now, see?" she asked tentatively, moving slowly toward her mother.

"Do you understand what can happen, Rapunzel, if we relax our vigilance for just one moment, if we become careless?"

Rapunzel nodded as soon as the first word escaped her mother's mouth. "I do know, and I'm very sorry. I missed it somehow. It won't happen again."

Her mother suddenly pulled her into her painful embrace, nearly smothering Rapunzel with her overbearing fright. "No, it must not happen again. You *know* the consequences."

Rapunzel nodded against her mother, mainly with the objective of trying to find a pocket of oxygen. As suddenly as Gothel grabbed Rapunzel, she then released her. "Why this sudden interest in Cook?" her mother asked suspiciously, all concern forgotten.

Rapunzel stumbled at the sudden freedom. She put a hand against the countertop, regaining some balance in the shift. "Well, Mother, it's just that this is my whole world, this room. I've never seen the rest of the house. I have no idea what it looks like. I don't know who else works here, because all I ever hear about is Cook. I don't even know our *address*." She couldn't keep the exasperation from her tone.

Her mother pushed up against her, her face inches from Rapunzel's own, a blaze in her eyes Rapunzel had never seen before.

"Why would you need to know the address here, Rapunzel? What difference could that possibly make to you?" Rapunzel cowered against the sharp edge of the counter. Suddenly her mother relaxed and soothed her hands down Rapunzel's arms in a frantic petting motion. "You don't need to worry your little head about such things. Must you be such a burden? Just forget about your silly, unimportant questions."

She turned toward the door, scooping up the folder on her way past. At the door, she turned back, eyes narrowed, empty smile pasted on her face. "Rapunzel, put thoughts of a cure from your mind. There is no cure."

With those words she left the room, leaving a stunned Rapunzel trying to figure out what had just happened. She looked around at the dismal gray walls that seemed to loom closer than ever. She'd lived within these walls as long as she could remember. The thought of never stepping outside them, never seeing another person's face besides that of her mother . . . of never even knowing who lived or worked within her home overwhelmed her with sadness. How was she supposed to continue on without hope?

She turned to her computer and the one person who had become her refuge. He was offline, so she decided to leave him a message.

My mother leaves for her trip next week. Do you want to

She stared at her flashing cursor. She stood and walked back out into the main room, then into the other alcove with the window. She opened the window, surprised to see Angel perched in the tree. The bird turned her head toward Rapunzel and chirped, leaving her perch to land on the windowsill.

"I'm sorry, Angel, I don't have any seeds for you." She turned an empty palm over to show the bird, who hopped over until she resided on Rapunzel's palm. She pecked lightly at her palm twice before settling down, wings tucked under. Rapunzel grinned as she cautiously brought her second hand up. When she first stroked Angel's head she expected the little bird to flit away. Instead, the bird closed her eyes as if in pleasure. Rapunzel continued stroking, and Angel sat still, turning her head occasionally from side to side as if to encourage Rapunzel to not miss a single spot. Then, chattering, the bird flew off. Rapunzel laughed, her mood suddenly lifted.

With renewed determination, she walked back to her computer and finished her message.

> *My mother leaves for her trip next week. Do you want to come over one night?*

She clicked the send button without trepidation.

chapter

7

Seriously? You want me to come over while your
mother is away?

Rapunzel realized how her request must sound.

*If you're uncomfortable coming over without a suitable
chaperone, I will understand.*

Uh . . . that's not what I meant. Are you uncomfortable
without a chaperone?

She wasn't sure how to answer that. What was proper
in this situation? She hadn't really thought her request
through. She'd only been thinking that she wanted to talk
to someone else in person. Even if it killed her.

I promise your virtue is safe with me.

Rapunzel's cheeks burned.

*Oh, I didn't question that. Is it okay that I asked you over,
or is that a strange request?*

Not a strange request at all, and one I've been hoping
for. I've wanted to meet the mysterious Rapunzel G for

a while now. Not related to Kenny G, are you?

Who? And please don't ROLF at my ignorance.

Well, since I don't have a LAUGHING FLOOR to roll on, I think I can manage to refrain.

Rapunzel's laughed at herself.

Oops. I meant . . . well, you know what I meant.

Yeah, I do. And please, please know I'm grinning as I happily accept your invitation. When and where?

Her mind raced at the thought of having him here, in her rooms. A different face. Someone other than her mother.

She leaves Friday morning. Do you want to come Friday night? And here at my house, I suppose.

Friday night works well. Neither wrestling nor basketball has started yet, so I still have a few free minutes in my life. I do have practice after school but I could come around 8. You want me to bring a pizza? And FYI, I have no idea where you live. An address would be helpful for that.

Rapunzel suddenly realized she *really* hadn't thought this through. Not only did she not know her address, she wasn't sure how she was going to get him into her room. Obviously he couldn't just march up to the front door and come in.

Hold on a minute.

She hurried over to the window and, after looking around to make sure no one was near, opened it. She looked down. The ground was at least twenty feet below.

While the turret was built of rough stone, she doubted he *could* climb it. He *could* climb the tree, but then how would he get from the tree to the window. It was six feet away.

Her eyes fell on the outbuildings. There might be a ladder in one of them, but she had no way of knowing for certain. Frustrated by her discovery, she huffed out a breath. A bird tweeted nearby, catching her attention. Angel flittered overhead. As Rapunzel watched, the bird flew just below and landed on the trellis that hugged the side of the house.

"Hey, Angel," she called. "Wish I had time to play, but I have Fane on hold." Angel chattered loudly at her. Rapunzel pulled her head back inside, placing her hands on the bottom of the window to close it, when she realized what she had just seen. She stuck her head back out the window, glanced down at the bluebird, and laughed. "Angel, you're genius."

She went into the kitchenette and grabbed a handful of sunflower seeds from her drawer. She ran back to the window and scattered them on the ground below. Angel chirped and dove down to the proffered treats. Rapunzel closed the window and walked back to the computer.

> *I'm back. Can I ask how you you'd feel about climbing a trellis?*

> You are always full of surprises. That's nowhere near any question I've ever been asked before. And I'm kind of curious what it has to do with pizza and your address.

Before she could type a reply, a new message from him popped up.

> Wait! Are you saying I need to climb a trellis to get to you? Awesome!

> *Yes. I can't let you in the front door, so you'll have to climb up to my room. If I can discover my address, then I'll tell you where to find the correct trellis. There might be more.*

> You GENUINELY don't know your address? Huh. Weird. Okay. Maybe I can find you by your last name if it's not common.

> *I know the name of my house. Does that help? It's actually my own last name.*

> Your house has a name? Can't be too many of those, so maybe that will help. Especially if it's also your last name and your last name isn't Smith or Lee.

Rapunzel took a deep breath, then plunged.

> *My last name is Gothel. I live at Gothel Manor. Do you know where it is?*

The cursor flashed for so long without response Rapunzel thought he'd signed off. It showed him as still online, though. Maybe he was Googling the information. She smacked her forehead. *Of course.* Why hadn't she thought of that all this time? She probably could have discovered her own address in that same manner and not had to let him know that she didn't know where she lived. She moved her mouse to open a new tab for that very purpose when his message came.

Sorry. Just a bit stunned, here. Are you saying you live at GOTHEL MANSION??? THE Gothel Mansion? I'm having a hard time believing that. You've been playing me this whole time? Is that the reason for all the secrecy? I'm just kind of feeling . . . disbelieving, I guess.

Rapunzel stared at his words. Was her home well known? Why did he call it Gothel Mansion instead of Gothel Manor? And why did he think she was kidding about living here?

My mother calls it Gothel Manor, so maybe that's different?

No, Rapunzel. There's only one that I know of. It has to be the same. Are you telling me the truth here?

Yes, of course.

She made a decision.

Okay, time for me to stop being so "secretive" as you say. But I have good reasons for being so. I have a disease

She stopped and deleted the last four words.

I can't go outside because if I do I will get very sick. I live in a specific area of the house. It's the southeast corner. I only know that because I have a compass. I don't know my address because I've never had any reason to need to know it. I suppose I could have Googled it, but honestly the thought never crossed my mind. Is it weird that I live here?

There was no response again for a few minutes before he answered.

No, not weird, just . . . never mind. So you live in the tower?

Uh, the tower? I don't know. Is it a tower?

Yes, it is. I know where it is. I'll be there Friday at 8.

Rapunzel sensed the difference in his tone. Something wasn't right.

Rapunzel, promise me one thing.

Okay.

Don't Google your house.

chapter

8

Rapunzel's mother joined her for breakfast as usual on Friday morning. Rapunzel's entire being thrummed with nerves with the anticipation of both her mother leaving and her scheduled visitor.

"It's only six days, Rapunzel. You'll be fine." She handed Rapunzel a small phone. "I'll call you every day. Do you know how to work this?"

Rapunzel shook her head. Of course not. She'd seen them on the Internet and in some of the movies she'd watched but had never held one. Her mother took a matching phone from her purse and pushed a button. The phone in Rapunzel's hand vibrated, startling her.

"Push this button here," her mother pointed. She did so, and after a few moments her mother guided it to her ear. Gothel mirrored the gesture and when she spoke Rapunzel heard her words echoed in the phone. "This is how we will stay in communication." Her mother pushed another button, showing Rapunzel what to do to end the call. "I'll call you every evening at six. Now, Rapunzel, you remember what we spoke about?"

"Yes," she said, repeating the words that had been drilled into her daily since her mother first told her she'd be going. "Brush my hair each night in seventy-two strokes, stay away from the window, and keep my rooms clean."

"Yes, that's a good girl." She stroked Rapunzel's hair before pulling her into a quick, awkward embrace. "Stay safe. There's much riding on you."

"I know," she answered. As her mother left, Rapunzel turned back to the rooms that had always felt comforting and familiar. They now felt empty and cold. She shivered and went into the alcove to complete her homework. Once she finished with that, she opened the movie streaming site. She searched through the main page until she found one that looked interesting.

It downloaded quickly and she tried to concentrate on it, she really did, but Rapunzel couldn't keep her mind off Fane. They'd talked every night on Facebook, but it felt restrained somehow. She wondered if it was his nervousness of their impending meeting . . . or if it was something else.

She was just about to shut the movie off when the two main characters began kissing. She leaned back in the chair and watched, touching her own mouth as she watched the action. Would she ever be kissed? Probably not. One kiss could kill her. As the two characters pulled away and gazed into one another's eyes, she felt the pang of loss. No one would ever look at her that way, no one would ever hold her like that. She snapped the computer off and strode from the alcove, brushing her tears away.

She scrutinized the room, making sure it was perfectly clean and sterile. On a whim she decided to bake cookies.

Two hours later, the room once again sterile but aromatic with the scent of fresh baked cookies, she walked into her bedroom. She sat at her vanity and looked at herself.

She'd watched a movie recently in which a plain girl was made beautiful by making herself up, subsequently wanted by the movie's hero. She wished she had some makeup to make herself look better, but it wasn't allowed. She touched her plaited hair. She pulled the heavy end up and released the tie, fingering the braid until the strands hung free. She brushed it until it gleamed.

She looked at the clock on the microwave. 7:45. Her stomach tightened. She moved to the alcove, opening the window in case he came early. There wasn't any light in the alcove. It was dim enough she felt safe standing there waiting. She saw him when he came around the corner of her house and her nerves, already taut, felt as if they would snap.

"Rapunzel!" he called in a loud whisper.

"I'm here," she called back in the same manner. She leaned forward a little so he would see where she was. He waved.

"I'm coming up."

She watched as he tugged against the trellis, testing its security. As he started to climb, she pulled the mask from her pocket and secured it around her ears. Her quick breathing pressed loudly behind the mask, and she could hear her heart pounding. At the last moment, as his hand touched the windowsill, she made a decision, ripping the mask from her face and shoving it into her pocket.

As his face came into the window, she could see the outline of him, but it was too dim for details. Still, her pulse sped up. In just moments she'd be seeing another person up close, other than her mother, for the first time in her life.

"Hi," he said, and she could see his stark white teeth against the darkness.

"Hi," she answered.

He pulled himself over the ledge, half falling into the alcove with a laugh. "You have a light in here?" he asked. She closed the drapes, leaving them in deep darkness before she clicked the dim lamp on, creating muted light. As he got his first look at her, he stopped moving. His mouth dropped a bit as he gazed at her. For a moment Rapunzel wondered if this was a mistake, if she'd made a horrible error in judgment by allowing him in. Then he swallowed, loudly.

"Wow, you're really . . . beautiful," he said slowly on an exhaled breath.

Her cheeks heated up, and she raised her hands to touch them, vaguely worried about why they suddenly felt so warm. She lifted the corners of her mouth in a small smile, embarrassed by his words.

"Um . . . thank you, I suppose," she said quietly.

He shook his head as if trying to rid himself of something, then continued to his full height. Now it was her turn to be stunned. She'd had some idea of what he looked like, of course, from his photos on Facebook. He was tall, as she'd known. His dark hair was pushed back from his forehead, a thick lock falling onto one temple, landing above a short sideburn. His eyes were dark in the muted light, lips full above a patch of dark whiskers on his chin. She came to just below his shoulder. He was trim but substantial some-how, broad shouldered. He had on jeans and a long-sleeved polo shirt pushed up to just below his elbows, revealing muscled arms. As handsome as she'd thought him in the photos, he was even more so standing before her.

"Would you . . ." she began nervously, sweeping one hand toward the sitting room. "Would you like to come in?"

He finally tore his eyes from her face and looked beyond her. "Sure," he answered, walking past her. As he did so, she inhaled deeply the scent of another human being. She wasn't sure how to describe the smell: clean, musky, something altogether different than anything she'd smelled before—and very, very pleasant.

"Wow," he repeated as he stepped out of the alcove into the seating area. "This is some setup you have here."

She looked around. It looked the same to her as it did every day, as it had every single day of her life. He stopped next to the bookcase and turned back toward her. She stood next to the opening to the alcove.

"So, what's the deal?" he asked. "You said you can't ever go outside. Why not? What happens if you do?"

"I'll die," she answered simply. His eyes widened and she understood that she had perhaps spoken too abruptly. "I mean," she tried to backpedal, "I have a disease—"

He stepped away from her, a small motion, but obvious nonetheless. "What kind of disease?" His voice sounded tight though clearly he tried to sound normal. "Is it contagious?"

"No." Her answer was firm. She knew for certain

that it wasn't *her* that was the danger. It was the world that threatened her life. "I have SCIDs—which stands for Severe Combined Immunodeficiency. It's an immune system deficiency I was born with. If I'm exposed to any germs or bacteria, my body will be unable to fight them, and I'll die."

His look became even more worried. "Isn't it dangerous having me here? Who knows what germs I brought in with me?"

She shook her head. She had considered that possibility before she had asked him over. The invitation hadn't been extended lightly. "It doesn't matter," she said lightly, eyes turned to the floor. "I've been here alone for so long that sometimes I think it's worth the risk, exposing myself, just to spend a few hours with someone."

He relaxed his worried pose, now looking sympathetic. "That sucks," he said.

She grinned and laughed when he added his grin to hers.

"I suppose that's one way to put it," she said.

"So you just sit here, all day, all alone?" His tone was incredulous. She only nodded in answer as she moved forward into the room and the full light.

"Whoa!" he exclaimed, seeing her hair. "I have never seen hair like that."

She self-consciously pulled a long strand around to the front and played idly with it as she lowered herself into the chair. He sat across from her on the sofa.

"It's pretty heavy to lug around all day. It's never been cut," she said.

"That's amazing." He leaned forward. "Can I touch it?"

She shied back for a moment, then realized he couldn't hurt her by *touching* it. "Okay," she said. He stepped around the oval table that separated them. He crouched down next to her and almost reverently reached out. Taking one thick strand between his thumb and finger he slowly pulled downward until he had nearly reached the end before letting go.

"It's so soft," he murmured. She was glad she had taken the time to so thoroughly brush it before his arrival. Her eyes dropped to the patch of hair on his chin. She'd never seen facial hair before. He reached up and lightly scratched his fingers through it. "Do you think my mom's right about shaving it?"

She shook her head. She brought one hand halfway up. "May I?" she asked, looking at him for permission. He nodded and she touched the tips of her fingers to the bristly, wiry strands. She hadn't felt anything like it before, rough and scratchy. She pinched a small chunk, amazed at the thickness of it. Her eyes came to his in amazement.

He glanced up at her from beneath long, dark lashes, and her breath caught in her throat. She'd never been so close to a boy before. She'd never been so close to *any*one before besides her mother. His eyes dropped to her mouth, and she unthinkingly licked her lips, remembering the kiss she had watched in the movie earlier. His eyes came back to hers, and something within their depths, something intense and hungry, sent a skitter down her spine. He slowly lifted his face toward her. The movement caused her to draw a breath. As if that broke whatever spell held them, he blinked and backed away from her. He moved back to the sofa, and she felt the loss of . . . something. She just wasn't sure what.

He shrugged and held out his empty hands. "I didn't bring pizza."

"That's okay." She smiled. "It might have been kind of difficult to climb up carrying a pizza."

"It was kind of tough climbing up *without* carrying a pizza."

Her smile fell. "I'm sorry. I didn't consider that. It wasn't fair of me to—"

"Hey," he interrupted. "I wasn't complaining. Just stating a fact."

"Oh." She lifted the corners of her mouth temporarily, returning her gaze to the floor.

"So . . . this is awkward, huh?" he asked.

She shrugged, then remembered the cookies. "Oh, I made some cookies. Do you want some?"

"I never turn down cookies." He stood and followed her to the kitchen area. "Wow," he said yet again. "Your hair is the most incredible thing I've ever seen. How long is it?"

"I think about fifteen feet," she said, blushing.

"That's gotta be some kind of record. You could probably be in the *Guinness Book of World Records*."

"That would require someone coming in to measure it, right? And that isn't allowed. I don't think they'd just take my word for it," she said.

"Oh, yeah, right." He sat at one of the bar stools at the counter and she put the place of cookies in front of him. "So this is like, your apartment?"

"I suppose," she said, turning to the fridge. "Do you want something to drink?"

"Sure, whatcha got?"

She looked into the cold interior. "Milk, lemonade, or water."

"What goes better with cookies than milk?" he asked with a grin.

She filled two glasses and sat next to him, taking a cookie.

"These are fantastic," he said around a mouthful of cookie. "Did you make them?"

"I did." She couldn't help the flush of pride at his genuine pleasure.

"I have to tell you," he said, "I was pretty skeptical about coming here."

She didn't know how to respond to that, so she just nodded.

"Not because of you," he said. She could feel the weight of his gaze, so she turned to look at him. "I couldn't wait to finally meet you face-to-face." She felt her cheeks heat up but held his gaze. "It's just that I honestly didn't believe you were who you said you were."

"Thought I was a creepy stalker, huh?" she teased, and he laughed, breaking the tension.

"You're definitely not creepy," he said. "It remains to be seen whether you're a stalker."

She laughed. "Kind of hard to stalk from my . . . tower."

"The girl in the tower," he murmured. "Who woulda thunk it was the truth?"

chapter

9

After Fane finished half the plate of cookies—to Rapunzel's amazement—he stood and looked around.

"So, do I get the grand tour?"

"Uh, sure." She led him to the alcove where her computer sat.

"Is this where you sit when we're talking? Or chatting, or whatever you want to call it," he asked, stepping in and looking around.

"Yes."

"Cool. Now I'll be able to picture you. Before it was like just this weird . . . *void* when I tried to imagine you or your surroundings." He looked at her. "What did you picture about me?"

Rapunzel glanced up at the second lock of hair that escaped his brushed back hair, framing his face. "Pretty much like you look now, because you look very much like your pictures. Maybe better." He grinned knowingly and she dropped her eyes. "I guess I just picture the area where you sit as the same as mine."

He placed a hand against the rough stone wall and rubbed it, his hand vibrating across the uneven surface. "No rock walls in my house," he said casually.

"Oh." She really didn't know what to say to that. Was it abnormal to have walls of stone? They were only in the two alcoves. In the other rooms the walls were sheet rocked and painted. "Well, this is where I do my school-work." She turned and exited the alcove. He took one more look around before following. She led him into her bedroom, and he let out a low whistle.

"I know a lot of girls who would *kill* for a room like this," he said. Rapunzel scanned the room. It felt normal to her, but since she'd never seen another room she couldn't really compare. He walked over to the bed and ran a hand down one of the four thick posts that sat on each corner. He leaned in and peeked up at the white gauzy material that draped in a large X from corner to corner. He sat on the edge of the mattress, which he could easily do without having to hop up onto the bed as she did, and bounced up and down a few times. "Holy . . . is that your bathroom?" he asked incredulously, leaning forward. Without waiting for an answer he stood and walked into the room he spoke of, flipping on the light switch. The white marble floors and counters gleamed.

"That sucker is huge!" he exclaimed, eyeing the sunken tub. "You could swim laps in that thing."

"I hardly ever use it," she admitted. "It seems like a waste to fill it with so much water for one person. Plus, it's much easier to wash my hair in the shower."

He looked at her hair again, reached out and touched

a strand almost unthinkingly, then turned in a half-circle. "That's where the magic happens, huh?" he asked, indicating the glass enclosed shower. She didn't know what magic he meant but nodded anyway. He ran his hand along the marble countertop the length of both sinks, opening one drawer just the smallest bit before pushing it closed. His brows raised in humor at the monogrammed towels.

Rapunzel watched his reflection in the mirror as he circled her bathroom. He seemed curious about her space, which felt odd to her. He lived in the world where he saw all kinds of things, not shut in like her in a limited world. How could any of this be interesting?

They exited back into the main living area. He stopped, looking around expectantly. "So, what's upstairs?"

"Oh," she said, surprised he'd care about such a small room. "Just my exercise room."

"Cool. Can't wait to see that."

Rapunzel shrugged and led the way up the narrow set of winding stairs to the small room barely large enough to contain the stationary bike, weight machine, a treadmill, and a very small patch of floor where she could stretch.

"This is it?"

Rapunzel shrugged again. "Yeah. It's all I need." Fane looked at her oddly, eyes squinted, head cocked. "What?" she finally asked.

"This tower is huge, Rapunzel. You're telling me that out of all the space available, this is your entire living area?"

She looked around her at the stone walls that

completely enclosed the exercise room excepting the open doorway. "Well . . . yes. Why?"

"There are two stories below you, and three above you. If you're stuck inside, why not give you all of it?"

Rapunzel was stunned. She'd known there were probably two stories below, but she had no idea there was that much above.

"Well, my mother has to have somewhere to live," she said. "If she has those floors and the space I can see outside, it's probably not that much more than I have." *Well, except for the three stories above me that I didn't know about,* she thought.

Fane just stared at her mutely for long moments. Finally, he said, "You really haven't ever been outside your room, have you?" She shook her head, now feeling embarrassed. "Rapunzel, I read your house is like, twenty or twenty-five thousand square feet I think. How big is your room? Maybe one or two thousand of that? That leaves a *lot* of extra house for just your mother."

Rapunzel's mouth dropped. Her home was that large? She shook her head. He had to be exaggerating.

"Haven't you ever been curious about what's outside your room?"

She hadn't questioned it, really. She'd always been told her life depended on staying in her rooms and hadn't thought about what lay outside her door, knowing only it had the potential to be fatal to her.

"Haven't you ever peeked outside your door, even?" he asked. When she just stared at him, he swept past her, grabbing her hand as he did so and half dragging her back to the living area. He didn't stop until they were at the door, his hand placed on the knob. She watched his hand with a thrill of fear lighting her belly. "Shall we?" he said.

Swallowing over the lump in her throat, she nodded. He twisted the knob and—

Nothing. The door was locked.

"That's weird," Fane murmured. He tried twisting it again. "It doesn't make sense," Fane said, turning to face her. "Why would you need to be locked *in*? I mean, I can see why you might want to lock others *out* to keep yourself safe, but this . . ." He glanced at the door, trying the knob once again. "This is weird."

Rapunzel tried to make sense of it. She knew her mother used a key each time she left, but she assumed it was only to let herself out. Which of course didn't make any sense because then it would reason that Rapunzel would need a key as well. A thought struck her.

"Maybe there's a key here," she said.

Fane's face lit. He began searching around the door, running his fingers across the top of the frame. Almost immediately Rapunzel knew it was futile. She kept the place clean—sterile, actually—and knew every nook and cranny. There wasn't any place it could be that she wouldn't have found it.

"Fane," she said, tugging at his arm to pull him up from the carpet. "It's no use. If there were a key here, I'd know it."

"Hmm," he grumbled, stumped in his exploration. Suddenly he grinned. "Got a screwdriver?"

"No," she said, shaking her head. "Why would I have one of those?"

Fane shrugged, thwarted in his determination. "Okay, how about some cards? I can teach you poker and corrupt your innocence."

Rapunzel laughed. "Cards I have."

They moved back toward the sofa, Fane veering toward the kitchen. "May I?" he said, indicating the bowl of apples on the counter.

"Of course," she said, walking over to the fridge to get another apple to replace the one he removed from the bowl. She found her deck of cards and handed them to Fane, who watched her strangely as he bit into the apple. "Something wrong?" she asked.

"Uh . . . no." He gave a small laugh and took the cards from the pack, shuffling them as they sat across the coffee table from one another. After discovering she didn't have anything that satisfied Fane as usable for what he called "poker chips," he decided to teach her a game called "Go Fish" instead.

When he finally deemed it time for him to go home, Rapunzel felt a deep disappointment. She'd had more fun than she'd expected. It was amazing to spend time with someone besides her mother. As he swung his leg over the window ledge, she quickly said, "If you want to come back . . . sometime . . . I could make us dinner."

"That sounds good," he said. "How about Sunday?"

Rapunzel's heart soared at the thought of having him here again so soon. She was slightly disappointed at having to wait two days.

As he began climbing down the trellis, he suddenly popped his head back up over the ledge.

"Hey, Rapunzel?"

"Yes?"

"I knew you were hot." He grinned. Rapunzel laughed, and he scaled down. She hurried to the window and watched him anxiously until his feet safely touched the ground below. She waved. He returned the gesture and jogged to the corner of the house. He turned back and she saw the gleam of his teeth in the darkness again before he disappeared around the corner.

chapter

10

Remind me to set you up on Skype tomorrow.

Rapunzel's brows pulled together at his message.

Skype?

C'mon, you don't know about Skype?

Uh...

We can talk by video rather than by text. Since there is no longer any secret about who you are or where you live, I'd rather talk to you face-to-face—even if it is virtually.

Rapunzel felt worry gnaw at her. While she also would prefer to look at Fane while she spoke to him, she worried about possible ramifications.

I'll think about it.

What's to think about? Seriously, Rapunzel, after I've seen your hotness in person, you want me to be content NOT seeing your face?

She knew he was just baiting her. Since he discovered

how much it embarrassed her when he referred to her as hot, Fane went out of his way to do it as often as possible. She knew he didn't mean anything real by it. Still, her heart jumped with excitement each time he did.

Do you think your false flattery can convince me? It's a sad, pathetic attempt.

It would be if it didn't work.

Rapunzel laughed.

You must think me a silly girl to fall for such shallow trickery.

You're the least silly girl I know, although one of the most amusing at the same time. You're an enigma. A HOT enigma.

Okay, change of subject, please.

I have something for you.

Oh? What?

Sorry, it's a secret. I could tell you but then I'd have to kill you.

She stared at his words. Surely he was joking, but she didn't know what to make of them.

Oh, man, sorry again. I forget you're a pop-culture satire virgin. It's a saying, usually found humorous and not meant seriously at all.

Oh. Okay. Well, that's too bad because you could probably kill me with a kiss.

As soon as Rapunzel hit the send button, her hand

flew to her mouth. Why did she write such a thing?

Is that an invitation?

Her hands shook as she saw Fane's message. After a moment, she laughed. Of course he didn't take her words seriously, nor did he mean his words to be serious.

You wish.

You have no idea. Promise me a kiss and I might tell you what I have for you.

As tempting as your offer is, I think I can manage to restrain my curiosity until tomorrow.

Buzzkill.

As Rapunzel puzzled over yet another strange phrase, he suddenly typed

So I just got a text from my friend I was supposed to hang out with tonight. There's been a change of plans and suddenly I'm free. If you're going to be home (hardy-har-har) I could come by tonight. If you don't have any plans, that is.

She stared at the screen, her face lighting with a smile.

What is "hardy-har-har"?

Just a cheesy way to say "ha-ha."

Oh. I was planning a trip to Paris, but I might be persuaded to put it off.

Paris is overrated anyway. Late notice so I'll bring dinner.

How do you think you're going to bring dinner, and my surprise, and still be able to climb my tower?

I have my ways . . . Be there at six?

Rapunzel looked at the clock. It was now 4:30. It could be 5:59 and it wouldn't matter. It wasn't like she had anything pressing or anywhere to be.

I'll be here.

* * *

Rapunzel stood at the window, holding Angel in her hand. The little bird had returned for more seeds and more neck massaging. She was glad not only for the companionship of her friend, but also for the excuse to stand at the window and watch for Fane. It was nearly 6:15, and she tried not to believe she'd been stood up. She couldn't stop the single tear escaping and landing on Angel. Angel shook the wetness free from her feathers, bringing a reluctant smile to Rapunzel's face.

Suddenly Angel took flight with a high tweet. Rapunzel watched her downward flight until she disappeared around the corner of the house. A brilliant smile lit her face as she saw Fane's dark head peek around that same corner. He looked left and right before glancing behind him. Finally his gaze found hers, and he lifted a hand in salutation.

He ran over to the bottom of the trellis and began his precarious climb, a lumpy bag on his back. He climbed over the windowsill with a grin, which she matched.

"Hey there, hottie," he said.

Rapunzel couldn't stop the blush infusing her cheeks, to which he responded with a laugh. Refusing to give him any further satisfaction, she responded, "Hey there, Fab."

"Ah," he said teasingly, "she finally understands my true nature."

"You really like yourself, don't you?"

"Yes. And so do you—don't deny it." His eyes sparkled with humor as he shrugged the bag off his shoulders.

"Is that what you brought me?" she asked, pointedly avoiding his question. "A bag to carry on my shoulders?"

"No, Rapunzel, I didn't bring you a backpack. It's what's inside the backpack that counts."

He strode into the kitchen area, Rapunzel following curiously. He set the bag on the counter and opened it, and she moved closer. He looked at her, suddenly stopping.

"Hey," Fane said. "You braided your hair."

"Yes," she said, fingering it self-consciously.

He walked next to her, touching it, lifting the heavy mass from where the tip of it barely brushed the floor. "That must take a while to do, huh?"

"It's not so bad," she said. "I braid it most days. It makes it much easier to maneuver."

"Yeah, I can see that," he said. "How heavy is your hair?"

Rapunzel gathered the bulk of it up and laid it on his arms to join the small amount he held.

"Holy crap! That's heavy. How in the world do you lug that around all day?"

"I'm used to it, I guess."

"Doesn't it give you a headache?"

"Sometimes." She shrugged.

Fane released the hair slowly, not letting it drop in one move. He placed his hands on both sides of her neck. A funny feeling zoomed its way up her spine at his touch. His hands were gentle as his fingers kneaded her neck.

"Good neck muscles, huh?" he asked, releasing her. Rapunzel couldn't answer, deeply affected by the sensations caused by his touch. Fane seemed unfazed, moving back toward his backpack. He pulled out a flat, greasy box. "The pizza's probably a little smooshed from being sideways, but it'll still taste good." He pulled out a smaller package wrapped in foil. "Garlic bread," he announced with a grin.

Rapunzel breathed in the intoxicating smell. She'd never tasted either pizza or garlic bread, but they smelled heavenly. She pulled two plates from the cabinet and set them on the counter. Fane opened the box and maneuvered the soggy mass back into a shape that somewhat resembled a circle. He placed a piece on each plate before unwrapping the foil and placing a piece of bread on each.

Rapunzel sat next to him and took her first bite of pizza. Her eyes widened as she glanced at Fane. A smile spread across her face as she quickly took two more bites, filling her mouth.

He laughed. "Like it?"

"Mm-hm," she mumbled around another mouthful.

"Taste the bread," he suggested.

She reluctantly set the pizza down and picked up the bread. Once again amazement lit her face.

"Fane," she enthused. "That's the best thing I've ever tasted!"

He grinned with satisfaction as she returned to devouring her treat. When she was full, she finished yet another slice of pizza and half a piece of garlic bread until she felt a little sick. It was worth it.

"Well," Fane said, "I'm impressed at the amount of food you managed to pack into that small body. Most girls would eat a dainty amount and leave the table still hungry to impress me."

Rapunzel turned horrified eyes on him. "I . . . I didn't—"

Fane laughed and held up a hand. "Please, don't apologize. It doesn't impress me when they do that. I much prefer to see my money well spent on a hearty appetite."

Rapunzel smiled uncertainly.

"Aren't you going to ask me?" He cocked his head and looked at her.

Her brows lowered in confusion. "Ask you what?"

"Why I was late."

"Oh, that." She shrugged. "You're here now, so that's all that matters, right?"

He shook his head in amazement. "You definitely aren't like the other girls I know." Rapunzel didn't know whether to take that as good or bad. "I'm going to tell you anyway. Since you're sitting here in oblivion, you may not know that your house is usually swarming with construction workers."

Rapunzel narrowed her eyes at him. "I do happen to know that, Mr. Obvious."

Fane laughed. "That's not . . . never mind. Well, what you might not know is that I had to wait for them to leave before I could sneak in. Apparently they work until six."

"Oh," was all Rapunzel could say. She hadn't thought about the workers when she arranged for him to come. Because she heard them but rarely saw them, they were almost a nonentity in her world.

"Ready to see what I brought you?" he teased.

"It wasn't the pizza?" She was surprised. The pizza was more than enough.

"No, I told you I was bringing dinner. That's not the surprise."

"So this is the thing worth killing me over if you told me prior to bringing it?"

"Absolutely." He reached into his backpack and pulled out a floppy, book-sized brown bag and handed it to her. She could feel hundreds of small discs inside.

"M&M's?" she read. When he didn't answer, she looked up to see him watching her with a stunned look. "What?" she asked.

"You don't know what M&M's are?"

Rapunzel looked back down at the package. "Should I?"

"Oh, my friend," Fane moaned. "You have been far too sheltered." He smacked a hand on the counter, startling her. "I've decided from now on, it's my privilege—nay, my *duty*," he punched the air with one finger lifted, "to introduce you to all of the wonders of life that you've been missing."

Rapunzel laughed. "Well, based on the pizza, I can hardly wait."

Fane took the package from her and tore a corner open. "This candy serves a double purpose. Not only are they delicious . . ." He took one of the candies and held it to her mouth. She opened and he popped it in. "They also make excellent poker chips."

Rapunzel chewed the chocolate candy and grinned at him.

"Like them?" he asked.

"Oh, yes," she said, holding out a hand for more. He dumped a small amount of the brightly colored discs into her hand but refused to give her more, claiming they needed them all for poker. They sat at the table and he explained the value of the different colors of candy—which fascinated her with how pretty they were—along with the rules of poker and how to bet.

Rapunzel found she had a knack for the game, and with mounting pleasure, she watched Fane become more and more frustrated. After an hour, he threw down his cards.

"Uncle!" he exclaimed.

"Uncle?" Rapunzel repeated.

"It means I give up. Are you sure you've never played this game before?"

"Never," she confirmed.

"Wait," he said, "where are all your winnings?"

Rapunzel glanced down at her relatively small pile of the brightly colored candy. "I ate them," she said.

"In that case I win," Fane declared.

"No, you didn't. I won and you know it."

"Look at my pile compared to yours." He indicated his pile, decidedly larger than hers.

Rapunzel picked up three more candies and tossed

them into her mouth. "I won," she stated. "And I ate my winnings. So really, I won twice."

Fane shook his head at her, scratching absently at his goatee. "You're kind of stubborn, huh?"

She shrugged. She hadn't ever had anything to be stubborn about before, had *never* argued with her mother. But she genuinely enjoyed arguing with Fane.

He sighed deeply, stood, and walked to his backpack. "I brought you one more thing."

Excited, she jumped up and hurried over to him.

"But I don't know if I should give it to you. I mean, unless you're willing to concede my victory."

"Never," she said, leaning intently toward him against the counter.

He sighed again, this time dramatically. "Fine. You win. Besides, this is just as much for me as for you. Maybe more so."

Rapunzel stood up straight, anticipation doubled. Fane pulled a screwdriver out of his backpack and held it up triumphantly.

"Voilà!" he exclaimed.

Rapunzel shook her head. "I don't get it."

"This is our key, Rapunzel. This is how we get out of this room and explore the house."

Rapunzel's eyes flew to the door, as if someone might be standing there listening. Her heart pounded wildly in her chest. She hadn't ever thought to step outside the doorway. Of course she also hadn't ever thought to have anyone besides her mother in her rooms. She returned her gaze to Fane's eager, questioning look. Did she dare?

chapter
11

"What about Cook?" Rapunzel asked.

"We'll be quiet," Fane said. He stilled next to the doorknob, looking at her. "Wait, is this dangerous for you, Rapunzel? Do you think you might get sick by going out there? Because it's not worth that."

Rapunzel hadn't even thought of that. She remembered the mask. "Hold on," she said. She hurried into the kitchen and pulled it from the drawer she stored it in. She walked back to Fane and held it out to him. He grinned.

"Brilliant." He took it from her, placing it over her mouth and nose, hooking the elastics behind her ears, and pressing the wire along the upper edge to conform to the shape of her nose and cheeks. "There, now you look—"

"Yes, hot, I know," she said, voice muffled, eyes rolling.

Fane smiled. "I was going to say like a doctor, but if you think you look hot, then ya know, who am I to argue?" he teased and then added, "A *hot* doctor."

Rapunzel's face suffused with heat. Thankfully the mask covered a good portion of her cheeks, hiding her discomfiture.

"Ready?" he asked. She nodded, and he turned to the knob. After a short time, he tugged the knob, pulling it out. Rapunzel gasped as he pushed the opposite side out, the knob falling with a quiet *thunk* on the opposite side. There was a small hole where the handle had been. He stuck a finger in, pushed something, and the door clicked open. He glanced back at her and, holding her gaze, pulled the door open.

Panic crawled up Rapunzel's throat as she gazed at the gaping hole where her door should be. Beyond the opening was a carpeted hallway with a wall on the opposite side, which explained the lack of noise when the handle fell. Ambient light came from an unknown source. Fane stuck his head out the door, and she felt the overwhelming need to pull him back inside. He glanced both ways and turned back to Rapunzel with a wide grin.

If it hadn't been for that grin, she would never have had the courage to grasp his proffered hand. She held on tightly as he stepped stealthily across the threshold. She stopped short before taking the same step, and he glanced back with a question on his face. She took a deep breath, pulling all of the courage she could find, exhaled, and stepped out of her room for the first time in her life.

Fane squeezed her hand twice, as if he understood what it took. He turned and moved down the hallway, Rapunzel following, trembling wildly. When they came to the end, there were stairs going up and down. He listened for a minute then turned back.

"Up or down?" he asked.

Rapunzel knew that down was likely Cook, so she said, "Up."

Disappointment lined Fane's face, but he ascended anyway. Going up with hands held was awkward, but Rapunzel doubted she could continue without holding on to him. The stairs spiraled upward, the shadows deepening as they climbed. Upon reaching the top, they faced a heavy wooden door. Fane grasped the handle, which turned easily enough beneath his grip, but the door didn't budge. He was forced to let go of her hand in order to push with his shoulder. He gave several shoves before stopping.

"Won't open," he stated the obvious. He pulled his phone out of his pocket, pushing a button to light it up. With the small amount of light they could see the lock that bolted from the opposite side. "Well, I don't think my 'key' is going to open this one. I guess we go down." He pushed past her, grasping her hand once again as they descended.

They passed her open doorway, and Rapunzel had a momentary urge to go inside and close the door, to regain a feeling of safety. Instead, she continued to follow Fane down the next flight of winding stairs. The landing opened into a larger hallway that led from a small hallway similar to the one across from Rapunzel's rooms. Light streamed up the stairs from the lower floor, so Fane led her down the wide hallway, going slowly and listening carefully.

They eventually came to a T, the hallway continuing to the left and right. What lay ahead stunned Rapunzel. The railing at the head of the T overlooked a large room that began on the floor below them and soared a dozen feet above where they stood. The walls were painted with some kind of pattern that gave them depth, almost made them feel alive. A rock fireplace ran the height of the room. Overstuffed couches and chairs and elegant tables and lamps filled the floor space.

Filled bookcases lined the wall on either side of the fireplace. The wall to the right was mostly made up of six windows that must have been fifteen feet tall altogether.

"Wow," Fane breathed, keeping his voice to a whisper. "It's really beautiful, but it's so . . . *normal.*"

Rapunzel looked at him. "Should it be different?"

He looked away, as if searching for words. "Well, no, it's just . . ." He shook his head. "No, it just doesn't look how I expected. C'mon." He tugged her hand, and they continued down the hallway, passing the wide, elegantly tapered stairway leading down to the big room. Soon they were enclosed in another hallway, which had rows of doors on each side. Six to the left, and six to the right. Fane led her to the first door and placed his ear against it before twisting the knob and slowly opening the door.

The room was empty. The walls were painted and the floor carpeted, but other than the window there was nothing to break the monotony of the stark whiteness. They soon discovered that all twelve rooms were identical in that way.

"Is *that* normal, to have empty rooms like that?" Rapunzel asked, indicating the twelve rooms.

"Uh . . . I'm not sure. In a house this size, maybe." His words were hesitant, and she felt he avoided a straightforward answer.

They exited the last room and rounded a corner in the hallway. Another descending stairway sat in front of them. Fane took her hand and led her toward the stairs. As they began their descent, they heard a voice and froze. The blood drained from Rapunzel's face, fear trilling along her spine.

"Tell me about it," a woman's voice came to them. "But I'm planning the day off tomorrow." Pause. "Yeah, I know, but how is she going to know I'm not here? The kid has been taking care of herself, making her own food. Why do I need to just sit here all day, every day?" Pause. "She'll call at 6:00 a.m. as usual, then I'll go. I can be to Mom's by eight." Pause. "No, I just have to forward the phones to my cell so that I can answer when she calls in the evening. I won't need to worry about being back until Monday." Pause. "Nothing's going to happen. I'll set the alarm." Pause. "Okay, sounds good. I'll see you tomorrow, then. Love you."

They heard her move around, and her shadow fell across the light at the bottom of the stairs. Rapunzel and Fane darted back up the stairs, Rapunzel's heart pounding so loudly that she was sure the woman could hear it. Once they were down the hallway and on their way back up the winding staircase, Fane turned to her with humor in his eyes.

"That was close," he said, laughing. Rapunzel stared at him. How could he be so casual? She felt as if she would choke on the panic suffusing her. When they returned to her rooms, she hurried inside, relief flowing through her.

"I'll put this back together," he said, picking up the handle and screwdriver. He stepped outside while Rapunzel took some calming breaths. "Hey, Rapunzel?"

Fane called a moment later, confusion lacing his voice.

"Yes?" she answered through the mask she still wore.

"You might wanna see this."

Reluctantly she moved to where he kneeled in the hallway. She stepped outside the room and peered around the doorway, following his gaze. He fingered a dangling hook-looking mechanism and looked at her with worry.

"What is it?" she asked.

"A latch."

"A what?"

"A lock."

"Oh." She couldn't figure out why a lock had him worried. They'd known the door was locked.

"It's on the *outside*," he emphasized. She shrugged, unconcerned. "Rapunzel, this lock was put here to lock you *in*. As in, you couldn't possibly get out even if you had a key. You could only get out if someone let you out. Why would you need to be locked in?"

Rapunzel's eyes returned to the lock as her mind processed his words. He was right. Why would she need to be locked in, any more than she already was with the handle? "I don't know," she muttered, returning to her room.

"Luckily it was not hooked, or we would never have gotten out of the room."

Fane quickly reassembled the handle, leaving it unlocked. He came to where she sat at the counter, her mind going over that lock. There was something just so . . . *wrong* about it. She pulled the mask off, crumpling it beneath her hand.

"That was a blast," Fane said as he sat next to her,

grabbing an apple from the bowl. She stood and moved to the fridge, getting another out, and replacing it. Fane grunted and she looked at him. "Why do you do—" He stopped when he noticed the look on her face. "Are you okay?"

She gave him a halfhearted smile. "Oh, yes, I'm fine. Just thinking about those empty rooms," she lied.

He shrugged. "Yeah, kind of weird. But considering how much of the house we didn't see, I'm sure that there are plenty of *non*-empty rooms."

"How much of the house didn't we see?" she asked, suddenly feeling like she was adrift in an ocean. She thought she'd known her world but was just finding that there were things she had no idea about.

"A lot," he emphasized. "But, if we get started early tomorrow, we can probably see a lot more."

"Early tomorrow?" she repeated.

"Well, yeah," he said around a bite of apple. "You heard the woman downstairs. She's leaving in the morning and won't be back until Monday."

"But what about the other workers?"

"Well, I know for sure that the construction guys don't work on Sunday."

"How do you know that?" she asked, setting the plate of remaining cookies in front of him as he finished his apple. He grinned in gratitude, picking one up and taking a huge bite.

"Mmm, so good," he moaned. "Anyway, I know because *everyone* knows that. They work six days a week." His eyes flew to hers, as if he'd revealed too much.

Rapunzel shrugged. That sounded about right to work six days and have a day off. Right?

They played another round of poker, this time using Skittles that Fane brought. Rapunzel enjoyed them, though not as much as the M&M's, so when they finished she still had a respectable pile. He showed her another card game called Rummy. Finally, he told her he had to go.

"So, should I come back tomorrow?" he asked.

"Yes, definitely," she said, excited at the thought of spending another day with him.

"I'll come back in the morning, if you want, so we can have the whole day to explore the house."

The thought of more exploration brought a thrill of fear to her stomach. Then she thought of the lock on the other side of her door and decided she wanted nothing more than to discover this home she lived in—but really didn't live in. She hoped he was right that Cook would be gone the whole day.

"Sure," she said. "I'm up early, so come when you want."

"Don't eat breakfast," he said. "I'm going to introduce you to the wonders of an Egg McMuffin."

If it was anything like the foods he'd brought so far, she was more than happy to discover whatever else he wanted to bring.

As he put a leg over the ledge, he turned back and took her hand in his, tugging her closer.

"Thanks, Rapunzel. I had a good time today." He leaned forward and placed a soft kiss on her cheek. Heat flooded her cheeks, and she was grateful for the semi-darkness of the alcove.

She watched him descend safely, watching until he waved before disappearing around the corner. She walked back into the living area, holding a hand over her cheek as if she could trap the feel of his kiss there. She glanced toward the door that suddenly felt ominous to her. She wanted to question her mother about it, but how could she without giving away her actions today?

She sighed and went to her room, fingering the braid out of her hair as she thought about the day spent with her hand enclosed by Fane's. She grinned happily, fell back on her bed, and, for the first time in her life, went to sleep in her day clothes.

chapter

12

Rapunzel rose earlier than usual the next morning, unable to sleep any longer with the excitement of having Fane come once again. She showered, washing her hair that took a good amount of time. Without having time to dry it, she braided her hair while wet. She still waited for Fane to arrive for over a restless hour.

Finally he rounded the corner of the house. He hurried to the trellis and began climbing. The bulk of his backpack was larger than it had been the previous day. She smiled in anticipation, wondering what he'd brought today. As he neared the top, he looked up at her and grinned. A loud crack reverberated in the morning air. With horror, she watched as the trellis began to sag away from the wall. A squeak escaped her as she caught sight of his fear-filled eyes. She looked around her for something to help him with. At the sound of a second crack, she panicked and threw the end of her braid out the window toward him.

"Grab on!" she yelled. He hesitated for a nanosecond until the trellis tipped precariously away from the wall. He quickly grabbed the thick rope her braid provided and used his weight to leverage the trellis back against the wall. He tugged against her hair, and she grabbed it near the base of her skull with her hands to relieve some of the pressure. Using her hair as the rope she proffered, he scrambled up the wall and over the ledge, falling to the floor with Rapunzel beneath him.

He stared at her, his face inches from hers. They both breathed heavily in the aftermath of his near fall. Suddenly, he wrapped his arms around her and hugged her tightly against him. "Thank you," he whispered in her ear before standing, pulling her up with him.

Rapunzel felt shaky as relief washed through her. She laughed, unable to stop the sound. Fane stared at her before laughing along. He reached out and ran a hand down her braid. She tipped her head to watch the gesture before returning her gaze to him.

"Seriously, thank you," he said earnestly. "You saved my life."

"Oh, well . . ." She didn't know how to respond, glancing down shyly.

He put his hand against her cheek, caressing his thumb along her jaw. Her heart beat staccato, and she felt heat rising in her cheeks as it always seemed to do when he was near.

"Did you remember breakfast?" she asked with a tremor, meaning it to come out sounding nonchalant.

"How could I forget?" He grinned and, thankful he was back to his usual self, she led the way to the kitchen.

The breakfast sandwiches they ate, which had to be heated a little in the microwave, were yet another item

Rapunzel savored. It did give her a bit of a bellyache, but she'd never admit it to Fane. She decided her next grocery list would include English muffins, sausage, cheese, and eggs so she could make her own version.

"I have to admit," Fane said around a mouthful of the breakfast sandwich, "I never thought my life would be saved by someone's *hair*. That's definitely a new one for the books."

Rapunzel fingered her thick braid. "I didn't have anything else to throw to you. I panicked."

"Well, thank *heavens* for your particular way of panicking. Seriously. That was some quick thinking. I was panicking as well, but in a completely different way. Still, never would have thought to yell, 'Rapunzel, throw down your hair.'"

Rapunzel laughed at the image of him calling that. Had he done so, she probably wouldn't have thrown her braid out just for the sheer ridiculousness of the request.

"Ready to explore some more?" Fane asked when they finished and cleaned up.

"Yes, let's go," she said, walking to the door and opening it.

"Where's your mask?" he asked.

"I'm not wearing it today." When he lifted an eyebrow at her, she shrugged. "The air out there has to be the same as in here, right? I believe I'll be safe enough."

Fane wavered but finally followed her out the door. Rapunzel felt confident until they came to the same set of stairs where they'd heard the voice the day before. Fane recognized her hesitancy.

"It's okay. Her car is gone."

"Oh," Rapunzel said. She still felt a little frightened at the thought of going into this portion of the house. Fane took her hand in his as he continued down the stairs, and she felt some of her confidence return.

At the bottom of the stairs they turned left into a large kitchen. The large gleaming appliances, including *two* ovens, wide counter spaces, a fridge that was double the size of hers, and a six-paned window that allowed the brightness of the early-morning sun to wash the room in light awed Rapunzel.

"Cool," Fane said, running a hand across the granite counter. Rapunzel was afraid to do the same. She just clutched Fane's hand tighter.

They discovered a fully stocked pantry as large as Rapunzel's main living area. A door at the other end of the room opened to a high-ceilinged dining room with a long, elegant, dark wood table large enough to seat twenty people, but only had six chairs clustered at one end. Red brocade wallpaper covered the walls and a red and black oriental rug nearly covered the entire wood floor. A chandelier above the table dripped crystal that matched the sconces above the sideboard. An overly large bouquet of dried flowers dominated the center of the table.

From there they entered the foyer. Sunlight filtered through a tall wooden door with patterned stained glass windowpanes that caused panic to fill her belly again. On the opposite side of that door was the outside world that she'd only ever seen from her window high in her tower. She took one step toward the door as if to step into the world, but Fane tugged her lightly back. He pointed to the little white box affixed to the wall next to the door that flashed a red light.

"Alarm," he said. "If you open the door, it'll go off."

Rapunzel nodded, disappointed that she couldn't follow her instinct. A wide set of stairs led up to a landing, where the stairs then split in opposite directions. Rapunzel thought they might go up, but instead Fane led her around the base of the stairs into a darker area. He opened a narrow door. A set of stairs that descended beneath the others. As they went down, the house changed.

It was darker, the little light available coming from both the upstairs and small windows tucked up against the ceiling in the rooms that they passed, all of them with cement walls and floors, dust and cobwebs evidence of their disuse. Rapunzel shivered, not completely due to the chill pervading this area of the house.

They came across a set of wooden steps that led up. By mutual silent consent they followed them, only to find that they ended at a cement wall. There was no door, no hallway, just a solid wall.

"Huh," Fane said, not sounding all that surprised. The discovery stunned Rapunzel. What was the point of the stairway?

They descended, discovering several other sets of stairs, both ascending and descending that ended in the same manner, or sometimes at a door that opened to a wall. The more they found, the more the sick feeling in the pit of Rapunzel's stomach increased. Finally they found a set of stairs opening onto a narrow walkway. Fane pulled his phone out to light the path in the dark. Rapunzel could feel the soft, stringy pieces of webs sticking to her face and arms and, shivering, tried to push the thought of it from her mind. The path went on for some ways, and Fane asked her if she thought they should turn around.

"Maybe," she said. "What do you think?"

He thought for a moment then said, "Let's go a little farther and see if we find a way out. If not, we go back."

Rapunzel agreed and they soon came to a door. Fane put his shoulder against it and gave it a couple of hard hits. It flew open, spilling him into a room like the others that had light coming in through their dingy windows.

"Stairs," he said, pointing to the opposite side of the room. They went up, ending in a trap door above their heads. Fane pushed it open and stepped up and out of the hole. He looked around before turning to lean down and offer his hands to Rapunzel. She placed her hands in his, and he pulled her up and out into a brightness that hurt her eyes.

"What is this?" she breathed, looking around in awe at the room made of glass. Plants and flowers grew everywhere, even trees. Rapunzel reached out and reverently brushed her fingers over the pink rose nearest her. She took a deep breath, breathing in the fresh smells, a mixture of scents she'd never experienced.

"A green house, or nursery," Fane told her. "People use these to grow plants where they can bloom year round. That way they won't die in the winter."

Rapunzel walked down the aisle, wonder lighting her eyes. Fane dropped the trap door, causing her to flinch and look back. "Well, I guess I know how I can get out of the house tonight without risking my neck on the trellis that will probably fall when I climb on it."

Rapunzel hadn't even thought of that. She was just so glad he'd made it in safely it hadn't occurred to her to figure out how he could get back out. He jogged the short distance to catch up to her. He took her hand once again, and though she didn't need it for security, she was glad of the feel of his hand firmly in hers. This was all so surreal she half believed it was a dream, and welcomed something real and solid to hold onto.

Fane named many of the plants for her. Some of them she was familiar with, others she'd never even heard of. They soon discovered little wooden picks at the base of each plant labeling those neither of them knew. When they came upon an orange tree, Rapunzel breathed in the clean citrus scent with pleasure.

"This is all so amazing," Rapunzel said, rubbing a maple leaf between her fingers. "I haven't ever touched a live plant before."

"You don't ever have flowers or plants in your room?"

"No. Mother says they can bring in unwanted germs."

Fane looked at her with horror, his eyes encompassing the plants that surrounded them. "Maybe we should get out of here," he said.

"No way!" Rapunzel laughed. "Whatever happens, this is *worth* it." She turned a dazzling smile on Fane, and he returned it though the worry didn't completely fade from his eyes.

They spent more time exploring the plants until they came to the wide double doors at the end of the building. Fane ran his fingers around the edges of the door. "Huh," he said. "No alarm here." He glanced at Rapunzel. "Your mom must be unaware of the tunnel that leads from the house out here."

Rapunzel gazed out on the lush green lawn on the opposite side of the glass. She turned her head toward Fane. "I want to touch the grass," she said.

Fane shook his head. "I don't think that's a good idea, Rapunzel. I mean, we're already taking a chance with all the places we've been today."

"Fane," she said, turning to fully face him. "I've spent my entire life inside my rooms. My entire world consists of that small amount of space. A few years ago I opened the window, even though I'd been warned it could harm me. But I had looked out for so long that the temptation was too much." She shrugged and took a step closer to him, taking both his hands, trying to convey her feeling. "It didn't harm me at all. And it gave me something to look forward to. It's probably ridiculous to you that I would look forward to something as simple as opening a window, but it became very important to me." She took a deep breath and blew it out. "But the grass." She turned her head and looked out at the green expanse. "The grass has always been out of reach. I've spent a lot of time wondering about it, the smell of it, the feel of it, even the taste of it." She turned her eyes back on him. "*Please.*"

"Okay. We'll go out but only on one condition," he said. "You've gotta promise not to eat the grass. It'll *definitely* make you sick."

Rapunzel readily nodded, a smile lighting her face.

"All right, then," Fane said, giving her hands a little shake. "Let's go meet the grass."

chapter

13

"Are you getting hungry?"

Fane's question pulled Rapunzel from her fascination with the grass where she was lying, reveling in the soft, prickly feel of it beneath her, smelling the clean scent and basking in the warm sun that felt as if it cocooned her.

"Are *you* hungry?" she asked.

"Of course I am. I'm a teenage guy." He laughed. Rapunzel wasn't sure what he meant by his comment, but laughed anyway. The thought of the long trek back through the dim, dirty cellar made her cringe. That, and the thought of leaving the amazing grass and sunshine. She'd felt the sun on her face and arms before, but not all over her body like this. And the grass . . . it felt just as she'd imagined it would and smelled even better.

"Let's go eat, then," she said, breathing in one last lungful of the glorious lawn before standing.

Walking through the greenhouse, Rapunzel took deep breaths, trying to memorize the smell. They went back down into what Fane laughingly called "the dungeon." The return trip was much shorter, and in no time they were back to her rooms. They ate ham sandwiches—Rapunzel one, Fane three.

After lunch they went down the hall in the opposite direction, Fane carrying a heavy flashlight he had stored in his backpack and discovered an unlocked door that led to the lower floors of the tower. They crept through dark, cold, stone-walled rooms filled with dust and cobwebs. On the bottom level, they discovered a dark room with a door that opened to the outside on the opposite side of the room.

"I don't think this one will trip the alarm," Fane said, after running his fingers around the perimeter of the door.

"Why's that?" Rapunzel asked, shivering in the dank cold that penetrated her skin and seeped into her bones.

"No connections, no wires—nothing but a wood frame."

He twisted the handle and pulled. They flinched as the door hinges creaked and breathed a sigh of relief when no alarm sounded. Sunlight flooded the room and Rapunzel closed her eyes, soaking up the heat. She opened her eyes and glanced at Fane, only to see him staring over her into the tower room with a look of horror on his face. As she began to turn to see what caused his reaction he quickly grabbed her, holding her in place.

"I don't think you should look, Rapunzel."

She stared at him, trying to read his face. Finally she shook her head. "I need to look, Fane. This is my home, where I live. It can't be any stranger than what we've already seen, right?" She smiled, but Fane didn't return her smile. That strengthened her resolve to look.

Taking a breath for courage, she turned. The room was painted entirely black. A large, white, painted six-point star dominated the floor. Six repeating designs were painted on the walls in equal spacing. Sixes were hand drawn with chalk on almost every remaining available space, sometimes drawn as a number, sometimes the Roman numeral, and sometimes spelled out.

A blackened space in the center of the star on the floor indicated a fire had been burned there at some point. Rapunzel thought about what that meant, a fire burning below her on a wooden floor, she locked in her room with no escape. She looked up and saw the smoke marks on the ceiling.

The room felt even colder now that she could see it. The black walls and overabundance of sixes were overwhelming. A shiver ran through her, and Fane stepped closer. Looking at him, she could see it made him uncomfortable as well.

"We should get out of here," he said.

Rapunzel nodded her agreement, unable to speak. Her throat tightened with the bad feeling the room gave her. She waited for Fane to lock the door, then grasped his hand tightly as they speedily made their way back through the room. She felt as if shadows chased after them. They went up the stairs, Fane insisting she go ahead of him. Once back in the warmth of the hallway, Rapunzel shivered again, this time having nothing to do with being cold.

"I think we've explored enough for today," Fane said. "Should we go back to your room?"

Rapunzel didn't answer but led the way. Once there, Fane closed the door firmly behind them. Rapunzel glanced at her floor, picturing the room with a smoke-stained ceiling beneath her own made her feel insecure.

"Fane," she said, turning to see he was also staring at the floor. He glanced up at her voice. "The door to outside, was it locked?"

"Yes, it had a bolt." He shrugged. "That doesn't mean someone else hasn't been sneaking in and using the room."

Rapunzel shuddered at the thought of strangers sneaking into her home, setting fires two floors below. "There's no way I can tell my mother about it without her knowing I've been out."

"Do you think she'd be that upset you were out of your room?" Fane sounded a bit incredulous.

Rapunzel thought about it. It did seem odd that she'd be in trouble for leaving her rooms to walk around in her own home. And yet, something told her that the little freedom she'd obtained would be immediately taken away if Gothel knew what she'd done.

"Yes, I do. I can't tell her. She would wonder how I'd even gotten out of my room."

"Yeah, there aren't too many moms who would be happy their daughter has been sneaking a boy into her room."

Rapunzel didn't know if that was true or not. It was true for her because of her SCIDs, but she had no idea what was normal for healthy girls. She supposed she'd have to assume it was true if Fane said so.

He pulled a laptop out of his backpack. "I brought this

so I can show you how to use Skype," he said. "Oh, wait, I forgot you said the camera was broken. So I guess there's no point in setting it up."

Rapunzel still wasn't sure it was a good idea, but the thought of not being able to *see* Fane when they spoke on the Internet was enough to make her willing to at least try it.

"Um, well, actually . . . it's not broken." He looked at her, brow lifted, and she shrugged. "I didn't know you. I wasn't sure I could trust you. So I said it was broken so I didn't have to send a picture."

Fane laughed. "You're a quick thinker."

"You're not mad?"

"No. That was smart of you. Kinda like giving a stranger your phone number with one number off."

She scrunched her brows in confusion. Did people do that?

"Never mind." He grinned. "C'mon, let's set it up."

He loaded the program on her computer, linked their accounts, and showed her how to work it. She laughed when his face first came up on her screen from where he sat in the other room. His image was a bit jerky, and though she could hear his words clearly, his image sometimes froze for a second or two before catching up. Still, she thought it wondrous and was excited to talk to him using it.

He handed her a bag full of bite-sized candy bars, none of which she'd ever tasted—or even heard of for that matter. She tried one of each kind, her stomach grumbling at the chocolate overload.

"Take it easy," Fane said. "They're not going anywhere. You can save them and eat them later. You don't have to eat them all at once."

Rapunzel looked at the bag of candy, wondering how she could keep it. She couldn't explain it to her mother. She looked around, trying to spy somewhere she could safely hide such a treasure.

"One more treat," he said. "Sorry."

"Sorry? For what?"

"No," he said, grinning. He pulled a square box out of his bag, with the word "Sorry" printed in large letters across the top. "It's a game."

"Why is it called Sorry?" she asked.

"Because the game is all about cruelty and vengeance, so you end up saying sorry a lot."

Rapunzel was intrigued. Unfortunately she wasn't as proficient at this game as with poker, but she had fun—even if he beat her three times in a row.

She made him dinner. Contentment at having him here in her rooms while she did something for him filled her.

"I wish I could take you out," he said. "You know, to a real restaurant, where they cook for you."

"I can have my food cooked for me anytime I want," she said. "I prefer to cook myself."

"It's not so much about the food being cooked for you," he said, walking into the kitchen and leaning against the counter, watching while she cooked the stir-fry in her wok. "It's more about the people, the ambiance. It's about being out in public, seeing other people."

Rapunzel smiled at him. "Now *that* part sounds wonderful."

After they ate, they watched a couple of movies on Fane's laptop while relaxing on the couch, a delight that felt somehow devious. Fane popped her some microwave popcorn.

"If you keep coming over, I'm going to weigh five hundred pounds," Rapunzel said, tossing another greasy, delicious handful of the puffs into her mouth.

"That's such a girl thing to say," Fane said, elbowing her lightly as he dug into the popcorn himself.

"Well, I better go," Fane said later after the second movie. "If I'm not home by ten with school tomorrow my mom will ground me for sure."

Rapunzel dreaded him going, knowing she would be completely alone in the house. She wasn't sure why it bothered her since she never knew if anyone was here or not. She thought of the black room two floors below her and shuddered.

"Should I walk you down?" she asked.

"No," he said. "I've got the flashlight, so I can find my way in the dark."

Rapunzel was a little disappointed that he didn't want her to walk with him and immensely relieved that she wouldn't have to make the return trip alone. She had a feeling that without Fane by her side, her courage would fail.

"Be careful," she admonished as he stepped away from her room.

"Scouts honor," he said, holding two fingers up. The

words confused Rapunzel but she could sense the promise in them. She closed the door once he disappeared from view and ran to the window. Only then did she realize she wouldn't be able to see him leave from this side of the house. Still, she waited.

Eventually he came around the corner, his face turned toward her window. When he caught sight of her there, he waved, and she released a breath of relief, waving back. She closed the window and went to her computer. She pulled up her Facebook page and sent him a message.

> Thank you, Fane, for spending the day with me. I haven't ever enjoyed a day so much. I had fun with you. And, let's face it, the chocolate helped sway my opinion of you to the definite positive.

She shut the computer down and went to bed. Once tucked under her covers, she closed her eyes, wrapping her arms around her middle, pretending it was Fane's arms once again as it had been when he fell through the window. For the second night in a row, she fell asleep with a smile on her face.

chapter

✳ 14 ✳

That night, she dreamt.

She lay in a field of grass, green as far as the eye could see, the only thing breaking up the bright color were dots of pink roses, each one sprouting from the grass on a single stem. The sun warmed her skin, lighting her. As she inhaled the scents that had become dear to her in such a brief time, she laughed aloud in pure joy.

She heard him call her name. She pushed to her knees as she watched him jog across the emerald expanse. It occurred to her that if she stood, he might hug her again.

She placed her hands against the lush grass to do just that but stopped at the feeling beneath her hands. She looked down; the grass disappeared, replaced by a soft green blanket decorated with pink rosebuds. Her hands had formed into those of an infant. Unable to manage standing, she turned her head to search for him. Wooden slats replaced the expanse of lawn, and beyond that, the green color morphed into light pink walls. He was gone.

Confused, she rolled onto her back. Above her head a baby's mobile twisted, playing a song she could almost hear, but not quite. A pair of hands reached for her. Startled, she glanced beyond them to see a woman with soft blonde hair, her features indiscernible. She reached for the woman, wanting nothing more than to be held by her when suddenly everything vanished. She was lying on a hard wooden floor, staring up at a blackened circle on the wooden ceiling above.

Terror gripped her, and she abruptly sat up, grown again. The room's ghostly darkness and walls strewn with drawn sixes surrounded her. She lay, suffocating, centered on the black star splayed across the cold floor. She couldn't take her eyes off the smoldered circle above her head. A low murmur drew her attention. Six figures dressed in black capes pulled low over their heads swayed around the perimeter of the star, chanting in low tones.

Horror filled her, and she quickly stood, looking for the door. The figures all stood also, slowly, never breaking from their chant. She took a step forward, and the walls moved closer. She stopped, frightened by the strange occurrence. A second step brought the walls closer yet again, and a third. She didn't take a fourth. Her fear intensified with each breath.

"Mommy," she murmured. At her word, one of the figures stepped from the circle toward her. She tried to back away but was unable, as if a wall were at her back. The figure reached up to push the hood from its head. As the dark hair, eyes, and familiar face emerged, she opened her mouth and—

Rapunzel's scream woke her up. She was sitting up in her bed, tears streaming down her face, her chest heaving. Fear still squeezed her throat in spite of the fact that she knew she was safe in her room, in her bed. She pushed the covers back and stumbled to the bathroom, flipping the switch and flooding the room with welcome light.

She wet a washcloth and wiped her face with the cool cloth. Glancing at herself in the mirror, she laughed shakily. What a strange dream. She tried to think of the part that had woken her up, but it was lost. She remembered the walls closing in, though she was sure something had come after, something terrible.

That part was new, the part with the black room, but there was no doubt why it had infused itself into her dream. The beginning was also different and also easy to see why she had dreamed it. The middle part however, with her as an infant, was a dream she'd had repeatedly as a child. She didn't know how many nights she had woken up crying, though from a feeling of loss rather than the terror this new version inspired. It always ended with the woman reaching for her and her desire to be held by the woman. She hadn't had the dream for several years now.

She snapped the light off as she exited her bathroom, then quickly turned it back on when the darkness surrounded her. She decided it wouldn't hurt to sleep with it on for one night.

chapter
15

Fane came to Rapunzel's every day as soon as the workers left, staying for dinner, until the day before she expected her mother to come home. Rapunzel knew he wanted to explore the house more, could sense his restlessness, but every time she thought of it, thought of the room beneath her—of discovering more unsettling secrets—she couldn't bring herself to leave the room.

He'd discovered a back hallway that brought him up to her rooms without passing through the kitchen or family room area where Cook always seemed to be. Still, Rapunzel worried about him each time he came and left.

He brought a couple different games for them to play. Monopoly was one of her favorites, aside from poker. She was saddened by the thought of their meetings ending. Her mother had never gone out of town before so she had no reason to believe she would ever do so again.

"I guess tomorrow we go back to conversations on Facebook," she said to him as they ate her homemade chicken burritos.

"Not Facebook," he said. "Skype."

"Oh, yeah." She smiled. "I guess that's better. At least it will feel like we're kind of together." She took another bite, watching him as he devoured his own. "Aren't your friends upset you've been spending all your time here?" He'd told her about some of them.

He shrugged, looking uncomfortable. "I didn't tell them I was here."

Rapunzel knew that, because he'd promised not to tell. "Where do they think you've been?"

He glanced at her and quickly away. He cleared his throat and shifted in his chair. "Don't be mad, okay?" he said.

Rapunzel shook her head. "I won't be."

He lifted the lemonade to his mouth as if to take a drink, then sighed and set it back down without doing so. "I told them I'd met this hot girl who lived nearby, but they didn't know her since she doesn't go to our school."

"Okay," she said.

He just stared at her.

"Well, it's all true—except the 'hot girl' part," she continued.

"You're not mad?"

"Why would I be?" Rapunzel was genuinely confused.

"Because I told them about you."

"You didn't tell them who I am or where I live, right?" He nodded. "So, that's okay."

"Huh." He took another large bite of his burrito. "I think I've been dating girls who are way too high main-tenance." Rapunzel didn't know what he meant by that but didn't ask. He grinned at her. "And just so you know, the 'hot girl' part is true. You're one of the hottest girls I know."

Rapunzel shoved him lightly against his shoulder, laughing, her face heating as it always did when he teased her that way.

When it was nearing time for him to leave, Rapunzel felt a rush of sadness. They stood just inside the closed doorway, the one she wouldn't be leaving again for who knew how long. Suddenly she regretted not spending the time outside the room with Fane. She would have loved to see the greenhouse one more time.

"I'm going to miss . . ." she began, but lost courage and finished with, "beating you at poker."

"I'm not going to miss getting my butt kicked on a regular basis." He laughed. He stepped closer, lifting one hand to brush along her jaw. A shiver ran through her at his touch. "But I am going to miss you."

She swallowed over the lump of fear in her throat and braved the question. "Will you kiss me before you go?"

Fane looked stunned and took a step back from her. Rapunzel read the hesitancy in his eyes. Her heart plummeted, and she dropped her gaze. He tugged her chin back up until she was looking at him.

"It's not that I don't want to. But you . . . I mean, if I . . ." He blew a breath out. "It could make you sick, Rapunzel. It could kill you."

She gave him a tremulous smile. "Maybe," she conceded. "But I also thought it would kill me to be around strangers and to leave my room. It didn't. The thing is, I might never get the chance to see you again, or anyone else for that matter. I don't want to live my entire life wondering."

"Wondering if a kiss can kill you?" he asked.

"Wondering what it feels like," she answered.

Fane shook his head, the movement barely discernible. He stepped forward once again, his eyes locked firmly on hers, asking silently if she was certain. She answered with a tiny nod. His hand came up to her face once again, then the other, until her jaw was sandwiched between them. He leaned forward, never taking his eyes from hers. At the last second, just as he touched his lips to hers, he closed his eyes.

Rapunzel watched, a strange feeling flooding her from the top of her head to the tips of her toes. It was a feeling similar to when she lay on the grass and the sun enveloped her, warming her. She let her eyes drift closed and realized what she'd been missing by keeping them open. Now she could simply *feel*. His thumbs on the edge of her jaw, lightly moving up and down. His fingers wrapped lightly around the sides and back of her neck. His lips moving gently across hers felt unlike anything she could have imagined, soft and warm, the pressure slight but firm. His whiskers tickled her chin.

He slanted his head, urging her to slant her own in the opposite direction with the slightest pressure of his thumbs. The kiss changed, became more demanding. His mouth opened slightly, and she bravely followed suit. The sun-heat became scorching, and with her eyes closed she found the courage to slide her hands around his waist. He took her hands and placed them on his shoulders, placing his own on her waist and pulling her closer. She boldly threaded her fingers into the hair at the nape of his neck.

Rapunzel's pulse beat swiftly in her chest at their closeness. Finally he lifted his mouth from hers, and the loss was immediate. He wrapped his arms tightly about her, burying his face in the crook of her neck. She tightened her embrace, and they stood that way, silently, for several minutes. Peace swathed Rapunzel, something she couldn't remember feeling before.

Fane released her in slow degrees until he was a step away and holding both her hands. He smiled and said, "Wow." Rapunzel nodded, blushing furiously.

"Thank you," she whispered. He brought her hands to his mouth, kissing them as he backed out the door. Rapunzel stood in the hall until he disappeared from sight, twisted the lock on the handle before closing the door, then hurried to the window to wait. He always waved from below. This night was no exception, though tonight he also blew her a kiss. She smiled at the gesture.

After he was gone, she brought her fingers to her lips. She felt changed, renewed. Time would tell if the kiss would make her sick, but she didn't care. If she didn't wake up tomorrow, she'd be happy. She walked into her bedroom and sat at her vanity, staring at her image. She looked the same as always. She touched her lips again and marveled at the remembrance of the kiss, a smile behind her fingers.

The smile fell as she realized she would never be kissed like that again. She'd have the memory for her whole life—something she could think about, dream about.

She'd also have the memory to torment her.

chapter

16

Rapunzel's mother returned on the sixth day as promised. As much as she'd missed her, Rapunzel was almost sorry to see her come because it meant no more visits from Fane.

"Hello," her mother said, breezing into the room. It had been six days, but she didn't move to hug Rapunzel, nor did she say she missed her, which bothered Rapunzel.

"Hi, Mother."

"Was everything okay while I was gone?"

Rapunzel smiled. *Okay* didn't begin to cover it. "Yes, Mother, everything was . . . fine."

"Did you complete your homework?"

"Yes."

"Did you have enough food?"

"Yes."

"Did you brush your hair seventy—"

"Yes, Mother." Rapunzel couldn't keep the exasperation from her tone. "I brushed my hair each night. I brushed my teeth twice a day. I kept my room clean."

Her mother's eyes narrowed at her. "Why the attitude, Rapunzel?"

Rapunzel shook her head. "I'm sorry. I didn't mean it."

Her mother flicked her fingers her way, as if to dismiss her apology. For the first time she wished her mother would pay closer attention. She should delve further to understand why Rapunzel felt frustrated. Couldn't she see the changes that Rapunzel felt inside?

"Mother . . ." Rapunzel began as her mother carried in the food that Rapunzel was sure was prepared by Cook. "Do you think . . . ?"

When she didn't finish her thought, her mother glanced at her irritably. "Complete your sentences, please, Rapunzel."

Rapunzel took a breath. "Do you think, if I wore the mask, I could leave my rooms? Just go into another part of the house?"

Her mother blanched, then flushed red as anger suffused her face. "What are you talking about? Do you think I would risk your life like that? Rapunzel, you know of the prophecy. You know what is to be lost if you don't live."

Rapunzel cowered at her mother's words. She honestly didn't know exactly what would be lost, only that she was the key. She thought about spending the rest of her life inside these walls . . . never being kissed again.

"What if it doesn't hurt me? What if staying inside the house is okay? I just don't like the thought of spending the next fifty or sixty years in this room."

Her mother began pacing, wringing her hands. "You

know that isn't possible. The risk is too high. You can't leave here, Rapunzel. You can't do it."

Had her mother been yelling the words, Rapunzel might have continued pressing it. But the words came in a half-mumbled nervous rush, her mother's wringing hands trembling.

"You wouldn't just endanger me, you'd endanger everything. Do you understand?" Rapunzel didn't think she was talking to her anymore. Her stomach clenched with a different kind of fear. Suddenly her mother whirled toward her and seized her upper arms, pulling her close to her face. "Do you understand? Haven't I done everything for you? Haven't I protected you, kept you safe? I built this tower just for you." A vision of the black room covered in sixes flashed through Rapunzel's mind. "How can you question me now? All of this is for *you*."

She flung Rapunzel away from her and strode to the door, ripping it open. Turning back to Rapunzel, fury lighting her eyes, with a voice low and full of warning, her mother said, "Don't ever ask to leave again, Rapunzel." Rapunzel swallowed and nodded once.

Her mother slammed the door, and Rapunzel dropped to the floor. She wrapped her arms about her knees, burying her face as she rocked back and forth. A nervous trembling shook her body silently. She felt as if she'd just survived an earthquake—not that she knew what one felt like.

After a few minutes, she stood and cleaned up the uneaten dinner. She had no appetite. She sat in front of her computer, wondering if she turned it on if she'd find Fane on the other end. She lifted her hand to try, but stopped, her fingers hovering just above the keyboard. With a sigh she dropped her hand back to her lap. She couldn't tell him what had happened. She wasn't entirely sure herself what had happened. And what could he do, anyway?

She pulled a book from the shelf and sat on the couch. She never opened the cover. Her mind kept spinning through the events and her mother's strange words. She knew of the prophecy—or some of it anyway. It had been drilled into her for as long as she could remember. She'd always been told that she had to stay healthy and never cut her hair. She realized her mother had never said *why* really, other than the fate of the future depended on her, that the world would be destroyed if something happened to her. Her mother said that her disease was part of the proof that she needed to be kept completely safe and kept away from the rest of the world. Now she began to doubt the authenticity of it. After all, she'd survived having someone besides her mother in her rooms and being out of her rooms. Even outdoors.

She'd survived being kissed. She'd *enjoyed* being kissed.

She went into her room, glancing at the clock. Enough time had passed she doubted her mother would come back. She got ready for bed and brushed her hair. She pulled back her covers and climbed into bed. As she did, a thought struck her and she sat up. She glanced toward her bedroom door and the living area beyond.

She walked out of her room slowly, hoping. She approached her door and slowly twisted the handle, her heart pounding in her chest. It turned easily and when she tugged on it, the door opened. Her breath rushed out as she peered around the edge of the door.

She glanced back at the microwave. The time shone bright red in the darkness of the room: 9:56. She looked into the hallway, able to see the edge of light coming from somewhere else. Her mother was probably still up. Others might be up as well, like Cook, and . . . well, whoever else might live in the house. She quietly closed the door and walked into her room.

Instead of climbing back into bed, she pulled her nightgown over her head and dressed once again.

chapter

✴ · 17 · ✴

At midnight she felt safe to leave her rooms. She pushed aside the covers she'd been buried beneath—just in case her mother came back to check on her—and moved to the door. It still opened freely. She thought maybe her mother remembered and came back to lock her in once again. Beyond the door was darkness. She wished Fane had left his flashlight behind. Then she thought of the cell phone her mother hadn't retrieved, remembering how Fane used his to light the way.

Before crossing the threshold, she stopped. Nerves vibrated up her legs and down her arms. Her entire body trembled with the idea of venturing out into the house without Fane by her side. Unsure of the wisdom of her decision, she hesitated. Turned around. Turned toward the open door.

Taking a bracing breath, she moved into the hall, her hand running along the walls to guide her. She didn't dare use the light of the phone here. She only hoped her hands wouldn't leave a mark for her mother to discover. She went toward the tall room, as she thought of it, the one with the tall windows and fireplace. It sat in darkness, some ambient light filtering in from outside. She went down the stairs that took her into the room.

Moving slowly, carefully, so as not to trip over something and bring unwanted attention, she made her way across the room. On the opposite side, she found an opening into what she assumed was another hall. She walked down the hall, keeping her hands on the wall. Suddenly, she bumped into a solid wall in front of her. She moved left, then right, but found no opening. It just ended.

Huh.

She went back up the hall, then back down again, feeling both walls only to discover there were no doors, no openings, no escape from the hall. *Odd.* She braved the light of the phone and discovered it was as she thought—just a hallway with walls. She walked back toward the tall room and froze when she heard a noise.

Her heart pounded so loudly in her ears she barely made out the sounds. Then she realized it was a familiar voice—the same one she and Fane had heard their first night out of her room.

"The crazy old bat is holding one of her séance's again . . . No, I can't yet . . . She was particularly agitated after she was up in that tower . . . Yeah, who knows, some kind of . . ." Her voice faded as she moved further away.

Rapunzel pressed her hand against her chest. She peeked around the corner, but saw no one. Why was Cook walking around this time of night, talking on the phone? Rapunzel waited a few minutes, then crept back to the stairs. Instead of going up, she walked around behind them, finding another hallway as well as a second set of stairs that descended. She glanced down the stairwell, but it ended in inky blackness. Her last trip down a set of stairs didn't end anywhere good, so she bypassed them and continued down the hall.

She came to a closed door and pressed her ear against it. When she heard nothing, she pushed it open and looked inside. It was a bathroom, large but basic. She closed the door and went to the next. A linen closet sat behind that door. A few more doors revealed what appeared to be sparsely decorated guest rooms.

At the end of the hallway was yet another bedroom, but this one was different than the others; larger, though still sparsely furnished. She looked behind her and, assured she was alone, entered the room. She pulled open the closet doors and was immediately assaulted by a familiar smell. She gasped, realizing she stood in her mother's room. But why would her mother provide her such an opulent room and live in one so utilitarian?

She walked over to the bed, reaching out to touch her mother's pillow. Just before making contact, she quickly withdrew her hand. The bed was made perfectly, the sheets and blankets pulled tight, the pillows smooth. She had a feeling that her mother would notice anything out of place, even a small handprint on the pillow.

Suddenly afraid of being in this room, Rapunzel turned to the door to leave when footsteps padded in the hallway. Panicked, she looked around for escape. A window on the opposite side of the room beckoned and she hurried over. She pulled up the sash as the footsteps neared. Looking out, she saw a small balcony. She swung her legs over the sill and pushed the window closed quietly and quickly as she could.

She pressed herself against the outside wall, as if she could be invisible this way. A light turned on in the room. Cold sweat broke across her forehead as she shook with fear. Peeking around the edge of the window, she could see the tall shadow of her mother moving around within. She didn't know how long she stood in place before the light within went off.

She still didn't move for several minutes, paralyzed by the thought of being caught. Finally she peeled away from the wall and leaned over the railing. There were no stairs leading from the balcony, and she was still on the second floor.

She weighed her options. She could sit here all night and hope to sneak back in at dawn without being seen, or she could find a way down. Since the first option seemed the bigger risk, she decided to find her way to the ground. She supposed she could hang from the railing and drop but decided that might end in a broken leg. She looked up. Nothing there either. No trellises adorned the walls here. She was truly stuck.

She pressed herself back against the wall, wondering if she dared try to sneak back in this way. She didn't know how easily her mother woke. She shuddered at the thought of being caught in her mother's room in the middle of the night. Her hand tightened around the cell phone, useless for calling anyone other than her mother.

Except . . .

One day when Fane came to visit her, he showed her how to text. Of course the only person to text was him since no one else knew about her. She pushed a button on the phone and it lit up, bright as a spotlight to her petrified mind. She hunched over the phone to shield the light and began pushing random buttons, trying to remember how he'd done it.

By happenchance she found his last text to her. Now if only she could remember how to send a text to him. Through trial and error she finally discovered what she thought was the right way. She typed in

Fane, it's me, Rapunzel. I need some help.

The message showed on the phone, but she thought it was supposed to disappear. Then she remembered she had to send it. She found the little button below the send command and pushed it. Almost as soon as she did, she wished she could retrieve it. Fane would be asleep, of course. And even if he woke, he could hardly leave his home in the middle of the night to rescue her.

Her phone beeped, the sound loud in the night. She cradled it against her, breathing quickly as she waited to see if it was loud enough to wake her mother. When there was no apparent movement from within, she dared to look at the phone.

What's wrong? Where r u?

Rapunzel took a breath.

On my mother's balcony. Long story.
No way to get down. Any ideas?

On my way.

Rapunzel released the breath she'd been holding. She'd hoped he would come, *known* he would, even though she knew he probably shouldn't. Now she just had to wait.

chapter
18

I t felt like ages—though only fifteen minutes according to the phone—before Fane came. Rapunzel watched him scan the yard, then the upper walls, before spotting her. He crept over to stand beneath her.

"You okay?" he whispered. She barely heard him but nodded. He held up a single finger, then jogged lightly back across the yard.

Soon he was back, lugging a ladder. He carefully tipped it vertical and placed it against the side of the balcony. The aluminum rattled as it settled, and Rapunzel's breath caught as she pushed herself flat against the wall. Fane froze, hands on the sides of the ladder. Rustling came from within the room, as if her mother had stirred, or at least it sounded so to Rapunzel's ears. Long, tense minutes passed while they waited. Finally, Fane grinned up at her, his teeth glowing in the moonlight, and began his slow ascent.

When he reached her, he leaned his forearms casually on the balcony railing. "So, what's a nice girl like you doin' in a place like this?" he asked quietly in some weird accent.

She laughed and quickly slapped a hand across her mouth. She pushed his shoulder lightly.

"Come on," he said, leaning back to give her room to climb over.

"Don't you want to go down first?" she whispered.

"No, I'm going with you to make sure you don't fall."

"What if the ladder falls with us both on it?"

"Good point," he said. "Go slow, though. This isn't the quietest ladder ever invented." He descended and then held the ladder steady while she climbed over the railing. She was terrified as she looked at the ground far beneath her, secure that at least Fane would make sure the ladder was steady. When her feet touched the ground, she breathed a sigh of relief.

Fane pulled her into a hug. "You okay?" he asked.

She wrapped her arms around him tightly, closing her eyes. She nodded against his chest. A bird chirped nearby, startling them. Rapunzel wondered if it was Angel, and why she'd be out at night.

"Let's go," Fane said, releasing her. He carefully pulled the ladder back and eased it down. It clattered as it dropped the last few inches. Fane quickly pushed it and Rapunzel against the house beneath the balcony, flattening himself against her. A light came on above them, brightening as Rapunzel imagined her mother pushing the curtains back to peer outside. She heard the window being raised and imagined her mother leaning over the sill. Pressed against Fane, her head turned to the side, Rapunzel could only hope they were hidden from view.

After a few minutes, the window was shut, and soon

the light went out. But still they stood, Rapunzel pancaked between Fane and the rough stone wall. She became aware of his heartbeat against her ear, the feel of his arms pushed protectively around her, the feel of his heat against the chill. He dropped his head, rubbing his cheek against the top of her head, and she closed her eyes against the wonder of feeling that flooded her.

He moved back, the cold night air frosting her skin. He smiled down at her. "That was close," he whispered. She could only nod, her throat choked with emotion. He leaned down to retrieve the ladder, and she helped him carry it as he led her toward the greenhouse. They laid it on the ground, and Fane tested the doors, which opened easily.

He pulled his phone from his pocket to light the way and led her by the hand through the plants and flowers. Rapunzel regretted hurrying, wishing she could stop and smell them. They went through the dark tunnel beneath the house where she pressed closer to Fane, then up to the main part of the house. Fane slowly opened the door at the top of the stairs, creeping stealthily around the corner to look. He came back and took her by the hand, and they hurried toward her room, stopping at each corner to look first. Once they were in her room with the door closed, Rapunzel sank to the couch.

Fane sat next to her, pulling her hand into his. "So," he began, "is there a reason you were hanging out on a balcony in the middle of the night?"

"I . . . yes . . . no." She squeezed his hand. "I'm sorry for calling you so late. I didn't know what else to do."

Fane smiled. "You can call me anytime, though I admit I was shocked to see your message."

"I'm sorry," she said again.

"Please stop apologizing. I mean it when I say it's fine. I *am* curious how you got there."

Rapunzel sighed, tears pricking her eyes.

"Come here," Fane said, pulling her next to him and putting his arm around her. She relaxed into his embrace.

"My mother came home today. I decided to ask her if she thought I could go out of my rooms."

Fane stiffened. "Did you tell her you'd been out?"

"No." He relaxed at her answer. "She wouldn't even discuss it. I mean, I know she's worried about me, but she wouldn't talk to me about it. She got angry and we fought. She told me never to ask again. It was kind of . . . weird, her reaction."

"So you decided to go anyway?"

"Yeah, I guess so. I don't really know why. I think maybe I just wanted to see if it felt different, with her here, I mean."

"And did it?"

"It was different, but I think it had more to do with not being with you than her being here."

Fane's laughter rumbled beneath her ear. "Nice to know I'm loved," he teased. She smiled. "So. How is it you ended up on her balcony? You said that was her room, right?"

"Yes, it was. I found it while wandering around, and I was curious." She sat up and looked at him. "Before you came, I've never been curious," she said with wonder.

"Why do you think that is? Why haven't I ever wondered what was right outside my door? Or why didn't I wonder if I could survive out there?"

Fane shrugged. "I don't know really. Maybe because this was all you knew. I mean, you've only ever had your mom so why wouldn't you believe everything she said, right?"

Rapunzel shook her head. "I should have questioned at least a few things. I don't know a lot about money, but a house like this has to be a little expensive, right?"

"*Very* expensive," he confirmed.

"So why doesn't she have doctors or something up here trying to figure out how I can live a real life?" She stood, agitated. "Do I have to spend the rest of my life here, locked in these rooms? With nobody else? No friends, no husband, no children. No *life*. Just me and her. What happens when she dies?"

Fane stood and took her hands again. "We'll figure it out."

Rapunzel smiled at him. "You aren't going to be around forever, Fane. You have a real life."

He glanced at the floor, not answering. Then he said, "I'll always be your friend."

For some reason, his words caused an ache in her chest—small, but there nonetheless. "I honestly don't even know why I left my room tonight. I was in bed, and it suddenly occurred to me to wonder if she'd locked the door. When I discovered she hadn't, I decided to leave."

"Curiosity is a good thing," he said.

"I thought it killed a cat?"

He laughed. "Maybe sometimes. But not you."

She looked at him skeptically.

"I should go," he said, "before anyone gets up."

"Please be careful," she said.

He pulled her into another hug and she leaned into him.

"Hey, Fane?"

"Yeah?"

"Since you're here anyway, do you think you might . . ." She trailed off, stunned at herself. She was about to ask him to kiss her again. What was wrong with her?

"Might what?"

"Nothing."

He squeezed her. "Come on, I ran all the way over here, risking life and limb to rescue you, and you won't even finish a sentence."

"Nope," she said.

"Fine." He paused. "How about a kiss then?"

Her heart flip-flopped, and she grinned up at him. "I guess it's the least I can do." She lifted her face and he kissed her. She had to admit she honestly wondered if their first kiss was a fluke, amazing simply because it was new. But this kiss disproved that theory.

He left and she waited by her window as usual, not thinking he would really go to the effort to come around so she could wave to him. He did, and relief flooded her. She knew he wasn't completely out of danger yet—he still had to move the ladder and get safely out of the yard.

She undressed and climbed into bed, putting the phone in her drawer. She was counting on her mother's lack of technical know-how to keep her from figuring out she'd texted anyone. Fane had erased them from the phone, so she could only hope there was no way for her mother to still find them.

She closed her eyes and drifted into a restless sleep.

chapter

19

Rapunzel had no desire to sneak out of her room again, but she was curious whether she could if she wanted to. The next night, after her mother left, a twist of the doorknob revealed she couldn't. It was locked.

The locked door bothered her. It showed a marked lack of trust on her mother's part. She laughed at herself. As if she deserved her trust. Hadn't she been sneaking around? Okay, so trust wasn't the issue, but motives were. She wondered why her mother kept her locked up like a prisoner more than a quarantined patient. *I'm incarcerated with my mother as my only visitor.* She didn't have the freedom to *choose* for herself if she wanted to wander out of her room and risk her health—and maybe her life.

She went to her computer and pulled up Skype. Fane wasn't on. She went into her kitchen and got one of her hidden pieces of chocolate. She wasn't sure why, but the chocolate always made her feel better. She was restless, bored.

A sound came from her computer that made her smile. It was the sound of Skype ringing, and there was only one person it could be. She hurried back to her computer and hit the video button. Half a second later Fane's slightly unclear but smiling face was in front of her.

"Hey, beautiful," he said, the greeting she was certain he knew would turn her cheeks pink. It worked, of course.

"Hi, Fane."

"Not trapped on any balconies tonight needing rescue?"

Rapunzel laughed. "Nope, not tonight. Sorry."

"Too bad," he said nonchalantly, leaning back in his chair and putting his hands behind his head. "I kinda like the payment I get. I could get used to rescuing damsels in distress."

Rapunzel blushed furiously—she could tell by the amount of heat in her cheeks.

"Yes, well, don't get used to it." She tried for a casual tone but feared he could hear the tightness in her voice.

Fane laughed and leaned forward again, his eyes on his desk. Rapunzel knew this pose. It meant he was nervous. "So," he began, drawing the word out. "Halloween is coming soon."

"Yes, I know," Rapunzel said, confused by his demeanor. Did he think she was unaware of Halloween? Well, she'd surprise him. She'd been reading lately about things normal people did so that she wouldn't seem so innocent. "It's a strange custom, don't you think, to send children out dressed as monsters to knock on strangers' doors to ask for candy?" Rapunzel definitely thought it odd.

Fane gazed at her with a small smile. "Yeah, I guess, now that you put it that way."

"I mean," she continued, proud of her knowledge, "isn't it standard for parents to warn their children to *not* take candy from strangers? And then on this one night, it's okay. Doesn't that send a mixed message to children?"

Fane grinned openly now. "I suppose it does."

Trying to sound mature and knowledgeable, she said, "I suppose by the time one is our age then maybe it isn't quite so strange because we can understand that this is the only night it's allowed, but a young child wouldn't understand." Then, because she didn't really know anything about children, she added, "Would they?"

"You're very charming, you know that?"

Rapunzel felt herself blushing again. What was wrong with her? "What?" she stuttered.

"Wish I was there to see just how red your cheeks are."

"Fane," she admonished. "Stop teasing me."

He laughed. "Where would the fun be in that?"

"You know I can just turn you off if I want, right?" she said, holding one finger threateningly over the power button, knowing she'd never do it.

"Not possible," he said, waggling his eyebrows comically. When she didn't respond, he said, "Well, that was a wasted double entendre."

"What's a double entendre?" she asked.

Fane laughed. "Not something I'm going to explain, or I'll be blushing as much as you. Let's change the subject, or at least get back to the original one, which is Halloween."

"Okay," Rapunzel said, not sure why he wanted to keep talking about Halloween. Maybe it was important to him in some way. "What should we discuss about Halloween?"

He cleared his throat. "Well, there's this Halloween party I'm going to. It's a pretty big deal. One of my friends has it every year since Halloween is her favorite holiday."

"Oh, that sounds like fun," she said.

"Yeah, it is. And since Halloween is on a Friday this year, it's doubly good because the party is actually on Halloween."

Obviously it was important for Halloween to be on a Friday, though for the life of her Rapunzel couldn't fathom why. Not understanding, she didn't comment and just nodded.

"And I want you to come with me," he said.

Rapunzel's jaw dropped. "Wait, what? How could I go with you?"

Fane held one hand up. "It won't be easy, I know. I'll come get you after your mom leaves your room for the night."

"But, Fane, I can't . . . all those people—"

"I thought about that," he said. "I wouldn't have asked unless I had a plan."

Curiosity once again got the best of her. "What plan?"

"I was talking to one of my friends who works at a medical supply place. They have these masks used by people who are really sensitive to germs."

"You told him about me?" Rapunzel couldn't help but feel a little betrayed.

"No, of course not," Fane said. "I gave you my word. I won't tell anyone."

Rapunzel leaned back in her seat. She pictured it, a party with other people her age surrounding her. Talking to them as if she were normal. While intriguing, it also filled her with fear.

"Won't I look out of place, sitting there wearing a mask?"

"I thought of that also. It's a costume party. You go as a nurse or a doctor, or some kind of medical person. Then it will look fine." He leaned toward the screen again, and Rapunzel felt herself wavering, wanting to do this for him. "He claims it filters almost all germs. But if you think there's any risk at all, Rapunzel, then we won't do it. It isn't worth risking your life just for a party."

Rapunzel touched one finger to the bottom corner of the screen, where she knew Fane wouldn't see it. She'd much prefer to be touching Fane than the electronic version of him. She should be grateful she'd ever gotten to touch him at all.

She considered his request. Walking throughout her house hadn't made her sick. Lying outside on the grass hadn't either.

"I want to do it," she said.

"You want to come to the party?"

"Yes, Fane, I want to come to the party. You'll have to arrange for the costume, though. I don't have any way to get one." *Or to even know where to look for one*, she thought, *or what might be appropriate.*

"I can do that." He grinned. "I promise, Rapunzel, I'll keep you safe. If at any point you think it's not safe, I'll take you right home."

"I know you will. I trust you."

chapter

20

Fane brought a ladder to get her. It surprised her he'd found one tall enough to reach her window.

"Where did you get that?" Rapunzel whispered as she helped him over the windowsill.

"It wasn't easy," he said. "That sucker is heavy. And not exactly quiet for carrying across your yard."

"I'm sorry," she said.

"I'm not," he answered. "I'm completely stoked."

"Stoked?" she asked.

"Excited, thrilled, elated, overjoyed."

"Okay, calm down, Mr. Thesaurus." She laughed, holding her hands up in surrender.

Fane removed his backpack and unzipped it. He held up a piece of white material and handed it to her.

"What's this?" she asked, holding it up. It appeared to be a long shirt.

"Your costume. It's a nurse outfit. Haven't you been in the hospital enough with your SCIDs to have seen one?"

"No, I've never been in the hospital," she answered distractedly. "Where's the rest of it?"

"You've *never* been in the hospital?" He sounded incredulous at the thought. He took the costume from her and held it up. "This is the whole thing. It's supposed to be sexy."

Rapunzel's mouth gaped. "No way am I going anywhere in that, Fane." She grabbed it from him and held it against herself. It barely skimmed the top of her thighs. "Look how short this thing is."

Fane shrugged. "Well, you can't blame a guy for trying." He pulled another item out of his backpack, a thin, gauzy material that was an amazing shade of peacock blue.

"Wow," she said, taking one of the pieces. "That's beautiful." She held it up and looked at Fane through the sheer material. She raised one brow at him. "Really?"

Fane laughed. "There's more."

He handed her the other items he held and pulled more out of the bag. He explained to her how they all worked and she went into her room to put it on. Once dressed, she looked at herself in her mirror. Fane explained that this was a belly-dancers outfit. The pants were made of the gauzy material, loose and flowing. The top was long sleeved, but short enough to expose her belly. Strands of beads with flat metal discs dangled all around her mid-section as well as from her hips. Beneath the whole thing, she wore a long, one piece, flesh colored leotard that covered her from her wrists to her ankles. Without it, she would *not* wear the outfit. With it, she still felt exposed, but then when she placed the veil over her head and the scarf across the lower half of her face, she somehow felt hidden . . . safe.

She'd braided her hair up as tightly as she could and wrapped it around her head once beneath the veil so that it only hung to her knees. She stepped out of the room shyly.

"I'm ready," she said. When Fane didn't answer, she looked up at him.

He stared at her, one of the cookies she'd baked especially for him halfway to his mouth. His eyes scanned her. That look made her blush more than all the times he'd teased her by calling her beautiful.

"Where's the mask?" she asked.

He shook his head as if waking. He went to his backpack and pulled a white mask out. This one wasn't loose and floppy like the other had been. This was more form fitted. She slid it on beneath the scarf.

"Do you have a jacket?" he asked. His voice sounded funny, kind of choked. "It's a little cold."

Rapunzel went to the closet and pulled out a long jacket. It wasn't hers—it belonged to her mother. A few years ago she'd had it on when she came to see Rapunzel and she'd accidentally left it behind. Rapunzel had hung it in the closet, figuring she would come get it. She never had, and Rapunzel had kept it. Just in case. She put the jacket on, pulling it close around her.

"I think you should keep that on all night," Fane said. She looked at him questioningly.

"To cover my hair?" she asked.

"Among other things," he murmured. Fane led her to the window. "I'll climb down and hold the ladder for you."

Rapunzel watched his descent, nerves fluttering in her stomach. She'd watched him go up and down, but now that it was her turn, it seemed a very long distance to the ground. When his feet touched the ground he took hold of the ladder to indicate she should now descend.

She looked behind her. Fane had showed her how to arrange her pillows to look like she was in the bed. She doubted it would fool her mother should she come. They'd turned off all the lights other than the small lamp in the alcove. She considered what she was about to do.

It was one thing to wander around in her house. It was something completely different to think about leaving the house. Panic crawled up her throat as she glanced down at Fane. She thought about waving him away and going to bed. Then he grinned at her and she found herself putting a leg over the sill. Determined not to look down, she descended the ladder while looking up at the open window, her heart in her throat the entire time.

When her feet touched the ground, a trembling began in her legs. She desperately wanted to go back up the ladder. Instead she turned and threw her arms around Fane's waist. He stumbled a little under her attack but recovered and hugged her back.

"Are you okay?" he asked.

She nodded against his chest. "I just need a minute."

"Okay," he said, tightening his hold. After a few minutes her panic began to subside. She could do this. She released Fane and stepped back, smiling with embarrassment.

"Sorry," she said. "I just panicked a little at the thought of leaving."

"It's okay. I'd probably be a little worried if I were you

too, I guess. You've never been out." Concern crossed his face. "Rapunzel, is this too dangerous for you? If it is, then let's forget it. We'll hang out here for a while."

She was tempted. She remembered how much she'd enjoyed having him there, eating together, watching movies. She also remembered how excited he was about this party.

"No, we'll go," she said. "I want to."

He studied her for a minute as if to see whether she told the truth. Finally, he relented. "Okay, but we'll just stay for a little while, okay?"

She nodded, then knelt down to run her hands across the grass. It wasn't as soft as it had been before. She pulled up a few blades and sniffed them. It was beginning to hibernate and had lost much of its smell. Fane held a hand out to her. She placed her hand in his, following him across the yard, trying to push from her mind the fear of what she was doing.

Fane led her around the side of the house, the place he always came to wave to her. They stopped while he looked, then they hurried across the large expanse of lawn. On this side of the house there were a couple of large stone fountains and multiple empty flower beds. They ran to the gate. Just before they exited, Rapunzel turned to look at the house.

It was a monstrosity. She'd known it was large, of course, but she couldn't have fathomed the size of it. From the greenhouse she'd only had a view of the backside of the house and hadn't been able to see the whole thing. From here she could see the bulk of it. It was misshapen, with odd appendages, scaffolding leaning against one side. It was tall and imposing. She could now understand why Fane had been shocked at the size of her rooms. She realized they hadn't seen even a small portion in their wanderings.

"Everything all right?" Fane asked, squeezing her hand.

She nodded. "Yes. Fine. Let's go."

chapter
21

Rapunzel knew what cars were, of course. She'd seen them in movies, read of them in books, and seen them on the Internet. But she'd never seen a real one—since her window did not face any streets—let alone ride in one. Fane put the seat belt on her, and she was grateful once they began moving. The vehicle rumbled beneath her, the world speeding past outside the window. She wanted to look at that world, but each time she glanced out the window a new wave of terror engulfed her and she felt as if she would throw up. So she kept her eyes firmly planted on her lap, concentrating on her breathing so Fane wouldn't see her anxiety, afraid he'd insist on taking her home if he did.

When they stopped and Fane got out, she exhaled a loud breath, sucking another in deeply, trying to still her thrumming heart. Fane walked around and opened her door, which was a good thing since she had no idea how to open it herself. She climbed out of the car and looked at the house they were at.

Candles flickered everywhere, lining the sidewalk and

porch and scattered across the lawn. There were tomb-stones on the lawn as well. Rapunzel thought it odd that they would bury their dead in their front yard, but that could be normal for all she knew. Ghosts hung from the tree branches and carved pumpkins lined the front of the house.

Rapunzel could hear the music pounding from within the house. Fane took her hand as they stepped up to the door. Before knocking, he turned to her with a question on his face. She knew what he asked. This was the point of no return. She nodded.

A girl opened the door. Rapunzel could only stare as Fane introduced them.

"Rapunzel, this is my friend Marissa. Marissa, Rapunzel."

Marissa was exotically beautiful. She had stunning cinnamon colored skin, wide green eyes fringed with black lashes, long, dark brown hair that hung straight, and a smile that lit up her face. That smile was currently wel-coming Rapunzel. Fane led her into the house where she was assaulted by sounds and smells that were completely foreign to her.

Music played loudly, the noise of which was only outdone by all of the talking and laughter. People were crowded into every visible part of the room. Some were dancing, some stood in small circles talking, and others sat on various chairs and couches. Smells of food came from somewhere, a variety of foods all mixed together with an underlying smell of sweat. Rapunzel suspected if she didn't have her mask on the smells might be overwhelming.

"Great costume," Marissa said loudly to be heard over the music while taking Rapunzel's coat. Rapunzel simply nodded. Another girl walked up to them, looking similar to Marissa with dark eyes, bronze skin, and hair that fell in long curls. Her smile was as friendly and cheerful as Marissa's. She stuck a hand toward Rapunzel.

"Hi, I'm Ashlynn."

"My sister," Marissa clarified.

"This is Rapunzel," Fane said.

"Can't the girl speak for herself?" Ashlynn teased.

"Of course she can," Fane said. "But she's been sick so she's wearing a mask so she won't spread germs. You might not be able to hear her." Fane had told her ahead of time what he was going to say. As he'd predicted, they didn't question it.

"Cool costume," Ashlynn said. "Great way to cover the mask."

Marissa winked at Rapunzel, and she had a feeling Marissa was responsible for providing it.

"Come with us," Marissa said, wrapping an arm around her waist and leading her further into the chaos. Fane was left to follow behind. "Are you hungry? Thirsty?"

Rapunzel shook her head, glancing nervously behind to make sure Fane was still there. Marissa led her to a table with a padded bench that wrapped around three quarters of the table. She and Ashlynn slid in and scooted around, making room for her and Fane to join them.

"So how did you meet Fane?" Ashlynn asked.

Rapunzel glanced at him, not sure what to say. She decided to give them the truth.

"On Facebook," she said.

"Oh, Facebook." Ashlynn laughed. "I *love* Facebook."

"It's the best," Marissa chimed in. "But it can be obsessive. I have to limit myself or I'll spend all day on there reading people's statuses."

"And playing games," Ashlynn added.

Rapunzel couldn't stop staring at the two beautiful sisters. They seemed innately cheerful, as if they never stopped smiling. She wondered if one of them was Fane's girlfriend and that's how he knew them. Then she decided probably not since he sat on her other side, holding Rapunzel's hand. She doubted any girl would let her boyfriend do that, though she couldn't be sure.

Several others came over to say hi to Fane and to meet Rapunzel. There was no possible way she'd be able to remember any of their names, but she was enthralled by them all, and how different they looked in their various costumes. Ashlynn went and got her and Fane drinks. They were in cups that lit up from the bottom and had fog coming over the top.

"Root beer," Fane told her quietly when she looked askance at it.

She also brought a plate with small bat-shaped cookies and pumpkin cupcakes on it. Rapunzel really wanted to try the cookies, but knew it would be impossible with the mask on. She also knew it would be impossible to drink the root beer. Finally, she pulled the bottom of the mask up and slipped a cookie beneath it into her mouth. It was worth it.

"Wanna dance?" Fane asked.

She shook her head. "I don't know how."

"That makes two of us," he said, grinning. He stood and pulled her up with him. He led her out to the middle of the pack of people who were bouncing to the music. She looked around, afraid they'd laugh at her for her awkwardness. Fane began bouncing with them, comically. Rapunzel laughed and began moving—though much more restrained than Fane.

A few minutes later the song ended and a slower one came on. All around them couples fell into one another's arms and began swaying. Rapunzel laughed. Apparently when the song slowed down you just hugged someone. Fane held his arms out to her and she gladly went into them.

He pulled her close and began swaying along with the others. She rested her cheek against his chest, looking around the room as he turned her in slow circles. The house was dimly lit but that didn't seem to bother anyone. She saw people dressed in everything from monster costumes to ones that reminded her of the first nurse costume Fane had given her, laughing and talking, some doing the hug-sway, and others eating. Sadness dropped over her as she realized what she'd missed her entire life. She'd never have the freedom to stand around with a group of friends. She'd never have the freedom to *have* friends.

She was smart enough to know that Fane would grow bored of sneaking into her rooms and that eventually she'd be alone again. Her long, lonely future stretched out in front of her and the weight of it fell on her shoulders. Tears pricked her eyes and she hugged Fane tighter. If this was the only party she ever went to in her life, she was going to make the most of it so she'd have the memory to carry her.

When the music changed to an upbeat tempo, she released Fane and immediately began bouncing again. Ashlynn and Marissa came out and joined them, laughing with her. They began showing her a bunch of different dance moves, most of them silly, which she parroted—as did Fane to her amusement. They taught her what they called a line dance, where no one danced with a partner. Other than the hug-sway, it seemed people just danced anyway, whether they had a partner or not.

Fane found her a straw so she could drink the foggy root beer, which was delicious and tickled the back of her throat. She got hungry enough that she dared pull the mask down long enough to eat an orange roll and some chips. Fane shot her a worried look when she did that, but she smiled at him with a reassurance she didn't really feel.

Fane stayed by her side the entire night, his hand in hers. A couple of times some boys wandered over, and Fane would put his arm around her shoulders, pulling her close. Rapunzel wondered at the strange behavior until Marissa laughed and jabbed him in the chest with a finger.

"Jealous, Fane?"

"No," he said defensively.

"But you're not about to let her dance with anyone else, are you?" she teased.

He narrowed his eyes but gave a short, jerky shake of his head, which set both Marissa and Ashlynn off into giggles. Finally, after midnight, Fane told them he and

Rapunzel had to go. Rapunzel was disappointed. She didn't want the night to end.

In the car, she felt more relaxed than she had on the trip over and looked out the window at the darkened houses and buildings they raced passed. It felt like she was in a movie and that the places couldn't possibly be real, with real people behind those windows.

"Did you have fun?" Fane asked.

Rapunzel leaned her head back against the headrest. "It was a blast, Fane. Thank you for taking me. I'll remember it for the rest of my life."

He reached over and took her hand in his. She wanted to tell him to keep it on the steering wheel because it seemed like he would need both hands to control the speeding car. But it felt so nice to hold his hand that she let go of her anxiety. He gently rubbed her palm with his thumb.

"I'm glad you had fun." He turned worried eyes on her. "Are you sure you're going to be okay?"

"I feel fantastic," she told him.

"Fantastic?" he repeated with a smile. "Well, that's something, then, huh?"

"It's everything," she sighed.

He pulled her hand up to his mouth and kissed it. Rapunzel's pulse leaped at the gesture. "Time with you is never dull," he said.

They arrived near her looming house, and Fane parked the car on the side of the road. He quietly closed his door when he got out, then did the same with hers. They crouch-ran across the lawn and back around the house to where the ladder waited at her window. The house was as dark as it had been when they'd left.

"Want me to come up and make sure everything is okay?" he asked.

"No," she said. "If things *aren't* okay then I definitely don't want you there. I don't want you to get into trouble. And if things *are* okay, then there's no need."

"All right," he said. He ran one hand down her braid. "I'll get the costume from you some other time. Do you have somewhere you can hide it?"

"Yes." She turned her face up to his, hoping for a kiss. Then she realized he couldn't kiss her with the mask and scarf on. Boldly, she pulled them both down.

Fane smiled, placing one hand along her jaw, caressing lightly with is thumb. She closed her eyes at the sensation.

"That feels so good," she said. Her eyes popped open when she realized what she'd said, but he wasn't laughing at her as she'd feared. He was watching her lips, his eyes hooded. A tingling began in her chest as her heartbeat picked up. He leaned down, his eyes locked with hers as his lips lightly touched hers. His eyes closed as he tilted his head, deepening the kiss, and her own eyes drifted shut. She tried to memorize the sensation of his mouth on hers, the softness of his lips, his arm behind her back, his hand cupping her cheek.

He pulled back and smiled at her. She smiled in answer.

He held the ladder as she climbed up. Peeking over the sill, she saw that her room was as she'd left it. She climbed in as quietly as possible, turning back to wave at Fane. He slowly, carefully collapsed the ladder, pulling it away from the wall. It clattered loudly and they both froze. When nothing stirred, he picked it up and carried it back across the grass. She felt bad as she watched him struggle with the long, awkward weight, trying to keep it quiet. At the corner he flashed a grin back at her.

Rapunzel closed the window and walked into the living area. It was quiet. Too quiet. She went into her room and reluctantly removed the costume, scrubbing her face and getting ready for bed. She skipped brushing her hair. She tucked the costume into the back corner of her closet beneath a stack of pants. She climbed into bed and smiled.

She'd done it. And survived. Maybe her mother was wrong. Maybe she had a chance to live a normal life if she was careful. Hope suffused her as she drifted into sleep.

chapter

22

Rapunzel didn't know what was wrong with her. She felt achy in her arms and legs. She supposed all the dancing and climbing up and down the ladder might have something to do with it. But while she'd had aches before from exercising, this felt different somehow. Probably because she was also tired. She hadn't had much sleep the night of the party, coming home so late like she did. And though she'd slept long last night, going to bed early and not waking until her mother came in, she still felt like she needed a nap.

She walked over to the window and opened it. Angel perched in the tree branch in spite of the cold. She wondered how much longer the bird would be around before heading for warmer climes. Rapunzel leaned out, the cold air cooling her warm head. She held out her handful of seed, and Angel flew over, landing right on her palm.

"I haven't seen much of you lately, my little friend," she said to the bird.

Angel looked up at her, cocking her head side to side as if trying to puzzle out Rapunzel's words. A wave of dizziness hit Rapunzel, and she grabbed the sill with her other hand, steadying herself. *That was strange*, she thought. Angel chirped at her and flew back to the branch. Rapunzel scattered the remaining seed on the sill and closed the window.

She'd thought of cooking for her mother tonight but just couldn't muster the energy. She walked back into the room, still feeling overly warm as her mother entered with their dinner. Rapunzel went to help her carry the food in.

She sat down across from her mother and looked at the food. Chicken enchiladas. One of her favorites. Yet the thought of eating made her stomach churn. Suddenly she felt extremely cold and began shaking as her body broke out in goose bumps.

A look of alarm came into her mother's eyes. "Rapunzel, what's wrong with you?" She reached across the table, touched Rapunzel's hand, and then quickly drew her hand back as if burned, gasping.

"What?" Rapunzel asked, looking down at her hand. Was there something there that gave away her going to the party?

"Are you feeling . . . sick?" she asked, rising from her chair and placing a hand on Rapunzel's forehead. "Oh," Gothel exclaimed on an exhaled breath, the alarm in her eyes ratcheting up to panic.

"I'm okay," Rapunzel said. "Just a little tired." Although now that she thought about it, she did feel kind of funny inside. Her stomach grumbled, and her head spun. "I really, really need to lie down," she said, standing.

As she did so, the room spun in a sickeningly fast whirl and blackness crowded her vision.

* * *

Rapunzel was dying. She'd taken the risk, known the possible outcome, and now she'd pay. She just hadn't known it would be so utterly miserable to die. Her body ached deep in her bones, as if she'd been running and lifting weights non-stop for days on end.

Fire consumed her. She burned from somewhere deep within the pit of her belly. She wanted to beg someone to douse the flames, but when she tried to speak, her throat felt as if it had been jammed with rocks and sand, and the pain made it impossible to speak.

Someone had tied her arm down. She weakly tried to lift it, opening her eyes just a slit to see what was happening, and saw some clear plastic tubing binding her arm. She let it fall back to the bed.

"Rest, Rapunzel," she heard her mother say. She turned toward the voice but only saw an unfocused version of her mother sitting next to her, worry creasing her face. She let her eyes slide closed. Coldness suddenly penetrated her forehead and her armpits. Why her armpits? Within seconds a bone-deep cold replaced the fire. She shivered violently, the action abusing her aching muscles, and she wanted to beg for some warmth. She heard arguing but couldn't make the words out above her chattering teeth that knocked loudly in her pounding head.

If it were possible, she became even more chilled as icy coldness pressed against her again. She wished wildly for the fire to return and consume her, put her out of her misery. She heard a low moaning and realized the sound came from deep within her chest. The sound terrified her. She was helpless to stop it. Darkness pressed against her and she rose up quickly, gratefully to meet it.

* * *

Darkness pervaded the room when Rapunzel opened her eyes. She lay on her side, facing the wall. Her head throbbed, her body ached, and the strange plastic tubing was still stuck to her arm. But at least she wasn't burning or freezing, though her bed was damp beneath her. She decided to lie still until she knew whether moving was going to hurt. When she felt ready, she rolled over, facing her door where ambient light came into the room.

Voices filtered in from the next room. She felt as if she were listening to them from underwater. One voice belonged to her mother—she could recognize that. But the other was unfamiliar, deep and masculine.

"Why isn't she getting better?" she heard her mother ask urgently.

There was a pause, then the man spoke again, his voice much closer as if he'd moved closer to her doorway. She slammed her eyes closed. "You have to understand that she hasn't built up a normal immunity, being confined as she is. Flu and strep throat aren't easy for even a normal person's body to deal with."

"How did she get sick?" her mother hissed.

Again silence, broken only by rustling. She opened

the smallest slit and saw the man holding his arms away from himself, as if to indicate his confusion.

Her mother's head came into view, and she closed her eyes again. When she spoke, her voice was a harsh whisper. "She *cannot* die. Do you understand that?"

"Yes, I do, but—"

"There is no but, Henreich. Much rides on Rapunzel. If she dies, you know the consequences."

The man sighed, and a memory niggled at Rapunzel's memory. The name *Henreich* struck a note with her. Who was he?

"I'm well aware, Gothel. But perhaps it's time to reconsider your actions. It seems very unfair and potentially dangerous to keep the girl locked up—"

"You dare to question me?" Rapunzel flinched at the venom in her mother's voice. She dared to peek again and saw the man twisting his hands. "You have much to protect yourself by keeping the secret, Henreich. Or do you need to be reminded?"

Secret? What secret? Rapunzel felt nauseated, her stomach clenching at the words.

"Listen, Gothel, I appreciate what you've done. But now, perhaps—"

"You listen to me, Henreich. You will lose everything; your sons will lose everything. Do you think they will allow you to continue being a doctor?" Rapunzel suddenly had a vague recollection of him from when she was a young girl. He'd come once when she was young, but the memory was too unclear. "How is your family going to survive with you in prison? What will they think of you then?"

Henreich's shoulders drooped, and Rapunzel wondered what her mother was talking about. "It just doesn't feel right to keep her here, Gothel," he muttered so low that Rapunzel wasn't even sure she heard right.

"But?" Gothel prompted.

"But I'll keep your secret," he said.

"*Our* secret," she reiterated.

The man turned toward Rapunzel, and she quickly slid her eyes closed. She heard him move across the room and felt his hand on her forehead.

"I'm sorry," he whispered, and Rapunzel felt the words were for her. "Her fever has broken," he said more loudly to Gothel. Soon her mother's hands were on her, and Rapunzel slowly opened her eyes.

"Rapunzel, are you better?" her mother said urgently.

"It will take some time," Henreich said. Rapunzel's eyes moved to his. Sorrow reflected in his face, and something like guilt. "Don't worry," he said to her, "We're going to get you feeling better. You just relax and take it easy, give your body time to recover."

Rapunzel nodded and let her eyes drift closed again. She wanted to replay their conversation in her mind again, as if she were missing some key that she couldn't quite grasp. But lethargy overtook her, and she was unable to fight against it.

chapter

23

S everal days crawled by before Rapunzel felt strong enough to get out of bed unassisted. Henreich had come the day before and removed the tubing from her arm, explaining the IV and its function. She shuddered with horror as she watched the long tube sliding out of her, where it had been embedded beneath her skin.

She wanted to shower. Her mother or Henreich had been by her side constantly, and this was the first time she'd been left alone. Gratefully, shakily, she rose from the bed and slowly made her way to the bathroom. She avoided looking at herself in the mirror, having seen how awful she looked the last few times she'd been in here with her mother's help.

She dropped her pajamas from her sunken body and climbed into the shower, reveling in the feel of the warm water as it sluiced across her body. She stood for long minutes, letting it soothe her before beginning the arduous process of washing her hair.

Half an hour later she emerged, exhausted but

refreshed. She toweled dry and had just finished pulling on gym shorts and a T-shirt when her mother returned.

"Rapunzel! What are you doing out of bed?" Her mother hurried over, fluttering around her.

"I needed to shower," she said. "I feel much better now."

"You must get back to bed, right away."

"Can't I just sit on the couch for a while?"

"No." Her mother's tone didn't allow for argument. "You must rest and get better. You need to lie down. Cook will soon bring your dinner."

Rapunzel allowed herself to be led back to the bed. Her dinner came, which her mother stayed to watch her eat. She didn't have much of an appetite and wasn't able to eat much, but her mother seemed pleased and left her alone to sleep.

But Rapunzel didn't want to sleep. She was bored. She was restless.

She wanted to talk to Fane.

An hour later her mother returned and Rapunzel pretended to be asleep. Satisfied, her mother left and Rapunzel, betting her mother wouldn't return again, rose from her bed and made her way to her computer.

It took a few minutes for it to boot up. When it did, she quickly connected to the Internet and signed in to Facebook. He wasn't online.

She saw that she had messages and clicked on the little icon. Message after message from Fane appeared. They began with a lighthearted tone and quickly became worried.

Hey, Rapunzel, just wanted to say how much fun I had at the Halloween party with you. You were definitely the hottest girl there. (Yes, I can see you blushing.)

Just wondering where you've been? Guess we keep missing one another. Maybe we should set a time. Tell me when you can be on, and I'll be here. Anything for the hot girl.

Are you avoiding me? Cuz I know where you live, hahaha. Okay, sorry, that was a little creepy. But seriously, where are you?

Hey, are you mad at me? If I did something wrong, please tell me. I miss you.

Okay. Now I'm seriously worried. Did something happen to you? I kinda think if you are mad at me, you'd tell me. So now I think something might be wrong with you. Please, please, even if you hate me, let me know you're okay.

If you hate me and never want to speak to me again, that's okay. Just tell me so I know you're fine.

Rapunzel, I am seriously going to come break into your house to see what's going on.

Rapunzel counted. There were over thirty messages all together. She scrolled back up to the top one, surprised to see it had been ten days. *Ten days?* How in the world had so much time passed? She felt like it had only been a few.

Suddenly, her Skype window popped up, flashing to

show Fane was calling her. She quickly answered with video, then regretted it when her reflection in the tiny window showed her hair plastered to one side of her face and her pale, drawn visage.

Fane leaned toward the camera, and in spite of the not-quite-clear quality, she could see the worry etched on his face.

"Rapunzel? Is that you? Are you okay?"

She smiled, drinking in the sight of him. "Yes, I am now."

"Now? What does that mean?"

"I wasn't feeling well for a few . . . for a while. I was sick. But I'm better now."

Fane squinted his eyes a bit, examining her face. The worry never left his.

"Are you sure you're better? You look really . . . tired."

"I am," she said. "But I do feel much better."

Fane leaned back in his chair, twisting back and forth, arms crossed, chewing on one thumb. Finally he sat forward again. "It's my fault, isn't it?"

"What's your fault?" she asked.

"You. Being sick. What if . . . what if you had, you know, died or something?"

Rapunzel couldn't deny that she had thought she was dying, more than once. So she didn't answer that particular question.

"No, Fane. It's not your fault. It's mine. I shouldn't have lifted the mask."

"I shouldn't have taken you to begin with," he said.

"Don't say that," she said. "You're the only fun I've had

in my whole life. Even if I died tomorrow, I'd be okay with that. Fane, do you understand what my life is?"

He didn't answer, just looked down.

"I sit inside these walls, all day, every day, doing nothing, seeing no one, talking to a bird that lives in the tree outside my window. I don't want to live like that anymore."

His eyes came back to her. "What do you mean?"

She looked around, as if her mother might have snuck in and would overhear her. "When I was sick, I overheard my mother and my doctor speaking. It was really weird."

"Yeah? What'd they say?"

"I can't remember everything," she said with a sigh. "I was very sick and so I'm honestly not sure how much I really heard and how much I imagined. But he was telling her I shouldn't be kept inside so much. He said something about it being bad for the community."

"Bad for the community?" Fane's brows clashed together as his mouth tightened.

"I know. It doesn't make sense to me, either. But she told him that if he told her secret, he couldn't be a doctor any longer, and that his family would be ashamed of him." Tears pricked Rapunzel's eyes. She wasn't sure what it all meant. Somehow it felt deeply wrong that her mother had a secret involving her—a secret bad enough that a man would no longer be a doctor, that he would go to *prison* if revealed. She'd gotten to know Dr. Henreich as she recovered a bit, and found him to be kind and caring.

"What can I do to help?" Fane asked.

Rapunzel swallowed the lump in her throat. She'd known he would do whatever he could.

"I don't really know," she said. "Can you ask around, see if anyone outside has heard anything? Find out what I have to do with the community?"

"Absolutely," he said.

"And come see me soon," she said quietly.

Fane cleared his throat. "Do you think that's a good idea?"

She smiled at him. "I think it's the best idea I've ever had."

"But what if I make you—"

"*Please*," she whispered.

He stopped speaking at her plea. Then he nodded. "Okay. I'll try to come as soon as I can."

Rapunzel rolled her shoulders. She was still somewhat sore. "I'm really tired. I think I should go lie down."

"Definitely," he said. "You should definitely go lie down."

"Fane?"

"Yeah?"

"I'm glad you were on. Thanks for worrying so much about me."

"I'm glad you're okay," he said, his voice full of emotion.

chapter

24

Each day Rapunzel felt stronger until she finally finished taking the pills, *antibiotics* Dr. Henreich called them. She managed to be out of bed for longer periods of time, and soon her mother had reduced her visits to twice a day. This gave Rapunzel time to try to figure things out surfing the Internet.

She began by Googling SCIDs. She read about David Vetter, known as Bubble Boy, and was grateful she didn't have to live in the same kind of sterile environment he did. Although he at least was able to have some social contact with others instead of being shut up in a tower. She didn't know which was worse.

She was excited when she read about a vaccine or possible cure, then became disheartened when she read it was only for infants. She read about the possibility of bone marrow transplant or gene therapy but again realized these worked better on young children.

There were many sites relating to SCIDs, though most of them repeated the same information. The only hope she seemed to have was a site that talked about possible false negatives. She wondered if that were a possibility in her case, though her recent illness seemed to negate that. She could find a lot of information about causes and symptoms of her disease, but nothing definitive that said if she'd be safe going out in the general public if she were careful.

She thought of asking her mother about it, but knew there was no chance based on her recent illness. She remembered when she was six and first asked if she could go outside and play.

"No, Rapunzel, and you must never ask again." Her mother's tone was firm.

"But why?" her young self asked.

"Because, my dear, it was prophesied that you must live to save us. You must live, and you must never cut your hair."

"Why?"

"Because, Rapunzel," she said, voice full of irritation, "someone foretold of you before you were born. He told me I would have a child with golden hair who would be the savior of . . . humanity. He told me that you would live to save *everything*, and that your long, golden hair would be the beacon to light the way."

Rapunzel had no idea what any of those words meant, but they sounded ominous. And her mother had repeated the story to her over and over through the years until she'd memorized it. Confused how she was supposed to save humanity from her tower, she didn't want to cause the downfall of the world with her selfishness.

She shut the computer off—no chance of Fane being on during school hours—and twisted a strand of hair around her finger. She looked down at it, briefly considered cutting it, not for the first time, and knew she never would. She couldn't take the risk.

She walked over to her window with a handful of birdseed and saw Angel huddled on the tree branch. Gray and overcast, the skies promised snow soon. She didn't think the little bird would still be around, weathering the cold.

She pushed the window open, breathing in the fresh, clean, cool air. Smelling the outdoors was such a relief. She hadn't realized how much she missed it. Angel flew over and looked up at her, cocking her head as if to ask where she'd been.

"I've been sick, little one," she said. Angel seemed satisfied and pecked a seed from her palm. "I'm better now."

Angel ruffled her feathers and picked up another seed.

"I wish you could talk to me," she said. "I wish you could answer my questions. I wish *someone* could." As she said the words, Dr. Henreich flashed into her mind. She wondered if he would answer her questions or if he'd be as closed about everything as her mother.

"Do you think the good doctor would answer my questions?" she asked the bluebird. Angel fluttered her wings, then settled back down for more seed. "I don't know how to interpret that." Angel looked up at her, blinked, then bobbed for another bite. "Well, I suppose if I don't ask I'll never know, right?" Angel chirped and snatched one more peck of seed before flitting off to her perch.

Rapunzel released the rest of the seeds, leaning on her elbows and watching her friend. "You should go soon. It's going to snow before long. You don't want to get caught in the cold."

As if her words were the impetus needed, Angel flew off to the south. Rapunzel watched her go, saddened that she might not see her little friend again until the spring. She took a few more deep breaths and then closed her window.

She flopped down on her sofa, looking around at the area that had been her entire life—until Fane, that was. She thought again about the prophecy. Who had told her mother of her destiny? Rapunzel stood, intending to go back to her computer to research prophecies to see what she could discover. As she entered the cove where her computer was, she heard the door to her room open. She turned guiltily, as if she'd been about to do something wrong.

"Are you feeling better?" her mother asked with far too much concern in her voice. Rapunzel raised a brow at the false tone until she saw Dr. Henreich follow her mother in.

"Yes, I am," she said.

"I'd like to check you over, Rapunzel," he said. "I want to do a few tests just to make sure that we're not going to have a relapse."

Gothel's eyes widened. "Is that a possibility, Henreich?" she asked, the worry in her voice genuine now.

"Of course it is," he answered. "Though it's unlikely. However, due to the . . . unusual circumstances of Rapunzel's . . . uh, disease, we should make sure."

Rapunzel wondered at his halting speech.

She led the way into her room, followed by the other two. Dr. Henreich went through a series of procedures, listening to her heart and lungs, looking in her throat, eyes, and ears.

"I'd like to take some blood to run a few tests as well," he told her. She nodded, not sure how he was going to get the blood from her. When he pulled out the needle, she pulled back in fear.

"It's just a small poke," he reassured her.

Rapunzel looked toward her mother, opening her mouth to ask her to hold her hand. But her mother stared at the needle as if it were a viper.

"I'll just be out here," she muttered, quickly exiting the room.

Rapunzel's attention drew back to Henreich as he tied what looked like a large rubber band around her upper arm.

"It might help if you look away."

She nodded, took a bracing breath, and turned toward the door her mother had disappeared through. She felt a pinprick against the inside of her elbow, and a few seconds later the rubber band released. She looked at her arm and saw the blood flowing into the little vial that he had pushed onto the needle.

"That didn't hurt," she said, her tone reflecting her surprise.

"Good," he said, smiling warmly at her. Suddenly it struck her—she was alone with the doctor.

"Dr. Henreich, can I ask you something?" she asked quickly before her courage deserted her.

"Certainly." He pulled the vial away and replaced it with another.

"It's about my SCIDs." His eyes flicked nervously toward the door. She continued, "I'm wondering . . . do you think there might be a cure? Or something . . . some kind of way that I could maybe at least be okay enough to go outside, or see other people?"

Henreich pulled the needle from her arm, pressing a cotton ball against the dot of blood that welled up.

"Hold some pressure on this," he said. Rapunzel began to think he wouldn't answer her as he marked the little vials. "It's difficult to say, Rapunzel. There are some cures that are currently being used, but it depends on each individual case."

"Well, who would I talk to about that?" she asked excitedly.

Henreich cleared his throat and looked at the door once again.

"I don't think any of the cures would work on you," he said, his voice lowered. Rapunzel's heart plummeted. "But not because I don't think you can't be cured."

"What?" *What in the world did that mean?*

Henreich swallowed loudly, as if he were nervous. Rapunzel thought about the secret he shared with her mother. He glanced at the door again, and Rapunzel followed his gaze.

"Is there something . . . you know? About me?" she whispered.

Henreich's eyes cut quickly back to meet hers. He opened his mouth as if to speak, but her mother's voice from the other room cut in.

"Are you finished yet, Henreich?" she called.

He closed his eyes, clenched his jaw, then stood. Rapunzel felt as if an opportunity were slipping away.

"Please," she said, reaching out to touch his arm. "If there's something I should know . . ."

He froze at her touch, then placed a hand over hers as her mother appeared in the doorway.

"You're going to be okay, Rapunzel," he said, patting her hand, sounding like a concerned doctor. But his eyes bore into hers, seeming to want her to find meaning in his words. He squeezed her hand lightly. "You're *just fine.*"

"Well, that's a relief, isn't it?" her mother asked, coming further into the room. Henreich's face tightened as he turned away, placing all of his tools back into his bag. Rapunzel watched him, once again feeling as though she missed something that, if she could just figure it out, might change her life.

chapter

25

When you asked me about your disease and the community, is it possible you meant *immunity?*"

Rapunzel blinked. She'd been staring pretty hard at Fane through the computer screen as he regaled her with tales about school, and updated her on the beautiful sisters Marissa and Ashlynn. In all honesty, other than when he talked about the sisters she didn't really pay attention, just took the opportunity to look at him. She missed him desperately. She hadn't realized how lonely she was until he came along.

"Immunity?" she repeated.

"Yeah. I . . ." he trailed off, looking distinctly uncomfortable, eyes downcast. "I asked my mom what diseases had to do with the community." He glanced up at her as if to see her reaction.

"What did she say?" she pressed.

"A *lot,*" he grinned. "And after lots of listening to her talking about diseases that affect communities, she began talking about *immunity* and I suddenly wondered if that was what you'd heard."

"Could have," she said, nodding. "The two words sound similar."

"It would make more sense," he said. "Do you remember any more of what they were talking about?"

"Not a lot," she admitted. "It's all kind of fuzzy. Just something about being kept inside being bad for the community . . . or the immunity, I suppose. Makes sense as SCIDs is an immune deficiency disease, right?"

"That definitely makes more sense," he said, leaning forward excitedly. "I Googled some stuff after she said that, and I read in several places that babies who are kept inside don't have the chance to develop normal immune systems."

"Babies have to be exposed to the world to develop their immune system?"

"Yeah. I didn't know a lot about immunity, so I read some stuff. It's the . . . thing in your body that keeps you from getting sick. That's not quite right. It's like your body's defense system. It's how you're able to fight off viruses and bacteria and other things that make you sick. If a baby isn't exposed to some of those things when they're a baby, they don't have a good immunity, which means even the slightest exposure can get them sick—really sick."

Confusion swirled around in Rapunzel's head.

"Don't you get it?" Fane asked. Rapunzel shook her head. "Maybe what has made you unable to go outside is the fact that your mom has kept you inside your whole life. She was afraid you'd get sick. But now, because you don't have that immune system you need, that means you're more likely to get sick if you *do* go outside."

Rapunzel dropped her chin into her hands, keeping her eyes glued to Fane's face. Even all this baffling information couldn't dim her joy in seeing him.

"So how do I fix it?" she asked.

He slumped back in his chair. "I don't know."

Despair swirled around Rapunzel. "Then how am I supposed to—gotta go," she said quickly, shutting down the program as she heard her door handle turning. She pulled up the math page she'd been working on before Skyping Fane.

"Still doing homework, Rapunzel?" her mother asked as she breezed into the room. "You're going to cause yourself to relapse if you don't get more rest."

Rapunzel sighed. It had been nearly three weeks since she'd first gotten out of bed following her sickness. She felt completely normal, but her mother would have her lie in bed all day in her fear of a "relapse." Rapunzel almost considered faking one just to see if she could get Dr. Henreich to come back so she could question him again.

"I feel fine, Mother," she said, rising from her seat and joining her in the kitchen.

"Well, we can't be too careful, can we?"

Rapunzel didn't answer the rhetorical question. She slid into the seat opposite her mother and watched as she pulled the chicken, baked potatoes, and apple cobbler from the basket she'd used to carry it upstairs. Cooking was another activity her mother felt to be too strenuous and wouldn't allow Rapunzel to do.

"Can I ask you something?" Rapunzel said. Her mother didn't answer, but Rapunzel knew she wouldn't.

She always waited to hear the question before committing to answer. "Remember the prophecy you told me about? Can you explain it to me again?"

Gothel's gaze sharpened. "Why the curiosity, Rapunzel?"

Rapunzel heard the slight note of warning in her voice and her resolve wavered. She was determined, though, to know.

She dropped her gaze and shrugged. "You just haven't told me in a while. I want to be certain I have it right."

"What do you mean, have it right? Right for what?"

Rapunzel clasped her hands nervously beneath the table, feeling as though she were standing on a thin sheet of ice above dangerous waters. "I just spent some time thinking about it while I was sick, and I worry that I'm forgetting it, or not remembering it correctly. It's important, right?"

She slowly raised her gaze as her mother eyed her silently. Finally, she pushed her plate to the side and Rapunzel knew she would tell her.

"I suppose you're right. You're older now, and perhaps better able to understand the importance of what was told to me."

Rapunzel wasn't sure what she should do: to keep eating and pretend nonchalance to hopefully pull more information from her mother or to give her her full attention. She pushed her plate to the side and turned her gaze on her mother. Gothel's eyes took on a sort of glow, confirming Rapunzel had made the correct decision.

"I'd been to plenty of psychics before, but they were

all false prophetesses," she began, her voice taking on fervency. "However, I never lost faith that I would find someone who could answer my questions. And then, a couple years before you were born I found Vedmak." Rapunzel felt a jolt zing through her. She'd never heard the name before—or if she had, she didn't remember it.

"He *knew* things, Rapunzel, things he couldn't have possibly known about me. He knew of my hunger for a child. He knew about my parents and how they'd died so young.

"So I returned to him a second time, and then a third. Each time he knew things from my past. I asked about my future, the future of my daughter, and he told me about you." Gothel smiled, but it wasn't directed at Rapunzel, rather at some distant memory. "He said a golden-haired child, a girl, would come into my life. But that she wouldn't be an ordinary child. Oh, no. Not my child. My child would be *everything*, not just to me but to my daughter as well." How could Rapunzel be important to *herself*? It didn't make sense. "You're the one who is going to save everything."

A chill ran up Rapunzel's spine at hearing herself spoken of as some kind of extraordinary being, more than human. She didn't *want* to be some kind of . . . savior.

"Vedmak told me you would have beautiful hair, like spun gold, and that it would be magical. He explained that your hair would grow at an unusual rate, and that, much like Samson, it must not ever be touched by the sharpness of a blade. He said that doing so would drain your hair of its magic, and the consequences would be devastating." Gothel leaned forward, grasping Rapunzel's hand urgently. "*Devastating*, Rapunzel." She relaxed, releasing Rapunzel's hand.

"And then I found you," Gothel said.

Rapunzel startled. "*Found* me?" she asked, her voice high with surprise.

"*Had* you," Gothel said. "I *had* you. And you were exactly as Vedmak had described you, from your thick, long, golden hair to your big green eyes, and you smiled all the time. I knew it was you. I knew you were the one he had foreseen—my daughter restored."

Rapunzel's mind was flying. Her thoughts kept tripping over that one word: *found*. Her mother had corrected herself, but she couldn't get the word to stop spinning in her mind.

"When I brought you to him, he confirmed that you were the one foretold, Rapunzel. He recognized you immediately. And then he told me the rest of the prophecy.

"There was danger of being lost forever, he told me, and you would be the one to save her."

"Save *her*?" Rapunzel interjected. Panic suffocated her.

"Save the world, Rapunzel. Do you want me to tell you this, or do you want to continue to interrupt me?"

Her mother's eyes bore into her, and Rapunzel cringed. "I'm sorry," she murmured.

"Yes. Well." Gothel looked off again as she continued. "You are to save everything. He spoke of your hair. He told me that it was all tied together—your hair, your safety, and the safety of the world. That I must protect you at all costs, and that your hair must never be touched by the sharpness of a blade. And I've done that, Rapunzel, I've done all he's asked, and so far we've been protected from danger."

The gleam in Gothel's eyes unnerved Rapunzel. Still, she found the courage to ask, "And my SCIDs? Did he know about that?"

Gothel stood and turned away from Rapunzel. She walked over to the sink and leaned her hands on the edge of the counter, pushing her weight against her arms. "He told me you'd be fragile. He told me you'd need protection." She turned back toward Rapunzel. "So, yes, I suppose he did know."

Rapunzel nodded, feeling too shell-shocked by what she'd heard to form any further words. She'd been told the story many times over in her life, but never in this way, never with so much detail. She had more questions than when she'd asked. Her stomach churned.

"Rapunzel, I have to go away again, in a few days."

If there were words to pull Rapunzel from her sense of doom, those were it. Her mother gone meant she could see Fane again. She tried to keep the happiness from her face.

"Oh?" she managed.

Her mother came to her, taking her hands in her own. "It will only be for six days again. You seemed fine when I last went. Will you be okay again? If not, I can change it, I can—"

"No," Rapunzel said quickly. "Go. I was fine then and I'll be fine this time as well."

"I'll be certain food is cooked for you each day."

"It's not necessary, Mother. I can feed myself."

"We can't risk a relapse, Rapunzel. You understand the danger now."

"Which is why I should make my own meals, Mother. How will Cook get the food to me without exposing me to any possible germs she might carry?" Guilt plagued Rapunzel for playing the germ card, but she definitely didn't want a babysitter spoiling her slight bit of freedom.

Gothel thought about Rapunzel's words, then nodded in agreement. "Yes, I suppose you're right. Then make a shopping list and I'll bring you what you need."

Rapunzel dropped into bed an hour later, after messaging Fane with the news about her mother's pending trip. She wanted to get on the Internet and Google so many things her mother had told her, but she was too emotionally exhausted. More than that she wanted to talk to Fane about it, but should she? How could she explain the things she'd been told without him thinking that she and her mother both were insane? Would he look at her differently if she told him all she'd been told?

It wasn't a risk she was willing to take, not right now.

chapter

26

I mmunity: a state of having sufficient biological defenses to avoid infection, disease, or other unwanted biological invasion. It is the capability of the body to resist harmful microbes from entering the body.

Rapunzel read the definition several times until she could repeat it from memory. With SCIDs she definitely did *not* have a sufficient defense against biological invasion. She tried repeatedly to remember the overheard conversation between her mother and Dr. Henreich, but try as she might she couldn't recall specifics.

She read about the different kinds of immunity: the immunity acquired by being exposed to certain germs and bacteria in the world, and the immunity acquired by receiving vaccinations *against* certain germs and bacteria. She tried to remember if she'd ever been vaccinated but didn't know.

Her fingers hovered over the keyboard. She knew she could be opening a door better left closed—or what was that Greek thing she'd read about? Pandora's box? Fane had warned her. Her fingers touched the keys. She was tired of being the only one who didn't know anything about her life. She typed in "Gothel Manor."

The search popped up with *Did you mean Gothel Mansion?*

She clicked on the underlined words, stunned as pages of links came up. *The Mystery of Gothel Mansion, Gothel Mansion: Myth or Fact?, Gothel Mansion's Haunted Legacy, Gothel Mansion's Tower Ghost.* The titles almost all sounded sensationalistic, with only a few that seemed to stick to the historical. Taking a bracing breath, she clicked on one that seemed to avoid the sensational.

> Gothel Mansion, built in the early 1700s by pioneer Lawrence Gothel, was nothing more than a small, two-room cabin for him, his wife, Clarisse, and their eight children to live in as they moved into the northern California territory. A renowned fur trader, Lawrence's luck didn't extend to his family. Within a decade of their move, six of their children had died, along with Clarisse.

Wow, Rapunzel thought. *How horrible to lose six of your children* and *your wife.*

> The two remaining sons married, but only one had a child, a son.
>
> This downturn of luck continued for the Gothel family for over a century, until the Gold Rush of '49, when Lucas Gothel struck it rich. He built on to the cabin until it became a large home. The large home was for naught. Lucas also was only able to sire a single child, a son named Frederick.
>
> Frederick was a financial genius, and it is due to him that the family has prospered in the century and a half since. Frederick tied the family fortune up into profitable ventures, unable to be discontinued by any of his

descendants, which has ensured the continued prosperity of the Gothel fortune for many generations to come.

Currently, for the first time ever the home is owned by one not of Gothel blood. The last heir, Nigel Gothel, married Bonnie Higby, who came from a questionable background. There was some speculation as to the untimely death of Higby's parents. However, with inconclusive evidence, Higby was not charged with any crime. Gothel married Higby and then died in an accident three years later. Higby was again brought under question, but again there was no evidence proving she had anything to do with Gothel's death. She has since continually built onto the house, despite living there alone.

Unfortunately, the couple did not have any children, and with no other heirs the home and fortune has been left to Higby."

Wait, what? Rapunzel read the last two lines again. "No children . . . lived alone." *But then, who am I?*

Higby, who now goes by her legal name of Gothel, resides in the home. She has never remarried, and it remains to be seen to whom she will leave the fortune upon her passing.

Rapunzel finished the article, which had a few pictures of the outside of her house, including an aerial view. The older photos showed a much smaller house, and her tower was definitely missing. She went back and read again the line, ". . . the couple did not have any children." If she were correct, Bonnie Higby was the name of her mother. Her mother who had a "questionable" background.

Why didn't anyone know about Rapunzel? Was her birth a secret? She felt overwhelmed by what she'd read.

Then, deciding since she was already in this far, she may as well go all the way, she clicked the link called *The Mystery of Gothel Mansion.*

Shasta County, California, may not have an amusement park adorned by a talking mouse with big ears, but it has something much more sinister: Gothel Mansion. Gothel Mansion has a long legacy of less-than-sane owners over the years, with the curse of each heir only being able to produce one son to carry on the legacy.

Until now.

Now the Mansion and Gothel fortune are in the hands of accused murderess Bonnie Higby.

Rapunzel's mouth dropped. Murderess?

Bonnie Higby's parents died when gas in their home caused them to asphyxiate. There was no leak. The oven had been turned on, the pilot light extinguished. Bonnie happened to be spending the night at a friend's house. *Happened* to be. While it never could be proved that Bonnie killed her parents, there was much suspicion and speculation. There were rumors of heavy abuse by Bonnie's parents.

When she managed to snag über-eligible bachelor Nigel Gothel, the world was stunned. When three short years after their marriage Nigel died in a hiking accident with his wife in the Cascade Mountains near their home, Bonnie once again became a suspect. However, with no witnesses to prove he hadn't slipped as Bonnie claimed, she was once again released.

And that's when things got really weird.

After Nigel's death, and with no other heir apparent, the fortune fell to Bad Bonnie. Or perhaps it would be more appropriate to call her Mad Bonnie. Mad Bonnie, who lives like a hermit, consults mediums, and holds séances. There have even been rumors of witchcraft possibly being dabbled in by her. In between all of her extracurricular activities, Mad Bonnie builds.

Yes, that's right. She builds. There is always construction on the sprawling mansion. Rumors abound that the construction is almost constant and is also useless. A previous construction worker claims he personally worked on stairways that go nowhere and doors that open into walls. And always, he claims, with six workers total.

Clearly Mad Bonnie is obsessed with the number six. Six workers on crew at all times, working six hours, six days a week. Doors must have six panels, windows either six panes or six windows per room. Everything must be measured in increments of six. For example, a room must be twelve, eighteen, twenty-four feet across. Anything divisible by six. Ceilings are twelve feet. And those that weren't have been modified at great expense.

The biggest mystery is the great tower. Built eighteen years ago, this tower is rumored to house a girl—perhaps Mad Bonnie's daughter? Although no one knows of the birth of any child to the woman, other than the child she miscarried. Workers have reported seeing a figure in the high window on rare occasion. Perhaps she's a ghost of one of the past Gothel wives. There is much speculation about her, but not a thing that's been substantiated—much like Mad Bonnie's murders."

Rapunzel's stomach churned. It was too much. She might pass the whole thing off as complete bunk—if she hadn't been told the story by her mother about Vedmak.

If she hadn't seen the black room of sixes.

If she hadn't seen for herself the stairways and doors.

If she weren't the ghost girl.

She shut her computer off. Fane knew all of this—
he told her not to Google her house, which meant he'd
known what she'd find. She stood and left the cove. Her
gaze caught on the bowl of apples—the bowl that was
always required to have six apples.

She went into her room, passed through to the bathroom, and for the first time in her life, threw up.

chapter

27

Rapunzel ignored the repeated messages left on her Facebook page by Fane. He was worried again. She knew that and felt bad. She couldn't face him, not now, not knowing what she did. It was hard enough facing her mother, pretending all was well.

Her mother sensed something was wrong.

"You're feeling ill again, aren't you? That's it. I'm canceling my trip."

"No," Rapunzel said quickly. She needed some time alone. "Really, Mother, I feel fine." She smiled widely. "I'm just a bit worried about a test I have coming up. I'll use the time while you're gone to study and it'll be fine. I promise."

Her mother looked askance at her. Rapunzel perked up and acted as normal as possible for the next few days until her mother was convinced she was fine.

The day before her trip, her mother broached the subject of Cook.

"I'm giving her the time off. No sense in having someone in the house, spreading around germs unnecessarily."

She tucked a strand of Rapunzel's hair behind her ear, soothing her hair as she always did.

"That's a good idea," Rapunzel replied, not mentioning that it had been her own idea originally.

"Do you still have the cell phone?" Gothel asked, as if just realizing she hadn't taken it back previously.

"Yes." Rapunzel tried to still her hammering heart. Would her mother ask for it and see her texts to Fane?

"Good," she said. "Make sure you charge it. I'll call you each evening."

"At six?" Rapunzel asked facetiously, biting her tongue against the bitterness.

Her mother didn't comment, simply answered in the affirmative. Of course she didn't ask to see or check the phone. She had no reason to believe that Rapunzel would do anything else with it. Who would she call?

Her mother left after making sure Rapunzel was well stocked with food. The day she left, Rapunzel considered staying in bed all day. She was depressed. She pushed herself out of bed and walked to her only window. It was a Sunday morning in November, and the gray, overcast skies outside matched her mood. She hadn't seen Angel in a couple of weeks, and while she was glad the little bird had gone south, she missed her only friend—besides Fane. But she'd cut him out of her life now as well. She just hadn't expected it to hurt so much.

Moving back into the main room, she glanced at the door, wondering if it was unlocked. She was alone, after all, for six days. She could see the rest of the house, see for herself the craziness of Bonnie Gothel. She twisted the door handle—locked. Of course.

She tried to remember how Fane had gotten the handle off before with the screwdriver. Not that she had a screwdriver. Even if she did, she wasn't sure she could do it. She squatted and examined the handle. The screws had some kind of x-looking indent in the center.

She went into her kitchen area and pulled open the utensil drawer. Then she glanced down at herself. She still had her pajamas on. She couldn't wander the house in her pajamas. *And why not?* she thought. There wasn't anyone else here, what difference did it make? In fact, why did she ever get dressed, to only see her mother? Surely her mother didn't care how she appeared.

She sifted through the contents of the drawer, trying to find something that would work. She had nothing that mimicked the shape of the indent. She picked up a sharp knife, wondering if the pointed end would work.

Returning to the door, she knelt and stuck the point of the knife in, twisting futilely. Her head dropped, defeated, but snapped back up when she heard movement on the other side of the door. Had her mother decided to stay home after all? Or Cook? Or was it someone else . . . She scuttled away from the door, not sure what to do as she heard a scraping noise against the door. Her heart pounded wildly. She held the knife up defensively, then realized that if it were her mother she wouldn't be able to explain holding a knife like a weapon. She hid it behind her back as the door handle began to turn. She pushed against the wall, watching.

The door opened slowly. It wasn't her mother. Her mother never entered so stealthily—at least, she didn't think so. Heat flooded Rapunzel as her nerves jumped, and she brought the knife up again. A foot stepped past the door—a man's foot, and she caught her breath.

"Rapunzel?"

The sound of Fane's voice followed by his head coming around the door brought a tidal wave of relief washing over Rapunzel. She dropped the knife and ran forward, startling Fane who'd been looking the other way. She threw herself against him, nearly knocking him over. His arms came around her as she clung desperately to him.

"Whoa, Rapunzel! Are you okay? What's going on?" He pushed her away from him far enough to look at her, see the panic on her face before pulling her back into his arms. "What happened?"

She shook her head, realizing how ridiculous she behaved, and moved away from him, wiping the tears of relief from her cheeks. "Nothing. I'm sorry. I was just . . . why are you here? How did you get in?"

He lifted one brow. "How do you think? And the *why* should be equally obvious." He stepped forward and took both her hands in his. "I've been worried about you. Why haven't you answered any of my messages, or been on Skype? I thought maybe you were sick again. I thought . . ."

Rapunzel shook her head and pulled her hands from his. She turned away, moving to sit on the couch. He followed, but instead of sitting he squatted before her.

"What's going on, Rapunzel?"

She wanted to lie, tell him nothing was wrong. She wanted to tell him to go away and never come back. But she couldn't. She looked at him, overwhelmed with how much she'd missed him. She wanted to ask him to take her from this tower and hide her from her crazy reality instead.

"I thought someone was breaking in," she said. "I was scared."

"I'm so sorry. I told you I was coming, but maybe . . . I guess you didn't read my messages, huh?"

Rapunzel shook her head.

When Rapunzel didn't say anything, he continued. "I suppose you didn't want me to come, but I had to make sure you were okay. I'm sorry for scaring you. I should . . . I should go now." He stood and moved toward the door.

She should *let* him go.

"Wait!" she said as he opened the door. He turned back. "Don't go. Please."

"Are you sure?" he asked.

She nodded, and he walked back to sit next to her. "Are you mad at me for something?" he asked.

Her mouth dropped. "Of course not. Why would I be mad at you?"

"Well, you haven't answered any of my messages, and you seem . . . sort of distant, I guess."

She swallowed and decided to just tell him.

"I Googled some things," she began.

His face changed, understanding crossing his eyes. "You Googled your house?" he asked. She nodded. "You shouldn't have done that, Rapunzel. The Internet is full of lies and stories that people make up just to get people to read them."

Rapunzel shook her head sadly, glancing at her wringing hands. "They weren't all lies, Fane. You know that as well as I do." When he didn't say anything, she said, "You can go if you want. You must think . . ."

"I must think what?" She looked up at him. "Rapunzel, all of that crap is nothing new to me. Do you remember when you first told me who you were?" She nodded. "I didn't believe you because I believed all of that. But now I know that you aren't a ghost. That's when I figured most of those stories had to be untrue."

"You think they're untrue?"

He shrugged. "Well, some of them have to be. Right?"

"I don't know," she said honestly. "There are things . . . I mean, it's true about all the construction, and the stairs and doors that go nowhere. And the sixes. You saw the room. But there's more." Fane waited. "I didn't think anything of it until I read the stories." She stood and walked over to the bowl of apples, picking one up. "I'm required to always keep six apples in here. She comes every night at six for dinner. I have six forks, spoons, and knives in the drawer. Six glasses in the cabinet, and six plates and bowls. If she's in town, everything in the fridge and pantry are stocked in multiples of six." She stopped as a new thought struck her. "She's been out of town twice—for six days each."

Fane stood and crossed the room, pulling her into his arms again. She hadn't realized how much she shook until he held her.

"What can I do?" he asked.

"Help me find the truth," she said.

"Okay. I can do that. Or try, anyway."

Rapunzel relaxed against him.

"Rapunzel?"

"Yeah?"

"Why is there a knife on the floor near the sofa?"

She gave a dry laugh. "I was trying to use it to break out of the room," she said. "And then it was my defense when I heard you outside the door."

Fane's laughter rumbled beneath her ear. "Were you planning to scratch me with it?"

She shoved him away. "Don't make fun of me."

"We have *got* to get you a better arsenal." Fane sobered. "You wouldn't have gotten out, Rapunzel. Not only was the handle locked, the hook was latched."

Rapunzel thought about that, about what it meant. She'd been truly locked in. Why?

Suddenly she remembered she was still in her pajamas. Embarrassment flooded her and she brought her hands to her cheeks.

"What?" Fane asked at her gesture.

"I'll be back," she said, turning and hurrying into her bedroom. She closed the door and quickly dressed, brushed her teeth and braided her hair, cursing the amount of time it took to tame the heavy length. She felt much better when she reemerged from the room.

"How did you know it was safe to come into the house?" Rapunzel asked.

"I watched for your mother to leave."

"Oh." He must have been really worried, she decided. Someone worrying about her so much caused a little bloom of warmth in her chest. "Did you see anyone else here?"

"No. There were no other cars here, anyway. If someone is here, they weren't in any of the places I passed."

"My mother told me she was giving Cook the time off while she's gone. I assume that no one will be here all week. That means we can explore the house more."

"You sure you want to do that?"

She nodded. "I need to find out everything I can."

chapter

28

"This must be part of the original house."

They'd crept down the stairs and walked through the house a bit before determining they were alone. The alarm was set on the doors. Silence greeted them in every room. Rapunzel ran a hand across the wood log wall in the room they'd just entered. The ceiling in here was lower than anywhere else in the house. It looked very much like the inside of an old log cabin, so she believed he was probably right. Other than an old iron woodstove taking up the bulk of the corner and a fireplace covered with a metal screen, the room was empty.

"She left this part of the house intact," Rapunzel said. "I wonder why."

"It would have been left this way from previous owners," Fane said. "They built around this. She isn't the first one to have built onto the original house. She's just the first one to have, you know, gone overboard."

"How much of the house was here when she moved in?"

"I'm not sure," Fane said. "But we can probably find out."

Rapunzel paid close attention to detail each place they'd been, which consisted of about twenty rooms today before coming upon the log room. Each room was built with six window panes, six panels in the doors, and six light bulbs or sources in each light in each room. Except for this part of the house. The more they looked, the more questions she had. Who was this woman who was her mother? She felt like a complete stranger.

"Check this out," Fane called from the next room. Rapunzel passed through a small doorway that led into what must have been the original bedroom of the cabin.

A large log bed covered almost the entire floor space. A big red quilt covered a lumpy mattress. In the middle of the quilt lay a small baby's quilt. While the big quilt was clearly aged, the baby quilt didn't look so old. Faded pink material covered in purple elephants indicated it as not quite new, but definitely not as old as the red one. Looking at the quilt, a sense of odd déjà vu struck Rapunzel.

She walked over and picked it up. Before she turned it over she knew what she'd see on the backside—green material with little pink rosebuds.

"I think this must have been my baby blanket," she said. "I remember it."

"I doubt it," Fane said. She looked at him questioningly and he pointed to the bottom corner. "It has initials embroidered into it. 'S. R.'"

"Oh. Maybe not, then. But I remember it, so maybe it was someone else's and then my mother used it for me."

"Maybe," he conceded. "I wonder who S. R. is."

"I have no idea," she said. "Let's get out of here." She

spread the blanket back across the bed, able to put it in the same spot since it was the area with no dust. The rest of the house was kept very clean, but these two rooms from the original cabin were a little dusty. As she turned to follow Fane from the room, her toes bumped against something beneath the bed. She leaned down and saw an old trunk beneath the bed. "Fane, wait."

He came back into the room, kneeling to see what she looked at.

"Score," he said with a grin.

An hour later they still hadn't been able to open it. The trunk was old, but the lock on it was new—and very sturdy.

"I don't think we're going to get it open."

"Not today, anyway," Fane said.

"What do you mean?"

"We just don't have the right tools," he answered.

They pushed the trunk back beneath the bed and left the room.

"How many rooms does this place have anyway?" Rapunzel said as they wound down another hallway. This part of the house was in good repair though definitely older than the parts they'd been in previously, and dusty like the log rooms.

"I'm not sure," Fane said. "No one seems to know exactly. Rumor is somewhere around a hundred and fifty, but I'm not sure how true that is."

Rapunzel stopped walking. "A hundred and *fifty*?"

Fane also stopped and came back to her. "That's just a rumor, Rapunzel."

"But probably true, right? Like all the other rumors?" Panic climbed her throat.

"I'm surprised your mom left you, you know, with Thanksgiving and all."

"What?" Fane's strange comment took her mind off the number of rooms.

"Thursday. It's Thanksgiving."

Rapunzel hadn't realized it was Thanksgiving already. But he was right. Hurt wound its way around her heart at the fact that her mother left with the holiday this week. They'd spent every Thanksgiving together. She hadn't even left Rapunzel a turkey.

"I didn't realize it was . . ." Tears filled her eyes and she blinked them back, refusing to cry in front of Fane. It seemed he saw anyway and stepped closer.

"I'm sorry. I didn't mean to make you cry."

"It isn't you," she said, smiling through her tears. "It's her. She's the one who left. Mother always made such a big deal about the holiday, telling me it was the most important one because we have so much to be thankful for."

Fane put his arms around her, and she tried not to feel sorry for herself as she leaned into him.

"You should come to my house," he said.

"What?" she sniffled.

"On Thursday. Come to my house for Thanksgiving."

"I can't do that," she said. "I don't know your family."

"And you never will if you don't meet them," he said. "We have some relatives coming over, but it'll be fun."

"I doubt your family will want me to come. You haven't even asked them."

"I guarantee my mom will love to have you there. I know her well enough to know that. She's all about having big groups of people over for holidays."

"Big groups?" Rapunzel asked, her voice quivering.

"Smaller than the group at the Halloween party." Then, as if remembering what came after the party, he said, "Maybe that's not such a good idea. I mean, you got sick after that one. I don't want you to get sick again."

"Fane," she said. Her shoulders dropped, and she smiled at him. "I don't plan to live the rest of my life inside my tower."

"What do you mean?"

"I mean, I've thought a lot about it. Do I want to stay closed up in my room for the next fifty or sixty years just to stay healthy? Or do I want to *live*? I'd rather die in two years than live a hundred inside that tower."

"Rapunzel, don't say that. You can't—"

"Of course I can," she interrupted. "I just can't *yet*. I can't make my own choices until I'm eighteen, which is in seven months. Maybe my mother will be angry and kick me out after that. It's incredibly selfish of me, I know, but—"

"Wait, why is it selfish?"

Rapunzel chewed a nail as she debated telling Fane. There was a good chance he'd never return if she told him. There was also a good chance he'd stay. After all, he knew about the rest of the insanity, and yet here he was.

"Let's go back to my room," she said. "I'll make us lunch and then I'll tell you a story."

"What kind of story?"

"Do you believe in prophecies?" she asked. He didn't answer but followed her as she led the way back to her room.

chapter

29

Fane listened without interruption while she
related the whole bizarre tale her mother had told
her. It sounded even stranger to her as she said
it aloud. Still, she told it to him exactly as it had been
related to her.

When she finished, he sat quietly. She became nervous, wondering if he just realized what a crazy situation
he found himself in. Crazier than he'd even suspected.

"So, what do you think?" she asked.

"I think the *Twilight Zone* exists."

"Twilight Zone?" Rapunzel asked. "As in, the books?"

That brought a small smile from Fane. "No, not the
books. No sparkly vampires in this story. At least, not yet."

Rapunzel sighed. "I was raised believing her story,
though I didn't have all the details of why she believes it.
I just accepted it as truth. Now . . . I don't know. It seems
a little . . . farfetched."

Fane shrugged. "I can't really say one way or another.
I've never talked to a psychic or prophet or whatever before,
never really even considered them and whether they're real

or not. Maybe we should research them. Or find one and go see her. Or him."

Rapunzel turned worried eyes on him. "What if they confirm what she told me?"

"What if they don't?"

"Yes," Rapunzel said. "What if they don't? That means my whole life has been a lie. I don't know which would be worse."

Fane nodded. "I wish there were an easy answer for you, Rapunzel. It seems like the more we discover, the less we know."

"Exactly," she said. "I wish I could just ask my mother, but if I do, she'll be angry with me."

"Well then, we'll find out what we can, so that when you do ask you at least know the right things to ask."

Tears stung Rapunzel's eyes again. She didn't know what was wrong with her that she felt like crying so much as of late.

Fane jerked at the tears. "Uh . . . are you . . . I mean, did I say something wrong? Did I make you cry?"

Rapunzel laughed through the tears. "No. I don't know why I keep crying. It's definitely not you. At least, not in a bad way. What would I do without you, Fane? If I hadn't met you, I'd probably still just be sitting here in my tower, content with my non-life."

"I don't know if I should apologize, or . . ."

"Don't apologize. Please. I'm grateful."

* * *

By the time Thursday came, Fane and Rapunzel had

explored a lot more of the house. Fane didn't have school because of the holiday, and Rapunzel caught up on her homework online quickly with his help. They hadn't been able to open the trunk.

Fane had brought her a screwdriver and a flat, stiff plastic ruler the thickness of a paper and showed her how to remove her door handle, and how to slide the ruler into the space between the door and jamb to lift the latch.

"See? It's pretty easy. Now you try it. Wait, let me go out and re-latch it."

She could now get out of her room anytime she wanted. She felt much safer. Being locked in scared her with the burnt room of sixes two floors below.

Rapunzel rolled out of bed on Thursday with nerves thrumming. She wasn't worried about whether she might get sick again. She worried about how Fane's family would perceive her. She had no idea how to behave in a social setting. The Halloween party had been fairly easy because with the loud music, there wasn't much required of her. She had a feeling there wouldn't be any music blaring today.

She decided to wear the only skirt she owned. She'd worn it once when she'd first gotten it. She didn't have a reason to have gotten it, just a desire to have one. However, it was really inconvenient to wear for just hanging around her rooms. Since she didn't have to go down a ladder today, she figured she may as well wear it.

She met Fane downstairs. It felt different waiting for him in the sizable living room rather than hiding in her tower. It felt as if she were starring in one of the movies she'd been watching where the hero picked up the heroine for an actual date—something she'd never experienced. She supposed the Halloween party might be considered a date, but still. Something about not having to climb down the ladder made it feel more like a real date. Of course, they'd still have to make their way through the dark tunnel. It didn't frighten her anymore since they'd been through it a few times. Now it just felt . . . familiar.

"Wow."

Rapunzel startled and turned at the sound of Fane's voice behind her. She hadn't heard him enter. His eyes swept her hair, where she had wrapped a braid crown-style, then used a few thin braids to lead from the crown to the thick braid that ran down her back. His gaze then dropped to her powder blue sweater atop the white skirt. She wore white tennis shoes. She knew that probably wasn't what fashion dictated she wear with a skirt, but she didn't have anything other than slippers and flip-flops. The cold weather negated the intelligence of wearing flip-flops. His eyes traveled back up her hair, and Rapunzel felt her face flush at the look in his eyes.

"You look beautiful," he said, his words heavy with feeling and a bit awed. His sincerity felt sweeter than when he teased her about her "hotness." She wanted to laugh and brush his words off as she usually did but couldn't this time.

Fane stepped forward and took her hand in his, gaze locked on hers. He brought her hand to his lips, the gesture somehow more intimate than all the times he'd done so before—more intimate than the kisses they'd shared.

"I kinda think we should stay here today so I don't have to share you with anyone," he said, grinning. But his words carried a serious undertone.

"Isn't this an important holiday for families?"

Fane grunted. "Yeah, I guess my mom would never forgive me if I didn't show up."

"Really?" Rapunzel was fascinated. His mother would forever hold a grudge for missing one day with the family?

Fane laughed. "No, not really. She'd be mad, but she'd get over it. However, I don't want to hurt her, so we'll go. Where's your mask?"

Rapunzel shrugged. "I don't want to wear it."

Worry filled Fane's eyes. "But, Rapunzel, you've been sick. What if—"

"Please, Fane, I don't want to meet your family that way. I want to be . . . normal."

"Normal isn't all it's cracked up to be," he muttered. Yet in his eyes was a sort of understanding. He didn't argue further.

He helped her put her mother's old coat on, then led her by the hand through the house and tunnel, walking slowly through the greenhouse to allow her time to admire and touch all of the flowers and plants. Outside the air was crisp and chill with low dark clouds.

The car ride was still a bit terrifying, even with her hand held firmly in Fane's. He pulled into the driveway of a house similar to the one they'd gone to on Halloween. Only instead of being populated with carved pumpkins, there were a few un-carved pumpkins on the front porch atop a hay bale. A stuffed animal that looked like a smiling turkey with a pilgrim's hat also perched there.

Fane parked and once again opened the car door for her. She could feel the tension in his grip and knew he was concerned about her. She was surprisingly calm. She didn't particularly want to be ill again but she couldn't find it within her to worry about it either. She'd decided that whatever fate had in store for her would occur whether she wore a mask or not. After all, hadn't she gotten sick while wearing one?

He took her hand once again and led her up to the front door. He opened the door and amazing smells drifted out, engulfing her. She recognized the smell of turkey, but there were other unfamiliar smells. It smelled delicious. She'd been expecting the noise of a lot of people, but it seemed fairly quiet other than some music playing quietly. She wondered if it were a tradition to be quiet on Thanksgiving.

The room they stood in was similar to Rapunzel's living area with two sofas, a coffee table, and an end table. However, this room had a large TV taking up most of one wall, the bookcase filled with DVDs and video games.

"Mom!"

Fane's yell startled Rapunzel. A woman came from somewhere at the back of the house and entered the room. She was tall and thin, and her eyes were the same golden brown as Fane's. She had red hair pulled back into a messy bun at the back of her head. She wore an apron with a terrified looking turkey inside an oven emblazoned on the front and the words, "Okay, who's the wise guy who told me this was the sauna?" beneath it. Her youthful look surprised Rapunzel. She was quite beautiful.

"Rapunzel, this is my mom. Mom, Rapunzel."

The woman took Rapunzel's hand in hers, as if in a handshake, but then she enclosed Rapunzel's hand with her other so that it was a more intimate gesture. She smiled warmly.

"Hi, Rapunzel. Great name. My name is Beth, by the way." She threw a squinty-eyed look at Fane as she said that, as if to remind him of his poor manners. "Welcome to our home. I'm so happy you came."

Rapunzel couldn't help but smile back at Fane's mother. Everything about her, from her smile to her eyes to her body language, added sincerity to her words.

"Thank you for having me," she said.

"Fane said your mom had to go out of town for a family emergency?" She phrased it as a question, and Rapunzel glanced at Fane, grateful she didn't have to try to make up her own excuse.

"Yes."

"That's too bad. Hopefully everything will turn out okay."

"Where's Dad?" Fane asked.

"He went to pick up Grandma and Grandpa. He'll be home soon."

"I'm going to show Rapunzel my room," Fane said, taking her hand and leading her to a hallway.

"Door open," his mom sing-songed as she exited through the doorway she'd just come in through. Fane rolled his eyes, grinning at Rapunzel as if she should be in on the joke, but she didn't get it.

Rapunzel followed Fane down a narrow hallway. The ceilings were much lower than any of the ceilings in her house, other than in the area where the original house was. She fought the urge to duck a few times. It almost felt claustrophobic. He opened the door to his room and stepped back for her to enter ahead of himself.

His room was very different than Rapunzel's. A narrow bed, covered with a dark blue quilt dotted with white, sat against the opposite wall. His walls were covered with posters of groups of people, movies, and a couple that depicted guitars. A dresser in the corner held a few trophies on top and a stack of books. His backpack sat on the floor next to the dresser.

"Oops." He darted in front of her and shut his closet door, flashing her an embarrassed grin.

On his desk sat his computer where they'd probably first met through Facebook and where she Skyped with him. She glanced at the area behind his computer. His bed was behind it, and a couple of the posters on the wall above that. She hadn't ever looked close enough to notice the posters—probably because she always kept her gaze so intently on him.

"Who are the people on the posters?" she asked.

"Bands I listen to," he said. "This one is Linkin Park, my favorite. Do you know them?"

"No."

"Well, that's just a travesty," he teased sarcastically. He walked over to a white box that had speakers with a smaller square object sitting on the front. "iPod," he said, pointing to the little square. "It holds all my music." She thought it odd that something that small could hold all his music. He must not have much. He pushed a button a couple of times and music blasted into the room. He quickly swirled his finger on the front of it, and the volume lessened.

"Have a seat," he said, pointing to the rolling desk chair. "You're gonna love this." He indicated the iPod. She sat on the chair and he sat on the bed. She turned the chair to face him, feeling shy sitting in his room. She wasn't sure why that should be. She'd spent plenty of time alone with him in her rooms. There was just something about sitting here in *his* room.

"Nervous?" he asked.

She nodded. "It's quieter than I thought it would be," she admitted.

"Just wait. Once all the aunts, uncles, and cousins come, you'll be wishing for the quiet. Enjoy it while you can."

Rapunzel's stomach tightened at his words. "How many are coming?"

"Let's see," he said, turning his gaze skyward and counting on his fingers. "I think probably around thirty."

Rapunzel's mouth dropped. "*Thirty?*"

Fane shrugged as if it weren't a gigantic number. "My parents are the only ones in the family who only have one child. My dad has two brothers, and my mom has one brother and two sisters. My dad's brothers have three and four kids, my mom's two sisters are coming and they have three and five kids. My dad's parents and my mom's dad, plus the four of us is somewhere around thirty people, right?"

Rapunzel's head spun from the numbers. She couldn't begin to count them based on his speech. "How will I ever remember their names?" she muttered.

"My mom thought of that," Fane said. Rapunzel blushed; she hadn't meant to speak aloud. "She's making everyone wear name tags that also tell you how they're related. Should be interesting to see if my cousins actually keep the right ones on." Fane laughed.

"Oh," Rapunzel said, overwhelmed. She preferred to be a bit more invisible, not have everyone do something unusual to accommodate her.

"My granny—my mom's mom—died a couple of years ago. It's been really hard on granddad, so don't be surprised if you see him tearing up now and then." Then, as if he'd just thought of it, "Do you have any grandparents?"

"No." Rapunzel shook her head. "If the stories we read are true, my mother's parents died under suspicious circumstances, and my father's parents died before he even married."

"Oh. Yeah. Right." Fane sounded sorry for asking, but Rapunzel was caught up in her words. She hadn't ever really thought of her father before. She'd never really questioned his existence—or lack of existence, until she'd read about him in the articles. It seemed strange that there had been a man who had fathered her, who would have been a big part of her life had he lived. She wondered if he truly had slipped off that cliff, or if—

"You okay?" Fane leaned forward, looking at her with concern.

"I just realized that I have—or *had*, I should say—a father. And grandparents."

"Yeah, I guess that would be weird if you'd never known about him. Or them." He smiled and took her hand in his. "You'll love my grandparents. And they'll love you as well."

Rapunzel looked at their hands. Fane idly rubbed the back of her hand. His hand was larger, darker, compared to her thin, pale, frail-looking fingers. While she was sure the gesture didn't mean much to him, it did funny things to her belly.

"So, why do your parents only have you?" she asked, voice trembling.

Fane shrugged. "My mom almost died when she had me. She had a stroke when she was only six months along. They managed to keep her pregnant for a couple of weeks, but then she had me. I only weighed a pound and a half."

"Really?"

Fane lifted and flexed one arm muscle—impressively—and joked, "From a one-and-a-half pound weakling to a one-hundred-eighty-five pound Hulk in eighteen short years." Rapunzel couldn't tear her eyes from his arm. Finally he dropped it. "After that, they told her it was too risky to have another baby. She could've died. My dad said it wasn't worth the risk. So I'm it."

"Do you miss having siblings?"

He shook his head. "I'm pretty close to my cousins. Plus, I have a lot of friends. So I've never missed having brothers or sisters. Besides, I pretty much always get my way since there's no one to argue with me."

Rapunzel thought about that. "I don't have anyone to argue with, either, but I don't get my way. Everything is my mother's way."

Fane nodded. "Your life is definitely a little different than mine, huh?"

"You think?" Rapunzel said, using one of Fane's phrases. They looked at each other and laughed.

"The world is a poorer place for not having you in it, Rapunzel. It's a shame to have you locked up in that tower."

"Thank you," she said, meaning it. At least one person in the real world was aware of her.

chapter

30

It didn't take long for Rapunzel to discover that Fane was right about the noise. As soon as his relatives arrived, it became very loud in his house.

"Hey, Rapunzel, when are you going to get rid of this jerk and go out with a real man?"

Rapunzel looked up at Kevin, Fane's cousin. It wasn't the first time he had made a similar comment. He'd been teasing Rapunzel about dating him since he'd arrived at the house. He was the same age as Fane, older by two months, a fact he never let Fane forget.

"You should date a real man, like me," he continued.

"I'm not dating Fane. We're just friends," she said.

Kevin punched Fane in the shoulder. "What's wrong with you, bro? You have a gorgeous girl like this hanging around and you're not dating her? You must be *loco*. See what I'm talking about, Rapunzel? If you were with a real man, like me, I wouldn't hesitate dating you."

Rapunzel glanced at Fane to see his clenched jaw ticking and a spot of red in his cheek. Was he angry at Kevin for insinuating that he should be dating her? Rapunzel's attention was drawn away from Fane and Kevin by Ava and Liv, Fane's eleven- and twelve-year-old cousins who were braiding the back of her hair.

As soon as they had come into the house and spotted her hair, they squealed in delight and begged her to let them braid it. She left the crown braid in but let them loosen the back, which they had since braided into a bunch of smaller braids. They were now taking the smaller braids and twisting them into a single braid down her back.

Their mother, Sandy, came into the room. "Are you still torturing Rapunzel's hair?" she asked the girls.

The girls completely ignored her, but Rapunzel smiled at Fane's aunt. "It's okay. I don't mind. It feels kind of nice having someone else do my hair for once."

"You do your own hair?" Sandy sounded surprised.

"Yes, my mother did it when I was little of course, but she hasn't done it for several years now. I usually just braid it in a single braid so that it doesn't drag on the floor."

"I've never seen hair that long on a person so young," Sandy said, "In fact, I don't think I've seen hair that long on anybody of any age."

Rapunzel wasn't sure how to respond to that, so she just smiled.

"Can we put ribbons in your hair?" Ava asked.

"Where do you think you're going to get ribbon in a house that has only one teenage boy and no young girls?" Sandy asked.

"I wouldn't be surprised if Fane *does* wear ribbons in his hair," Kevin interjected, "since Fane is not even man enough to ask a girl on a decent date."

At that, Fane tackled Kevin around the waist, pulling him to the floor. Rapunzel stood in alarm, but Fane's Uncle David calmly walked into the room and said, "Take it outside, boys."

Kevin took off running, slamming his way out the front door, Fane hot on his heels. Everyone scrambled to the front windows to watch the spectacle, laughing and making bets on who would win. Rapunzel wasn't sure what to make of the whole situation. Weren't they afraid that one of them would hurt the other? But as she looked out the window she saw that Fane and Kevin laughed as they wrestled. Finally Fane straddled Kevin, holding Kevin's arms above his head. Kevin laughingly yelled, "Uncle! Uncle!" Rapunzel glanced over at the uncles, surprised that none of them heeded his call.

Fane stood, reaching a hand down to pull Kevin to his feet. Kevin slung an arm around Fane's neck, scrubbing the top of his head with his knuckles. Just then, Kevin and Fane both stopped and glanced toward the sky.

"It's snowing!" Kevin yelled. Fane's eyes came to Rapunzel's, and he grinned at her. In that one look she knew that he understood she'd never been outside in the snow before.

"Come out," Fane mouthed to her, waving her out with a gesture.

Within moments the house had emptied of nearly every person as they all stood outside, looking up at the sky and the flakes drifting down. Fane came to Rapunzel and took her hand in his. His hand was icy cold. A worried look came across his face.

"You probably shouldn't be out here. You're going to get sick," he said.

Before she could answer, Beth stuck her head out the door. "You all get in here, out of the cold. Dinner's ready."

That brought a cheer, particularly from the men, and they all stumbled over one another, pushing their way back into the house. Fane and Rapunzel held back. She lifted her hand as a snowflake landed in it and immediately melted.

"I've felt the snow outside my window," she told him, "but I've never stood outside in it."

Fane brought her hand to his mouth and said, "Let's go eat until we're sick, and then I'll find you a decent coat and some gloves and we'll come back out."

"We have to eat until we're sick? Why?"

Fane just laughed and led the way into the house.

* * *

Rapunzel was amazed at how Fane's family had multiple, loud conversations going on throughout dinner. She wasn't sure which conversation to follow and didn't attempt to jump into any of them unless she was asked a direct question. It could have easily been overwhelming. Instead, Rapunzel found herself completely enjoying the chaos. She'd never been with any family members other than her mother.

There was also more food than she'd ever seen in one sitting. Fane's uncles ate so much food, she felt sure that their bellies would explode. Rapunzel realized that Fane had only been half teasing about eating until they were sick.

While they ate, the snowstorm had increased in intensity, until the world turned white by the amount of snow falling from the sky. By the time they finished eating, there was a good base of snow on the ground. Fane kept true to his word. He placed one of his mom's thick winter coats on her. It fell to her knees, puffy with feathers, and felt as warm as a cocoon. He gave her a knit cap and some thick gloves to wear. His mom lent her some sweatpants to put on beneath her skirt to keep her legs warm, and a pair of her boots that were only half a size too large. They went outside, followed by Kevin, Ava, Liv, and the rest of the cousins. It was colder than she'd expected, but she quickly warmed up as they all began chasing one another around in the snow. Liv taught her how to make a snow angel, and some of the other cousins attempted to build a snowman, but the snow was too wet and there wasn't quite enough of it yet.

Soon, another of Fane's aunts came out and called them in for hot chocolate. Rapunzel thought they would refuse since they had just eaten such a huge feast, but they all went running in as if they hadn't eaten for days.

Rapunzel moved to follow them until Fane took her hand in his and laid a finger on his lips, indicating that she should be silent. As soon as the last cousin disappeared through the door, he led her around the side of the house. He looked furtively left and right and then quickly led her out of the front yard and down the sidewalk.

Rapunzel had no idea where he was taking her but trusted him enough to follow. After a few minutes they came to a wide expanse of snow-covered grass. Several trees populated the area as well as some benches and children's play areas. She had seen play areas like these online and in movies but had never seen one herself.

"What is this place?" she asked in awe.

"It's a park," he said. He pointed. "Those are the playgrounds. I guess you've never been to one, huh?"

Rapunzel didn't answer but pointed to the playground. "Can we see those closer?"

"We can do better than that."

They walked over to the play area and Fane stopped next to a tall structure that had long chains dangling down with slices of rubber between each set of chains.

"Have you ever swung before?" he asked.

"Swung?" she echoed.

"Oh man, you're in for the ride of your life," he said.

He showed her how to sit on the slice of rubber and where to hold the chains, then moved to stand behind her.

"Hold on tight," he said, placing his hands on either side of her waist and then backing up, dragging her with him until her feet were off the ground. "Keep your feet up," he cautioned as he let her go.

Rapunzel's stomach dropped as she flew forward with the motion. She panicked for just a second, but then sensation overtook her and she laughed. Fane continued to push her higher and higher while she clung tightly to the chains, her legs sticking straight out in front of her the entire time.

Fane jumped onto the swing next to her and pushed backward, setting himself swinging alongside her. He showed her how to pump her legs to keep the motion going. However, Fane, being much more experienced, soon swung much higher than her. After a few minutes, he released himself from the swing, landing about ten feet in front of the swing set.

"Wanna jump?" he asked.

"No thanks." She laughed. Fane slowed her down and said, "You've gotta try the slide."

Fane showed her what each piece of equipment was for and how to use it. The "monkey bars," as he called them, were beyond her ability to hold onto with the thick gloves. She climbed up the top instead and sat atop the metal contraption.

Standing beneath her, Fane dramatically called, "Rapunzel, throw down your hair," with his hands clasped dramatically in front of his chest.

Rapunzel laughed and dropped it through the bars.

"Wrap it around the bar twice," he said.

She did as he asked, confused. He grabbed hold the end of it and began climbing as if it were a rope. The bar took his weight on her hair, only tugging slightly against her scalp as he climbed. At the top he grabbed the bar to hold his weight and said, "Lean down."

She did so, and he pulled himself up, kissing her through the bars. Then he dropped back to the snowy ground. Rapunzel, enjoying the game, said, "Climb up again," this time leaving her face near the bars. Showing off, Fane did pull-ups when he reached the top, kissing her each time he pulled up.

Finally he dropped back to the ground. "Come down. It'll be much easier to kiss you down here." Rapunzel was happy to comply.

The merry-go-round made her feel ill, but the teeter-totter was her favorite. She knew that Fane did most of the work to keep them moving up and down on the teeter-totter. The sensation of flying into the air and then dropping back to the ground gave her endless pleasure—even more than the swings.

Finally, he decided they better return to the house before his mother "called out the National Guard." When she asked what the National Guard was, he told her it was kind of like the military police. Knowing that police would surely tell her mother that she had been out of the house, she practically ran back to Fane's house. When they arrived, Rapunzel was stunned to find that it was time to eat yet again. Pie, this time.

After a couple hours and football games—which seemed pointless and violent to Rapunzel—the relatives began leaving. Rapunzel was sad to see them go. As Kevin left he hugged her and said, "As soon as you're ready for a real man, just give me a call." He laughed as Fane growled and shoved him away from her.

Fane and Rapunzel settled in front of the TV to watch a movie with his parents. The snow began coming down in earnest again, and Beth glanced worriedly out the window at the dark skies.

"It's getting bad out there," she said. "Maybe you should just stay the night here, Rapunzel, and Fane can take you home tomorrow when the roads have been plowed."

Apprehension tightened Rapunzel's stomach at the thought of not being home in her tower, where she belonged.

Then she realized that her mother would never know she hadn't spent the night at home. Also, it sounded incredibly appealing to stay here in the warmth and comfort of Fane's home. She agreed and Beth gave her some dry sweat pants and a sweatshirt to wear to bed. She also gave her a toothbrush and washcloth. Fane showed her to their guest room.

"You'll have to share the bathroom with me," he said, pointing to an open door down the hallway. "Sorry if it's full of boy stuff instead of the things you're probably used to having in your own bathroom."

"I don't mind," Rapunzel said. "It's really nice of your mom to let me stay here."

"Let me know if you need anything like more blankets or pillows or—"

"Fane, everything is great. Don't worry about me."

Fane shuffled uncomfortably and Rapunzel laid her hand on his arm. "Thank you, Fane, for sharing today with me. I never imagined how great Thanksgiving could be. Your family is really amazing."

Fane cocked a brow at her. "So . . . what did you think of Kevin?"

"He's really nice. I can see that teasing runs in your family."

"Yeah, but did you think he was, I don't know, cute, I guess?"

"Well yeah, of course," she said. Disappointment colored Fane's face until she said, "I thought all your cousins were cute, especially Ava and Liv."

Fane grinned. "So you don't think you would date him?"

Rapunzel shook her head. "I can't date anyone, Fane. You know that."

Fane looked frustrated. "But if you *could*?"

"Why would I date him? I like . . ." Heat suffused her face at what she'd been about to say.

"You like?"

Rapunzel looked away, embarrassed, and mumbled, "Someone else."

Fane smiled. "I'm the only 'someone else' you know."

Rapunzel looked up at him "So?"

Fane didn't answer, only bent his head to kiss her. Rapunzel wrapped her arms around his waist and held him tightly. When he lifted his head he said, "I like you too."

Later, as Rapunzel lay in a strange bed in a strange house, she'd never felt more at home.

chapter

* 31 *

Rapunzel opened her eyes and quickly sat up, startled. For a moment she didn't know where she was and then remembered she was at Fane's house. A knock sounded on the door and she said, "Come in." Her face melted into a smile at the sight of Fane standing there.

"Good morning," Fane said.

"Good morning," she answered.

"There are towels and things in the bathroom if you want to shower or anything."

"Thanks."

"I have an idea," Fane said, "for getting into the trunk."

"Really?" Hope filled Rapunzel.

"After you get dressed, we'll have breakfast and I'll tell you my plan."

Two hours later, they walked through the greenhouse. They went up to Rapunzel's room so she could change out of her skirt. Fane had come armed with some tools. They made their way down to the old log cabin and pulled the trunk out.

"That's what I thought," Fane said, pointing to the

tiny screws on the hinges. He pulled out a little screw-driver and proceeded to remove the screws. He looked at Rapunzel and said, "Are you sure about this?"

She nodded and he lifted the lid. Inside the trunk they saw stacks of papers, some old, some which looked a little newer. Rapunzel shuffled through some of the papers, not really looking at them. A wedding dress, wrapped in tissue paper, rested beneath the papers. She pulled it out, careful with the fragile, yellowed mate-rial. The dress was clearly old but beautiful. There were a few old pieces of jewelry in the bottom and some pho-tographs. While she looked at these items, Fane went through the papers.

"Uh, Rapunzel, you might want to take a look at these."

"What are they?" she asked.

"It looks like some of these writings might be from your mother."

"What?" Rapunzel asked, dropping the ring she had been examining back into the trunk and reaching for the papers.

Just then, they heard a noise from the floor above them. They both froze. Fane raised a finger to his lips and then waved for her to stay put while he went to investi-gate. He walked over to the door and slowly turned the handle, opening it just the smallest of cracks to look out. He listened for a minute or two, then closed the door and returned to Rapunzel's side.

"It sounds like maybe your cook has come home."

"What are we going to do?" Rapunzel whispered,

terror filling her mind, making it impossible to think clearly.

"We'll have to sneak upstairs," Fane said, moving to put the papers back in the trunk.

"No," Rapunzel said, "I'll take those up with me so I can look at them later."

"Okay," Fane said. Rapunzel replaced the other items inside, and Fane carefully replaced the lid, reattaching the screws to the hinges. He placed the stack of papers inside his shirt and tucked his shirt inside his pants to carry them hands-free. They carefully slid the trunk back beneath the bed. Fane took her hand and led her to the door.

Fane listened again and then apparently decided it was safe enough. He pulled the door open and led Rapunzel from the log room. They crept down the hallway, stopping to look around the corner. Rapunzel's heart beat so loudly she was sure that Cook—she assumed it was Cook that was in the house—would surely hear it. They made it to the first set of stairs and went up. Just as their feet touched the top step, they heard a voice. Fane quickly dropped to his belly and down a few stairs, pulling Rapunzel with him.

They quietly crawled back down a few more steps and then froze as Cook came into view. It was the first time Rapunzel had ever seen the woman who'd been providing food for what she assumed was her whole life. She was younger than expected, looking to be somewhere around her mother's age. She was average looking—brown hair, average height, and thinner than Rapunzel would have expected a cook to be.

Cook was talking on her phone, pacing back and forth. After a few minutes, she disappeared down one of the hallways, still talking on her phone, having never glanced their way. Sweat beaded on the back of Rapunzel's neck at the fear of being caught. As soon as Cook disappeared, Fane took her hand, and they quickly ran up the stairs and then in the opposite direction. As quietly as possible, they hurried into her room.

"Whew," Fane said, leaning against the closed door. "That was close."

"How are you going to get out of here?" Rapunzel asked worriedly.

"I'll just have to be extra sneaky," Fane said. Then he patted his belly, rustling the papers, "Should we have a look?"

They moved to the counter, and Fane set the papers on its surface. They decided to split the pile in half and just start going through them one by one. Rapunzel began reading the top paper in her stack.

September 5: I am going hiking with Nigel tomorrow on another one of his stupid trips. I don't know why he thinks that I enjoy doing these things with him. I would much rather stay home and continue to try and commune with my lost baby. I don't talk to him about that anymore because each time I do he begins talking about my needing therapy. I DON'T NEED THERAPY! Why can't he understand that? How can he be her true father if he refuses to acknowledge her existence? I'm beginning to wonder if he wasn't her father. Maybe she was a gift to me from the spirits. I will have to find someone to talk to about that. Meantime, I'll join Nigel on his stupid hike. Wouldn't it be a shame if an accident were to happen and he didn't come home with me? ~ BHG

Rapunzel's head reeled. It seemed obvious that her mother wrote the pages. *Why loose papers and not a journal or diary or something,* she wondered. She knew about the baby, of course, from the news articles, but in all these years her mother had never spoken to *her* about the baby. She also couldn't get that last sentence out of her head. She remembered the speculation in the articles that her father's death had not been an accident. With some dread, she turned to the next page.

September 16: I was forced to withstand the affected sympathy of all the neighbors and other curiosity seekers at Nigel's funeral. I know that they were all just here to look at the house and to try and ingratiate themselves with me, perhaps hoping to get some of my money. I earned this money. It's mine. I paid for it with the blood of my daughter. I could hardly stand to play the part of the grieving widow when all I wanted to do was dance with joy that my scheme has worked. I am now free to do what is necessary to get my beautiful baby daughter back. ~ BHG

Rapunzel quickly flipped to the next page.

July 17: Good news, today I found Vedmak. He is genuine, not like all of the frauds who have come before. He knew all about my baby girl and how important it was to me to have her in my life again. He told me that I will have a golden-haired daughter who will be my savior. I am not sure how I will have another baby as I do not plan to be with another man again. However, if what I suspect about my baby girl is true, then I don't need a man anyway. I expect that I will soon be pregnant. ~ BHG

November 3: I have not yet conceived, though Vedmak assures me that I <u>will</u> have a daughter, that I must be patient. He has told me more about the prophecy, that not only will my daughter be my savior, but will be the tool to return my first daughter to me. At first, I thought maybe he was just saying these things to try and get more money from me. But he spoke with such earnestness that I now believe he is telling me the truth, and he has not taken any further money, which proves he only has my interests at heart. I will try to be patient, though my anxiousness to be reunited with my daughter supersedes almost all else in my life. ~ BHG

February 25: It is very late but I could not wait until tomorrow to write of what Vedmak has told me. He said that the reason I have not yet been reunited with my daughter is because there is something I must do first. He said the spirits are unhappy with how stagnant my life has become. He said they would be happy if I began construction on my house and that as long as I continue to build and expand the manor, they will remain pleased with me and will provide for my reunion with my precious, golden-haired daughter. It's required, though, that I oversee the work, according to Vedmak. I have spoken to a man who owns a construction company. He will come next week to begin work. I can feel how close I am to having my dreams fulfilled. ~ BHG

June 6: I SAW HER TODAY! My beautiful, golden-haired daughter. I now realize why I have not conceived. It is because I was meant to <u>find</u> her and today I found her. I was in the grocery store, a place I never go. I have others who shop for me, but today I felt compelled to go myself. Clearly, the spirits were trying to show me the way and it was there that I saw her. She is exactly as Vedmak described her. She has long, golden hair in spite of her young age. She looked right at me and I immediately knew that I had found the vessel that will bring my own baby back to me. I do not think it is a coincidence that today is the sixth day of the sixth month and that she is six months old. As soon as I realized I had found her I looked down to see that I had six apples in my basket. My own baby girl would have turned six on this very day. Clearly six is the number that my daughter is trying to show me. It must be connected somehow to her return. I understand and I will heed what she says. Six has always been related to the discipline that came from my mother, a number I related to pain. I can see now that she was only preparing me for this. Six will be the number that I will live my life by from here on. I must now plan. I must be diligent and cautious in order to bring my baby girl home. Tomorrow, I will speak with Vedmak and I am sure that the spirits will guide me in my endeavors.

Horror ran through Rapunzel. She looked up at the basket of six apples that sat on her countertop. With a rage born of realization she swept the basket of apples from her counter violently to the floor. Fane immediately reached out to touch her arm.

"Rapunzel? Are you okay?"

She looked at Fane but couldn't speak past the revulsion choking her. She could only pick up the paper and thrust it at Fane. He read through it, his expression mirroring her own.

"Do you think this is you she's talking about?" Fane asked. "It couldn't be, right? I mean that would mean . . . that's not possible. That would mean that she—"

Rapunzel spun away from him. She felt sick. It wasn't bad enough that her entire life was a lie and that her mother had possibly killed her father but now maybe her mother wasn't even her mother. Then . . . who was?

Fane came behind her and wrapped his arms around her. She turned and clung to him. She buried her face against his chest, squeezing her eyes shut, wanting to erase from her mind the words she just read. Fane led her to the couch and sat, pulling her next to him and holding her tightly. After some time, he spoke.

"What are you going to do?"

"I don't know. I have no idea what to do with this information. She'll be home tomorrow. Should I show her what I found?"

"I wouldn't just yet," Fane said. "Let's make sure that we have all of the information before we confront her."

Rapunzel looked up at him. "We?" she echoed.

"Yes," he said. "That is, if you want me to be here with you."

Rapunzel laid her head against his chest again and nodded.

"It's late. I better go," Fane said reluctantly.

Rapunzel sighed. "I know." She sat up and looked at him. "I'll go through all the papers, kind of put them in order, and read them all."

"How are you going to keep her from seeing them?"

She shrugged. "I'll hide them under my mattress, I guess. She only comes into my room to brush my hair so it should be safe enough." She looked at him. "Will you come back in a few days and help me decide what to do about all of this?"

"Of course," he answered with no hesitation. "Try not to stress about it too much until then, okay?"

She nodded, knowing that was going to be a difficult task. But it lifted the burden somewhat from Rapunzel knowing that Fane would be there for her and would help her decide what the best course of action was.

Fane decided to brave the trellis rather than risk being caught. Rapunzel tried to talk him out of it, but he felt like it would be safe enough—with her help.

He held to the end of her hair as he climbed out and took the first tentative step on the trellis. It began to sag away from the wall and Rapunzel quickly pulled her hair tight, reeling him back in with a squeak. He smiled at her though she could see the panic and relief mingled on his face. Holding tightly to her hair, he slowly made his way down. Once he reached the end of her hair, the trellis seemed to be solidly connected. Before releasing her hair, he pulled it to his mouth and pressed his lips against it. Rapunzel could swear she felt the kiss up through the strands to her scalp. He released her hair, and she pulled it back into the tower.

chapter

✦ 32 ✦

*R*apunzel was a baby. She lay in her crib batting at the mobile that swung above her head. A woman came into view but it was not her mother and yet this woman was more familiar than her mother, somehow. She had the same golden hair as Rapunzel and kind eyes. She reached down to pick up Rapunzel, but before she could reach her the crib melted away and Rapunzel sat in the black room surrounded by sixes.

There were six people in black hoods chanting, and Rapunzel was terrified. She didn't know who these people were or what they wanted. She only knew that the feeling she got from them was cold and empty. She wanted to run but felt trapped by the circle drawn around her.

Suddenly, her mother was there, only instead of being comforted by her presence, Rapunzel's fear spiked upward. As her mother stepped toward her, she said, "You are the key. Everything depends on you. My daughter depends on you."

A man came forward and Rapunzel cringed in fear. He was tall and dark, his eyes black and lifeless. He too wore a black hooded cape. He lay his hands on her head and began *chanting, the words foreign and strange. Rapunzel wanted to move away from him but was unable to.*

Rapunzel's hair began growing at an unearthly rate, surrounding her, binding her, choking her. She tried to escape but could not get free. She could no longer see the chanting people or her mother. She opened her mouth to scream but was stopped in her intention as her hair covered her mouth and pulled tightly.

Rapunzel woke with a scream. She lay on her bedroom floor, bound in her sheets. When she realized that she was safe, and not in the room of sixes, she began crying, relief flooding her. She lay that way for some time before disentangling herself and standing. She sat on the edge of her bed and glanced down at the mattress. Beneath the mattress lay all of the papers that she had spent hours reading.

Some of the papers were harmless, historical records of the Gothel family. It was the other papers, the ones written by her mother, that disturbed her. Or rather, not written by her *mother* but by the woman who had kidnapped her and now claimed to be her mother.

Rapunzel's entire world had jerked to a standstill and she barely hung on. She felt as though the only thing she was capable of doing was screaming. But if she started, she might never stop.

She stood and went into her bathroom, removing her sweat-drenched pajamas and stepping into the shower. The hot water was almost painful against her fragile skin. She turned it cold, and let the chilly water wash over her frayed nerves, numbing them.

After carefully making her bed and making certain that there was no evidence of the papers that lay beneath, she went into her main living area, picked up the basket and the spilled apples and replaced them on the counter-top. She poured herself a bowl of cereal but was only able to eat a few bites before her stomach rebelled. She poured the rest down the drain and washed the bowl. Then, deciding under her mattress might seem obvious, she went back and gathered all the papers. She took them up to her exercise room and stashed them beneath the treadmill. She then sat on her couch and waited.

When her door handle turned, her stomach tightened. She didn't think she could pretend as though her entire life hadn't been entirely changed less than twenty-four hours ago. Gothel stepped into the room and it was all Rapunzel could do not to sneer at the woman.

"Rapunzel, there you are," Gothel said. *Where else would I be?* Rapunzel thought, sarcastically. She stood as Gothel came near. "How are you? Did everything go well while I was gone?"

"Yes," Rapunzel answered shortly.

"Good. I always worry about you so when I have to go away."

"Do you?" Rapunzel asked disbelievingly. "Tell me, where did you go?"

"Uh, I went away for a work meeting, Rapunzel. You know that."

"What work?" Rapunzel asked. "What do you do?"

"Why I . . . What's with all the questions, Rapunzel? I'm gone for six days and I return home to receive the third degree? Is that any way to treat your mother? You were fine when I spoke to you on the phone last night."

Rapunzel laughed, scathingly. She strode away from her mother and stopped on the opposite side of her kitchen counter.

"What's with you today? You're acting very odd," Gothel said.

"Compared to what?"

"Rapunzel! I am your mother and I will not tolerate this disrespect."

Rapunzel hadn't planned it, but somehow found her hand closing around an apple, which she threw with impressive force across the room. Gothel's jaw dropped in shock.

"You are not my mother!"

"What?" Gothel's voice was soft with disbelief.

"I know all about you. I know you killed your parents. I know you killed your husband and I know that I am *not* your daughter. You *kidnapped* me. How could you do that? What kind of person are you?"

As Rapunzel watched, something in Gothel's face changed. A look of evil awareness replaced the shock. She moved slowly toward Rapunzel, and Rapunzel realized her mistake. She should have waited for Fane. She was out of her element here. She'd allowed her emotions to rule her actions. She backed away from Gothel's approach until her back hit the edge of the counter.

"You think you know me, do you?" Gothel said, her voice practically oozing from her. "You don't know anything, Rapunzel."

Rapunzel reached behind her, her hand closing on the drawer handle. She pulled it open, rooting around inside while keeping her eyes firmly locked on the woman in front of her, the woman who she'd thought was her mother but was now a stranger. Her hands closed on an item, and a small smile crossed her lips. She pulled the pair of scissors from the drawer, pulling her braid around front and placing the blades against the silken strands.

"No!" Gothel froze, hands held upward as if she could stop Rapunzel's actions. She then continued moving toward Rapunzel, speaking soothingly. "Rapunzel, you know the consequences of taking such an action. Calm down, sweetheart. Put the scissors down."

Fury ran through Rapunzel. "Don't call me sweetheart," she said through gritted teeth. She brought the blades together, cutting a slice in one side of her thick rope of hair.

"No!" Gothel screamed again, rushing forward and tearing the scissors from Rapunzel's hand. "You horrible, horrible, selfish girl," she cried. She flung the scissors across the room, raising a hand high and bringing it down stingingly against Rapunzel's cheek. Rapunzel was stunned by the action. She'd never been hit before. Gothel quickly bound her arms against her side with her own arms. Rapunzel struggled against a strength she hadn't known her mother had.

"Stop it, Rapunzel! Stop it now!"

Rapunzel ignored the screeching of Gothel as she tried to get away. Something stung her shoulder just as she freed one arm. She stumbled, the room spinning and tilting wildly.

"Wha—" she said, finding it impossible to form a

coherent thought as she fell onto her knees, one arm still held by Gothel. She tried to regain her footing but was unable as Gothel began dragging her. She saw the blurry vision of a syringe hanging from Gothel's opposite hand.

Gothel dragged her out of her rooms, out the door, and down the stairs, not caring that Rapunzel's spine dropped painfully from step to step. Blackness swirled at the edges of her vision. Gothel dragged her across floors and down more sets of stairs—some that Rapunzel and Fane hadn't even found in their exploration. At least, she didn't think so. She was having a hard time thinking clearly.

Finally they came to a dark, dank, cement room. The air was cold and damp. She dragged Rapunzel to the middle of the room and let her go. Rapunzel fell heavily to the floor.

"I swear, girl, if you've ruined everything with your stupidity, you'll pay," Gothel said, leaning down to thrust her face close to Rapunzel's. She glanced down at her hand as if just remembering that she held the syringe. With disgust, she threw it to the side. She turned and strode from the room, closing the door behind her, leaving Rapunzel in the absolute darkness. She heard the sound of a key scraping in a lock.

She slowly pushed herself to her knees, wobbling. Crawling toward the thin line of light beneath the door, falling a few times on the way, she reached up and turned the knob. She knew it was futile, had heard the lock being turned. Still, the reality of it refusing to budge beneath her hand was too much. Rapunzel collapsed against the door as tears streamed silently down her face.

* * *

Time passed, though how much time Rapunzel was unsure of. Her eyes had adjusted a little so that she could see vague outlines of shapes in the room, but nothing clearly. She was thirsty. More thirsty than she'd ever been. She even considered licking the walls to try to get some kind of moisture in her mouth, but was afraid of what else might be on the walls that would end up in her mouth.

She wondered if Gothel would find the papers beneath her treadmill. If she did, Rapunzel might never find her real mother. If she could backtrack through the clues, she might be able to discover where she came from. She could prove that Gothel had done all of the horrible things she'd been accused of.

She fingered the slice in her braid that she'd made. The hair was stiff and prickly. In spite of the fact that she felt Gothel was probably crazy, she still worried about the prophecy. She'd been taught the prophecy her whole life. She'd never had reason to doubt it. Letting go of the belief now wasn't easy even if intellectually she thought it was probably untrue.

The depth of despair surrounding Rapunzel felt insurmountable. The woman who was her *mother*, who had raised her, taught her to braid her hair, showed her how to cook, who was her only companion until Fane, was a lie. What did she have now? Nothing.

chapter

33

Rapunzel was cold. It hadn't been bad at first, but the longer she sat in the dark without food or water, the colder she got. She wondered if Gothel would let her die this way. Didn't that go against the prophecy?

She wished desperately for Fane and worried about him too. He'd snuck in before when her mother left, willing to take the risk just to see if she was okay. Knowing everything they now did, she had no doubt that he would try to get in once again for the same reason. Only this time Gothel hadn't gone anywhere. Rapunzel feared what Gothel would do if she caught him.

She heard movement outside the door and tried to stand but was too weak. She pushed herself to a sitting position against the wall as the door opened. Gothel stood in the doorway, a tray of food in her hand. Rapunzel's eyes dropped to the glass of water, unable to look away, never wanting something so much in her life.

"It occurs to me," Gothel said, "that I am not required to keep you in the lap of luxury as I have all these years. I am only required to keep you alive and keep your body healthy." She set the tray of food on the floor and without another word strode from the room, locking it behind her.

Rapunzel crawled as quickly as she was able to the tray. She desperately gulped down the water. When the glass was half empty, she forced herself to stop. She had no idea how long it might be until she might get more. She examined the other contents of the tray.

A sandwich and six baby carrots were on the plate. There was also a small container of pudding. She picked up the sandwich and took a bite. The bread was dry and stale and the turkey tasted slightly rancid. It was the best thing she had ever tasted. She ate the entire thing and the carrots but decided to hold onto the pudding, just in case.

She took the pudding and the half glass of water with her back to the opposite side of the room. At least if Gothel decided to take them away from her, she'd have to come further into the room than just the doorway.

Rapunzel felt much better now. She was still cold, but at least she wasn't hungry and thirsty. She lay down on the cold cement and let her mind drift back to the day she spent at Fane's house. The laughter and noise of having a family around her was something she longed for. She couldn't have ever guessed that she'd want that. Now that she knew how great it was, she wanted it. Badly.

She remembered the easy love between them all. Touches and hugs were easily given and received. Even wrestling and arguing were done with love. The comfort of Fane's home, his entire family, the simplicity with which they cared for one another was worth more than a lifetime of staying safely locked in a tower. As soon as she escaped, she'd do whatever she had to just to be in that same atmosphere for even one more day.

She closed her eyes and let herself drift into dreams, tears sliding down her cheeks.

Rapunzel sat on the teeter-totter across from Fane. The sun was bright and they were in a field of green grass. She was happy and content. When Fane pushed off and her side of the teeter-totter touched the ground, it disappeared and she was a baby once again on the same green blanket with pink rosebuds. Only this time, instead of being in a crib she was on the middle of a bed in the log house.

She waited for the blonde woman to come and get her, but instead Gothel entered the room. Rapunzel wanted to yell out but could not make a sound. Gothel took the blanket and bound it tightly around Rapunzel, covering her head. The dark was smothering. Rapunzel couldn't breathe. She struggled but was bound so tightly she could not move more than a fraction of an inch.

She felt herself being lifted and moved, to where she had no idea. But when the blanket was finally lifted from her head, she was in the center of the star in the black room surrounded by chanting people. She wanted to crawl away but was unable to move. She was too weak.

The black room melted away and she was now lying in a field of snow. All she could see was white wherever she looked. She started calling for Fane, knowing that he was the only one who could find her. But no matter how long or how loud she called, he never came.

chapter

✲ 34 ✲

The sudden light as the door opened roused Rapunzel. She pushed herself upright from where she lay as Gothel entered with more food. This time, instead of dropping the tray and leaving, she entered, carrying a lantern as well. She closed the door behind her and brought the tray halfway across the room. She set it on the floor, her eyes on Rapunzel as she did, then retreated to the door.

Rapunzel watched her warily, afraid to move. When she didn't, Gothel finally spoke.

"I'm not going to feed you, Rapunzel," Gothel said disdainfully. Instead of leaving, she sat in front of the door, placing the lantern by her side.

Rapunzel crawled toward the food, reaching out when she was within reach to pull the tray toward her. It scraped loudly against the cement floor. She dragged it back with her to her position against the wall. She gulped some of the water, then picked up the roll and began to chew it. The thought suddenly struck her that Gothel would poison her and immediately spit it out.

"You must eat, Rapunzel. Your body must be kept healthy." When Rapunzel made no further move to eat, she said, "If you won't eat willingly, we'll force-feed you."

Rapunzel didn't know who "we" was and didn't want to find out.

"Is it going to make me sick?" she asked Gothel. "Or kill me?"

Gothel rolled her eyes. "Why would I do such a thing? If we don't keep your body healthy, the procedure can't be completed."

"What procedure?"

"Eat," Gothel commanded.

Rapunzel jerked at the harsh tone and began chewing the roll once again. A piece of chicken on the tray proved to be much tastier than her previous sandwich.

"Why are you doing this?" Rapunzel asked.

"Because of the—"

"Prophecy," Rapunzel interrupted with frustration. "I know. But what does that mean? Why am I part of it?"

"Quite simple, really. You're the vessel."

"The vessel?" Rapunzel's appetite fled but she forced herself to keep eating. "A vessel for what?"

"Why, for the return of my daughter, of course."

Shock zinged through Rapunzel as if struck by a bolt of lightning. Now she did set the chicken down.

"Your daughter?" she repeated, her mouth dry, barely able to form the words.

"My daughter, Rapunzel. You know, I always thought you were fairly intelligent. Perhaps I overestimated. No matter, when she returns she'll continue the education you began and be as brilliant as I know she is."

Rapunzel picked up the water and swirled it around in her mouth, swallowing with difficulty. Tears stung her eyes, and she shivered against the cold.

"Do you mean the baby girl you had who died?" she finally asked.

Gothel's gaze shot to her as she rose quickly to her feet. She moved threateningly toward Rapunzel, who cringed against the wall.

"She did not die!" Gothel screamed. "Do you hear me? She did not die!"

Rapunzel nodded as tears fell, one arm held up defensively. "Yes. Yes, I hear you. She didn't die."

Gothel backed off at Rapunzel's words. She moved back to her sitting position near the door. She smoothed her hair, then glanced at the tray.

"You must eat some of all the items on the tray," Gothel said calmly, as if her outburst hadn't happened.

Rapunzel's eyes dropped to the tray. Chicken, the roll, string beans, applesauce, an apple, and the water were on the tray. Six items.

She took a bite of the items she hadn't yet tasted. Once she had, Gothel seemed much calmer.

"You told me I was the savior of the world," Rapunzel said.

"How else was I going to get you to take care of yourself?" Gothel spit out. "From the beginning it was clear that you are a bleeding heart, worried about everyone and everything else other than yourself. You wouldn't care enough about yourself to keep yourself healthy, but to save others you would."

Rapunzel bit her lip, thinking about the risks she'd taken with Fane and leaving the house.

"The preparation for all of this began years ago," Gothel said as if Rapunzel had asked. "When first I met Vedmak. He came with the others. I have a room, a special room, where we first began the ritual." Rapunzel shuddered as the black room of sixes came into her mind. "Vedmak taught me the chants, the ones needed to get the answers from the spirits. At first, we needed fire. Then, once you came, we only needed you."

Rapunzel thought of all the strange nightmares and realized they must be memories. "You had me in that room?" she whispered.

"Of course. We couldn't continue preparations without you there."

"Did you do something to my hair?" she asked, wondering if that was the reason it grew so fast.

Gothel's eyes burned as she shot a glare toward Rapunzel. "No, Rapunzel, that was *you*. You did something to your hair! You cut it. You were commanded not to, and you did anyway." Rapunzel sat silently, afraid to breathe. Gothel was terrifying in her anger. And then in a blink, Gothel soothed her hair, taking a deep breath. "Vedmak will be here soon. And then he'll know whether the damage is reversible." Her mouth tightened. "For your sake, you better hope so."

The silence stretched. Gothel didn't seem angry anymore. Rapunzel thought about what she'd revealed. She hated the thought that she'd been in that horrible room. She remembered the creepiness of the sixes all over the walls. "Why six?" she ventured quietly, afraid of causing another outburst.

Gothel clicked her tongue in irritation. "Enough questions," she said. "Take the tray back to the center of the room and move away."

Rapunzel pushed the tray back to the center of the room, then quickly scuttled back to her original position. She had no desire to be near Gothel, who seemed as if she were tenuously holding onto control as it was.

Gothel picked up the tray and backed toward the door, watching Rapunzel as she did so.

She opened the door and backed out, never taking her gaze from Rapunzel, closing the door and shutting Rapunzel into the darkness once again.

chapter

✳ 35 ✳

When Gothel came again, she brought pancakes. Rapunzel assumed that meant it was morning. Once again, she placed the tray in the middle of the room then moved to sit by the door. This time, though, she also brought a blanket that she left near the tray.

Rapunzel stood and picked up the tray and blanket. She wrapped the blanket around herself before sitting back down to the food.

"Thank you," she said, indicating the blanket.

"I can't have you getting sick," was Gothel's only response.

Rapunzel ate half of the stack of three pancakes, both pieces of bacon, and drank most of the water in silence. It made her edgy and nervous to have Gothel there, watching her eat. However, the silence was worse than anything.

"Why do you build so much on this house?" she asked.

"It's part of the prophecy, Rapunzel. Vedmak's spirits weren't happy with how I was living, obsessed with nothing more than the return of my daughter." Rapunzel shivered at her words. "I needed an activity to appease them.

The more I build, the more space it gives them to roam."

Rapunzel glanced around her worriedly, as if they were in the room with them.

"As long as I keep building, they stay happy."

"But why the stairs that go nowhere, doors that open into walls? It doesn't make any sense."

Gothel grinned, the expression completely lacking humor. "That's the beauty of it, Rapunzel. It confuses the spirits. They get stuck at the ends of the stairs, or inside the doors, because they don't know where to go. It's how I keep their numbers down."

Rapunzel's jaw dropped. *What?* That explanation made even less sense than the strange construction. For the first time Rapunzel realized that Gothel was truly insane, and fear crawled along her nerves. She pulled the blanket closer. "Six workers, six hours a day, six days a week?"

"Well, yes, of course."

Rapunzel gaped at her. She acted as though it were normal when she now knew that it wasn't. "Everything in sixes?"

"Why the sudden curiosity? You've never questioned any of this." Gothel sounded less angry than she usually did, so Rapunzel pressed on.

"You said I needed to be educated right?" She tried to remember any reasons Gothel had ever given her for the importance of education but couldn't recall any of them. It didn't matter, though, as a fanatical gleam came into Gothel's eyes. Rapunzel recognized the look.

"You're right. I've been instructed to make sure you

are educated before the time comes for the transformation. I've been remiss in that, haven't I?" She glanced at Rapunzel, her eyes narrowing. "It's just too bad she's going to look like you. There was a time when I thought you were beautiful, a worthy vessel, but now . . . now I worry that the ugliness of your heart will taint her."

Rapunzel could only stare at Gothel as she stood. Her words twisted like a knife in her heart. Gothel had raised her, was the only mother she'd ever known. She hadn't doubted that Gothel loved her. Now it seemed obvious that she didn't.

"We'll begin your education tonight," Gothel announced as she opened the door. She looked at Rapunzel harshly. "Take a nap. We'll need your mind to be clear." She closed the door behind her, not even bothering to take the tray with her.

Rapunzel's eyes welled up as she stared at the seam of light beneath the door. She didn't know what Gothel meant when she spoke of her as a vessel for her daughter. A vessel carried things. What was she supposed to carry?

"A vessel with an ugly heart, apparently," she muttered, unable to stop the hitch in her voice or the tears that followed.

* * *

Rapunzel was in the greenhouse. She walked slowly among the fragrant blooms, running her fingers lightly over the tops of them. She came to the beautiful rose bush and leaned down to breathe in the scent. As she did so, the thorns on the stem pricked her finger. She jerked her hand back, looking down at the tiny dot of blood that welled up. She glanced back at the rose, which shriveled into a bud and became the green baby blanket with pink rosebuds.

Unlike before when the blanket was nothing more than that, this time it became ominous as it grew and came after her. She ran, but the greenhouse never ended. There was no trap door, no door to the outside world, only rows of plants that stuck their branches out to slow her down as the blanket bore down on her. She hyperventilated as the blanket wrapped around her, smothering her, binding her, taking her away from—

"Rapunzel!"

Rapunzel jerked awake at the sharp sound of Gothel's voice. She was bound up in the blanket Gothel had brought her earlier and panicked for a moment as the dream's vestiges clung to her. It wasn't the baby blanket, though, and she definitely wasn't in the greenhouse.

She sat up, trying to shake the dream from her mind. Gothel placed the tray in the center of the room then left the room, leaving the door ajar. Rapunzel stared at the open door, shocked. Had Gothel forgotten? She stood, her mind already envisioning an escape as Gothel reentered the room carrying some papers.

Her shoulders slumped as she walked over and picked up the tray, returning to her place by the wall. Her stomach growled as she began eating, surprising her with how hungry she was. It was then, with her missed opportunity for escape and her growling stomach that she realized if she did want to have a chance to escape, she was going to have to keep herself healthy and strong. Refusing to eat and sleeping all the time weren't going to accomplish that.

If she could convince Gothel that she agreed with whatever this crazy scheme was, and get her to relax, she might have the opportunity again when she was stronger.

She devoured the food on the tray, then stacked it with the other dishes from this morning and placed them all back into the middle of the room. She calmly returned to her spot and gave her attention to Gothel, who was looking pleased.

"Because you asked about the sixes, we'll begin with that," she began. "Six has always been my lucky number. I was six years old the first time my mother taught me how much more important it is to live a strict, disciplined life. Prior to that I had been too carefree. I was care*less*. At age six I learned that the world is a harsh place and can only be controlled by self-discipline."

"How did she teach you that?" Rapunzel asked, confused.

Gothel looked away from Rapunzel into the darkness. "I'd been playing by the canal near our home even though I'd been warned against it. I fell in and nearly drowned. She pulled me out before it was too late and gave me six lashings for my disobedience, one for each year of my age."

Rapunzel gasped at the idea of hitting a child, let alone one who had just nearly drowned. "That's terrible."

Gothel's sharp gaze came back to her. "No, it isn't. It taught me that there was a reason for rules. They were to protect me. Those six lashings may have saved my life countless times."

Rapunzel's mouth dropped at the warped reasoning.

"After that, each time I stepped out of line, she or my

father gave me six lashings to remind me. Or they'd make me miss six meals. On time they locked me in the closet for six days for a particularly bad infraction. So you see, I learned. I learned to discipline myself and that has made me the woman I am today."

Rapunzel was holding her hands to the sides of her cheeks, stunned at the revelation. Her heart broke for the little girl Gothel who'd been treated so poorly by her parents. No wonder Gothel didn't understand true affection.

"My parents died on December twelfth. I thought it ironic when I later had time to examine what that meant. It was the sixes again. And then my beautiful baby girl was born on June sixth." Rapunzel was astonished again. Gothel's first baby was born on the same date as she had been? "When I met Vedmak, he explained to me the importance of the number six, and that it wasn't coincidence that when I found you it was the sixth day of the sixth month when you were six months old." She leaned forward enthusiastically. "The six is a hook." She pointed to one of the sixes drawn on the wall near her. "It holds all things together. It's about balance and order."

"And you found me on the sixth day of the sixth month."

"Yes!" Gothel's enthusiastic response indicated that she hadn't heard the despondency in Rapunzel's tone. "So now you begin to see. It's been a guiding force in my life. And soon, on your birthday, when you've lived three cycles, she can come back to me."

"She?"

Gothel stood, ignoring her question. "That's enough

for today. I brought you some things to read. If you manage to educate yourself on them by tomorrow, I'll bring you a pillow."

Gothel replaced the trays with the papers and her lantern and exited the room. Rapunzel wanted to ignore the papers. She didn't want to know anything else Gothel wanted to "teach" her, but the hard cement wasn't comforting to her head that still ached from where it'd hit the stairs when she was dragged down, and a pillow sounded almost better than water now.

She reluctantly picked up the papers, grateful for the lantern. They were all pages on the various meanings and significance of the number six. Some of them referred to Christianity, some to numerology, a few regarding demonology, and several referring to the number six in witchcraft. Rapunzel shuddered. She read through a few of them before deciding she didn't want a pillow badly enough to continue reading these papers. Not because of anything in the papers, but because she could only see lines that fed Gothel's craziness.

She put the papers to the side, then decided to exercise. She felt much better doing it with the small amount of light provided by the lantern. She jogged around the room a few times, tiring quickly. She did a few sit-ups, but the motion made her head spin. She decided it was too soon for that. She'd have to take it slowly.

She lay down on the cement, keeping the lantern near, grateful for it. She wrapped the blanket around herself and let sleep take her once again.

chapter

36

Gothel paced agitatedly in front of her. Rapunzel kept her eyes on Gothel while she ate her breakfast. She'd asked Rapunzel if she'd read the papers and when she nodded, Gothel accepted her answer and didn't press any further. Gothel's strange mood kept her from asking any further questions though she definitely wanted to ask how exactly she was a vessel.

Gothel didn't stay long, not even waiting for Rapunzel to finish eating before stalking from the room. Rapunzel wasn't sure if she was relieved or upset by Gothel's strange behavior. As she sat contemplating, the lantern began to dim, drawing her attention. She picked it up and examined it. It was hot, the little bags within glowing. As she watched, they continued to dim and after a few minutes, the lantern went dark.

Rapunzel cringed in the darkness. She'd been so happy to have the light and had assumed it would stay. Now it was gone. The darkness seemed even more pressing now that she'd had the brief reprieve. She wished for her computer so she could Google to understand why it went out and how to make it come back on.

She wished for her computer so that she could talk to Fane.

Pushing past her disdain for the darkness, she stood and began jogging lightly in place. She didn't dare move around too much without the light. She did a few sit-ups, noticing she didn't tire as easily as she had the night before, though she still had a pounding headache when she finished.

Boredom ruled her day more than the fear of the dark. She knew now that Gothel would come, with food and water, and that agitated or not she didn't seem interested in hurting Rapunzel any further. Not that Rapunzel doubted she would, just that she didn't think she would if not provoked. And Rapunzel didn't plan to provoke her sooner than she felt necessary.

When Gothel came in, she seemed surprised by the darkness.

"Why do you sit in the dark, Rapunzel?"

"The lantern went out."

Gothel clucked her tongue as she crossed the room to retrieve the lantern. She bent right next to Rapunzel, close enough to touch, placing the tray on the floor. Rapunzel glanced past her at the open door. It was too soon. She wasn't strong enough.

Gothel left, closing her into the darkness. Rapunzel waited for her return before touching the tray. She came back in with the lantern relit.

"You can't keep it on all the time. It runs out of gas. You need to turn it off when you're not using it."

"How do I turn it back on?" she asked.

Gothel came near once again, squatting to show Rapunzel how to turn it on and off, and the sparking button to push to light it. Suddenly she lifted her gaze to Rapunzel as if realizing what a vulnerable position she put herself in. Rapunzel forced a smile on her face, which was not returned by Gothel, who stood and moved away. Rapunzel began eating, trying to look as benign as possible.

"We may have to move the procedure up," Gothel announced.

Rapunzel put her fork down. "What procedure?"

"The transformation. We'd planned to do it on your birthday, but Vedmak thinks it may work just as well on December twelfth. At least, we're going to have to try since you sliced your hair. Who knows what magic you've drained from it by doing so. Hopefully enough remains to complete the transformation."

Rapunzel suddenly regretted eating the food. It threatened to leave as her stomach churned.

"What transformation?" she whispered.

"Have you been paying attention to anything, Rapunzel? Your transformation—the procedure to bring my daughter back using your body."

Dread filled Rapunzel at the implication. *Bring her daughter back?* Rapunzel knew she wasn't Gothel's daughter, of course, but she also knew Gothel's daughter had died. Many years ago.

"I don't understand," she said.

Gothel smiled as if she were speaking to someone

simple. "It doesn't really matter if you understand this part. This part isn't essential to who you will become." She tilted her head. "However, I suppose it can't hurt to tell you.

"You were brought to me to be the vessel for the return of my baby girl. Vedmak began the procedure as soon as you came. He knows magic, the kind of magic that others can only dream of. Why do you suppose your hair grows so fast?" Rapunzel fingered her braid, terror shaking her fingers. "Vedmak did that. He's the one who taught me how to prepare you. And when the time comes, he'll be the one to perform the procedure."

A tremor began in Rapunzel's hands, quickly spreading up her arms and down her back into her legs. "What is the procedure? What's going to happen to me?"

"Why, you'll go away, Rapunzel, and your soul will be replaced with the spirit of my *true* daughter."

chapter
37

Rapunzel had dimmed the lantern but couldn't bring herself to bring back the utter darkness. She hadn't stopped shaking since Gothel had left. The idea that she'd been taken from her family in order to fulfill some crazy fantasy of Gothel's to bring her dead daughter's spirit back by using Rapunzel's body as the "vessel" filled her with uncontrollable terror. Gothel hadn't given her details as to what they planned to do with her, only saying Rapunzel would "go away."

Her mind kept spinning with those words. Go where? She tried to imagine any number of scenarios where she might go, but nothing made any sense. She clenched her eyes shut and pictured Fane.

"Where are you, Fane? Help me, please," she pleaded quietly.

By the time Gothel returned with her breakfast, she was exhausted. She hadn't slept much, and what little she'd managed was pervaded by nightmares of the room of sixes and the chanting, hooded figures. Gothel, as if aware of Rapunzel's panic, placed the tray in the middle of the floor and retreated. Rapunzel glanced at the tray and then closed her eyes. She couldn't even muster the energy to crawl to the tray to get it.

"You must eat, Rapunzel."

"I'm not hungry," she said listlessly.

"That doesn't matter. You must keep your body healthy."

"I don't care." She turned away from Gothel, facing the wall and pulling the blanket closely around her.

She spluttered as cold water doused her head. She sat up quickly, tangling in the blanket in her haste. The tray clattered to the floor behind her. She looked at Gothel, who'd retreated and stood near the door, stunned.

"Why did you do that?" she demanded.

"You must eat," she repeated.

Rapunzel looked at the bowl of oatmeal sitting on the tray. Alone. Her gaze shot back to Gothel. One item? There were always six. She might have refused to eat if she wasn't afraid Gothel might take her lantern away.

Picking up the spoon, she took a bite. It was overly sweet, as if Gothel had filled it with as much sugar as oats. She grimaced as she swallowed it.

"It's too sweet," she said.

"Eat," Gothel commanded.

Rapunzel took another bite of the sugary concoction, swallowing with difficulty. "At least give me some water or something to drink with it."

"Four more bites," Gothel said, "then I'll get you the water."

Rapunzel took the required amount of spoonfuls,

though she took as small bites as possible. On the fourth bite, as she slid the spoon from her mouth, she felt it. A warm dizziness swept through her. She swayed a little, thinking she must be more tired than she'd thought. Until she saw Gothel watching her intently. She looked down at the oatmeal, then back at Gothel.

"What did you do?" she exclaimed, though the words came out garbled, barely understandable past her swollen tongue.

The room began to spin, and she was forced to lie down. She watched blearily as Gothel opened the door. But she didn't leave. Instead, a man entered. Rapunzel's eyes widened as she recognized the man from her night-mare. She tried to scream but was unable to. The room swirled down into the inky darkness she'd tried to avoid.

* * *

Rapunzel was cold again. She opened her eyes, con-fused why that should be. She realized she was lying on the cement floor again, only this time she had no blanket. She pushed herself upright, taking deep breaths to combat the dizziness.

She remembered Gothel bringing her the oatmeal, and then . . . what? She scrubbed her face with her hands, her sleeves falling down to her elbows. Wait, that wasn't right. She looked down at herself and saw that she was now wearing a long, white robe. But how—

And suddenly it came back to her. The dizziness after the oatmeal, the man entering the room as she passed out. Her breathing picked up as she tried desperately to remember what had happened between then and now. There was nothing, no memory to be found.

Tears spilled as she pulled the strange garment closer, trying to retain some kind of heat. The robe was made of some type of nylon material, thin and flimsy and no protection against the cold air. Why was this happening to her?

It wasn't long before Gothel returned with another tray of food. She brought it directly to Rapunzel, not noticing or caring about the tears that continued to flow.

"Eat," she commanded. *Fat chance of that*, Rapunzel thought. "I'll not give you any further lessons in this incarnation. Once the transformation is complete, I'll help my daughter to understand anything *she* needs to know."

She exited without another word. Rapunzel shuddered. They'd already begun the transformation. What did that mean for her? She couldn't fight it if she couldn't even remember what they'd done to her. She looked at the tray of food and kicked it away from her. It clattered across the floor, the glass of water shattering. A large chuck of the glass bounced next to her. She picked it up, examining the sharp edges. Forcing the consequences from her mind, she pushed the piece of glass against the corner of the wall behind her where it wouldn't be obvious from the door.

Sometime later, Gothel returned. She saw the overturned tray and the spilled food. Rapunzel waited for the explosion, panic suffocating her. She was sure the piece of glass behind her was as visible as she was, and that Gothel would see she'd hidden it.

Gothel walked over to the mess and picked up the

bottom of the broken glass. She turned to Rapunzel and stared at her for long, tense moments. Rapunzel swallowed over the dry lump lodged in her throat. Then Gothel turned back to the tray, picking up the items that had been spilled, including the broken pieces of glass. Without a word, she walked to the door and exited, not so much as glancing back at Rapunzel.

Rapunzel let out the breath she'd been holding. She pulled her knees up beneath the robe against her chest, trying to warm up. She felt like crying again but decided it wasn't accomplishing anything. She grieved the loss of the woman who she'd thought was her mother. She wanted to reverse time and go back to when she was in her tower, Gothel brushing her hair, not exactly loving but at least a caring companion.

Gothel returned hours later, during which time Rapunzel slept lightly. She was afraid of what might happen to her if she fell asleep too deeply. Gothel brought in another tray and placed it in the center of the floor.

"You *will* eat, Rapunzel. If you don't, we'll put a tube down your throat and force-feed you. Do you understand?"

Rapunzel nodded, having no doubt she meant what she said.

"The time nears," Gothel continued. "We need your body strong."

As she left, Rapunzel tried to calculate the time to know just how long she did have. She wasn't sure since the passage of time was fluid in this room. She had no outside lighting to determine days. The sporadic meals brought in from Gothel might indicate a new day each time she brought in a breakfast meal—or not. She couldn't count on anything normal with Gothel anymore.

She walked over to the tray, her legs shaky with weakness. She wasn't going to eat or drink anything provided by Gothel, she knew that. She couldn't subject herself to that blankness again. She also didn't want a tube down her throat.

She picked up the tray and walked to the furthest, darkest corner where she proceeded to dump the food and water. She placed the tray back in the center of the room and lay down once again. She couldn't afford to exercise now that she wasn't going to be eating or drinking anything.

When Gothel returned, she examined the tray with satisfaction. Rapunzel made certain to keep the lantern where the light would not reach the corner where she'd dumped the food.

"Good girl," she said, leaving once again.

This pattern repeated several times. Rapunzel was getting weaker, afraid that it wouldn't be long before she gave in and drank the water that she craved stronger than ever, or ate food to calm her rioting stomach. Most of her time now was spent talking to Fane, hoping that somehow he heard her.

chapter

38

Rapunzel shivered. It was a nearly constant thing now, shivering. Gothel had finally relented and given her a blanket, but only when Rapunzel told her she thought she might be getting a cold again. She'd hoped Gothel would bring Dr. Henrcich. Of course, it would be hard to explain why she kept Rapunzel in the dungeon. At least, that was what Gothel called it.

She fingered the shard of glass that sat next to her on the stone floor. The quality of the meals had depleted steadily, and Rapunzel wondered if Gothel made them herself, rather than having Cook prepare them. The broken glass rested beneath her fingers, taunting her, tempting her. Did she have the courage to try to fight for her freedom? For that matter, did she have the strength? She wasn't sure about either one. She wanted to stand as a warrior, to command her destiny rather than having it thrust upon her. She removed her fingers from the piece of glass and sighed dejectedly. She doubted even now, that she knew Gothel had kidnapped her as a baby and had been holding her a willing prisoner all this time—that she could cause harm to the woman who she had always known as her mother.

Rapunzel wrapped the blanket tighter around her. At some point she'd decided that she could tell night from day based on the temperature of the room. The sliver of light that came from the bottom of the doorway never changed, which must mean that it was a lighted hallway, rather than light coming in from outside. So as far as she could tell, it was now sometime deep in the night. The lantern had long since gone out, leaving her in the dark once again.

Gothel hadn't brought her any food or water today if she was correct in her time approximation. She was thirsty beyond belief, though no longer particularly hungry. With her lack of food, her body had adjusted to not eating so often. Doubting anything was coming this late, she let her eyes drift closed.

Noises outside the door woke her. It sounded like scratching, and at first she thought maybe it was a mouse or a rat trying to get in. She sat up, wondering how much time had gone by while she slept. When the scratching noises continued, it occurred to her that it wasn't Gothel. Gothel had a key and would have simply unlocked the door to enter. It sounded as though someone were trying to get in who didn't have a key.

Panic gripped her. She searched around until she found the shard of glass. Pushing herself painfully up from the floor, she moved until she stood next to the door. For one wild second, she imagined that it was Fane, but knew that there was no way he could have found her here.

Gothel had assured her that no one would ever find her.

She thought about her nightmares and the chanting people in the room of sixes and her missing time after she'd eaten the oatmeal and was suddenly filled with the surety that one—or all—of them had come for her. After long, tense minutes, the door handle was pushed into the room, clattering to the floor. And then she knew. It had to be Fane. That was the trick he'd used to get her out of her room the first time. The door slowly opened and a flashlight shone in.

"Rapunzel?"

At the sound of his voice, she dropped the glass shard, shattering it. The sound drew Fane's flashlight her way. She rushed forward and launched herself against him. His arms wrapped around her as he stumbled back, his hands running down her braid.

"Rapunzel," he said again, more surely. His arms tightened, lifting her, and he buried his face in the crook of her neck. He held her tight for several minutes before finally lifting his head and saying, "I can't believe I finally found you."

He kissed her then, wildly and urgently. Rapunzel met his fervor.

"How did you find me?" she asked.

"Not easily," he said. "I've been searching for you since I last saw you. I snuck in several times but couldn't find you anywhere."

"What time is it?" she asked. "In fact, what *day* is it?"

"It's been ten days since I saw you last," he said.

"*Ten* days? I've been down here that long?"

"Yeah, and I've been frantic. I'm so glad I finally found you. Oh, and I think it's about two thirty."

"In the morning?"

"Yeah. Let's get you out of here. Now."

Keeping one arm firmly around her shoulders, Rapunzel's arms wrapped around his waist, they stepped from the room into the hallway. The brightness blinded her eyes that had not seen light for so long. She wanted to ask Fane what day it was but decided that it was more important to get out of there before all of her questions could be answered.

The stone walls and floor were vaguely familiar from when Gothel had dragged her down, though she had no idea what route would get them out of the house. Now that Fane was here, she knew that together they could find their way. He led them toward up a flight of stairs when suddenly Rapunzel remembered the papers.

"Wait, Fane. We should get the papers from my room."

"Too risky," he said. "We'll have the police come get them." Fane released her long enough to cup her face with his hands. "You have no idea how good it is to see you." He kissed her quickly, then put his arm around her again and resumed walking.

"How very touching," a voice drawled behind them.

chapter

39

Rapunzel and Fane jumped at the sound of Gothel's voice behind them. They swung around to see her standing behind them with an evil grin on her face. Fane pushed Rapunzel behind him.

"I'm taking her out of here. You can't stop me," he said.

"Can I not?" Gothel pulled a strange-looking object that looked like the handle of a gun from behind her back. She pulled a trigger and some kind of wire shot forward into Fane. He immediately fell to the ground groaning, his body twitching and straining.

Rapunzel screamed and dropped to the floor next to him. "What did you do to him?" she cried.

"Don't worry, he'll recover. Maybe." Gothel stepped forward and, grabbing Rapunzel's arm, jerked her away from him. "However, his recovery depends on you, Rapunzel."

"What do you mean?" Rapunzel couldn't tear her eyes from Fane, who no longer twitched but now breathed heavily, his eyes rolled back in his head.

"Meaning, Rapunzel, if you want this boy to live, then you will do exactly as I say."

Rapunzel wished she'd kept her shard of glass. It wasn't much, but it was something. She looked up at Gothel, anger consuming her. "And if I don't?" she asked defiantly.

Gothel squeezed the trigger thing again and Fane's body stiffened and twitched, unearthly groans coming from him.

"Stop!" Rapunzel yelled, defeated. "I'll do anything you say. Just stop."

"Move away from him," Gothel said. Once Rapunzel had done so, Gothel stepped forward and pulled him into a sitting position. She pulled a knife from somewhere and laid it against Fane's throat.

Rapunzel moaned. "Please, Mother. I said I would do anything that you ask. Please don't hurt him."

"Who is this boy to you?" Gothel asked suspiciously.

"He's my friend," Rapunzel said.

"How did you manage to make a friend when you have never been outside of your room?"

Rapunzel knew that to lie to Gothel at this point would be to seal Fane's fate. "On my computer," she said. "I met him on the Internet."

"So this is the boy who has caused so much trouble for me." Gothel yanked Fane's head upward, pressing the knife more tightly against his skin. "I should just get rid of him now."

"No!" Rapunzel cried, holding her hands toward Gothel in supplication. "Please don't hurt him. I'm begging you."

Her gaze dropped to Fane's, and she saw that he was coming back around. His eyes met Rapunzel's, and he gave the tiniest shake of his head. Gothel also seemed to notice that he was nearly back to himself.

Gothel leaned close to Fane's ear and in a voice full of warning said, "Don't try anything." She gave a little tug on the wire thing, still attached to Fane's abdomen. "I'll drop you in two seconds flat. Nod if you understand."

"I won't leave her here with you," Fane gritted out angrily.

"I don't believe you have a choice," Gothel replied.

"Run, Rapunzel!" Fane said.

"No, I won't leave you here!"

"Go now," he said.

Gothel tightened the knife against his throat. "She won't run if she has any care for you at all."

"I'd rather die than see her left here at your mercy."

"Again, touching, but also futile. She has nowhere to go. You, however, I think shall go to your grave for all of the trouble you have brought into my house by coming here. Do you understand what you have done? Do you understand what will be destroyed if anything happens to Rapunzel?"

"You're crazy," Fane said.

Gothel pushed the edge of the blade into his skin, far enough to cause a line of blood to form. Fane grunted against the pain, and Rapunzel cried out.

"You care very much for this boy, don't you?" Gothel said menacingly.

Heart pounding, hoping against all hope that she was

making the right choice, she said, "Let him go, Gothel. If you don't, I'll take my own life."

Gothel's hand sagged a little, relieving the pressure of the knife on Fane's throat. As soon as she did, Fane shoved her hand away. Gothel struggled with him, trying to regain the upper hand. Her hand closed around the trigger again and in horror Rapunzel watched as Fane's body twitched into a straight line, his head hitting the floor. Rapunzel found a surge of strength she couldn't have imagined and struggled back to the dungeon, her hand on the wall to steady herself.

"Rapunzel!" Gothel screamed.

Rapunzel pushed into the hated room, searching desperately. There, in the far corner. She hurried over, her hands closing around the tray left earlier by Gothel.

"Rapunzel!" Gothel was closer now. As soon as Gothel burst into the room, she lifted the tray and brought it down on Gothel's head. In her weakened state, she didn't do the damage she'd hoped, but Gothel did stumble and go to her knees. Not waiting to see what she'd do next, Rapunzel ran from the room, back to Fane's side.

She dropped next to him. He looked ghostly pale, clammy and sweating, with eyes closed. "Fane, please, you have to wake up. We need to go!"

"You're not going *anywhere*," Gothel spit, coming toward them. She stumbled as she walked, blood dripping down her face.

"Fane, please," Rapunzel pleaded, shaking him but not taking her eyes from Gothel.

Gothel lifted the knife above her head, clasped with

both hands. Rapunzel threw herself across Fane.

"Now the boy dies!" Gothel yelled.

"Gothel, stop!"

Rapunzel turned at the sound of a strange man's voice. The man was tall, foreboding, dressed in a flowing black cape. His hair and eyes were as dark as his clothing.

"Why are you stopping me, Vedmak?" Gothel said to the man, halting but not releasing the knife.

Rapunzel shuddered at the name. This evil man was the one who'd fed Gothel's insanity. Looking at him, she doubted he was any saner than Gothel.

"You don't want to upset the girl, Gothel. If we're to complete the transformation, we need her happy. Move away from the boy."

Gothel seemed to remember Fane and looked at the knife. "I can't. In order for my daughter to return, he must die. There is too much at stake."

Gothel gripped the knife tighter and crouched, as if to get better position. She leaped forward, and a loud noise exploded. Gothel flew backward, slamming against the wall, stunned. Gothel's knife clattered to the floor. Rapunzel gasped and turned to stare at the man. He stepped forward and dropped to his haunches. "It's going to be okay now."

"Please," she whispered, glancing down at Fane.

"I'll make you a deal," Vedmak said. Rapunzel's gaze was drawn back to the man. His eyes were endless, dark swirling pools. "You cooperate with us, and I'll insist Gothel spare his life."

Rapunzel's thoughts were muddled. She knew that

they wouldn't let Fane live. They couldn't. As if he divined her thoughts, he said, "I can erase his memory, Rapunzel. He won't remember you. He won't remember this place. It will seem as a dream. I promise to let him go if you coop-erate." He leaned closer, and Rapunzel felt the pull of his eyes once more.

"Give me your word," she mumbled.

He placed a hand on her arm, every line of his body and face exuding empathy—except for his eyes, which remained cold and unfathomable. "You have my word, Rapunzel."

"No!" Gothel protested.

Vedmak's eyes moved beyond Rapunzel to land on Gothel. Rapunzel was amazed to see Gothel shrink back beneath his look.

"Say your good-byes," he told Rapunzel.

She turned back to Fane, leaning down to kiss him. He responded weakly, his eyes opening the tiniest slit. "I love you, Fane. I have since I first saw your picture. You made my life worth living, and I'll never forget you." A tear dropped onto his chin from her cheek. "Even though you'll forget me."

"No, Rapunzel," he said weakly. "It's a trap. Run."

His body suddenly stiffened, jaw clenched, groans rumbling in his throat as he spasmed.

"That's enough, Gothel," Vedmak commanded.

Rapunzel turned burning eyes on Gothel, who held the trigger. Suddenly the gun was ripped from her hands by an unseen force. Rapunzel screamed.

Vedmak stepped forward and bent to scoop up the

unconscious Fane. Rapunzel tried to hold onto him, but in her weakened state she was no match for the big man. He carried Fane into the dungeon that she'd occupied so recently. She scrambled to her feet and followed.

Vedmak laid him on the floor and turned to Rapunzel. "See?" he asked. "I'm keeping my word. I've removed the wires from him. He'll wake soon enough. I'll come back after we're finished and erase his memory as promised."

He ushered Rapunzel out of the room. She had no choice, it was the only thing she could do for Fane. She glanced back where he lay on the cold floor, his chest rising with his breaths. Vedmak bolted the door behind him, locking Fane in. He took Rapunzel's arm and steered her away from the room.

"Come, Gothel," he commanded as they passed where she still sat on the floor. She shot Rapunzel a glare so full of loathing and hostility that Rapunzel cringed away from her. After they passed, Rapunzel heard her rise and follow them.

chapter

40

Rapunzel cringed and pulled back forcefully when she saw that Vedmak led her to the black room of sixes.

"No!" she screamed. "No, please, not in there!"

Vedmak turned to her, calm. "Now, Rapunzel, I kept my word. Won't you keep yours and cooperate?"

Rapunzel shook her head frantically.

"For the sake of your friend," he added, his voice cold and firm.

Rapunzel froze and looked up at him. Threat was evident in his words. She immediately quit struggling.

Inside the room that invaded her nightmares was a black cot in the center of the star. He led Rapunzel to it and indicated she should lie down. Fear shook her as she did so.

"You've let her become weak," Vedmak chided Gothel as she entered the room.

"She refused to eat," Gothel complained.

"You should have taken control," Vedmak said. "After all, you are the mother."

Gothel's nostrils flared at the insult but remained

silent. "Shall I get the tube?" she asked.

"Only if you wish her to survive the procedure," he said.

Gothel left the room. Vedmak turned away from her, doing something on a black table against the wall she didn't recall seeing before. Rapunzel quickly moved to sit up and run through the open door. She was stumped in her intention by the straps that held her tightly bound. She stared at them. *What the . . . ?* She couldn't recall Vedmak placing them on her, yet the black straps clearly crossed her chest, stomach, and legs.

Vedmak clicked his tongue, his back still facing her. "You're making me question how well you plan to keep your word, child. Please keep in mind your friend's fate rests on you."

Rapunzel immediately stilled. Soon Gothel returned, and Rapunzel was forced to submit to a tube being shoved down her throat. She coughed and choked, tears running from her eyes. Once it was inserted, Vedmak hung a can on a pole next to her head and hooked it to the tube. She looked up at the can and read "Ensure" on it.

Vedmak followed her gaze. "Not to worry. It's nothing more than nutrition."

Tears continued to flow along with the thick liquid that ran into her stomach.

"When do we start?" Gothel whined. "You promised me my daughter."

Vedmak turned black eyes on her. "Patience, Gothel. Tomorrow she'll be stronger and the others will be here. We can't continue without them."

Rapunzel had a pretty good idea of who the "others" were. Her nightmares were becoming clearer by the moment.

* * *

Gothel sat silently next to her throughout the night. When the can of liquid nutrition emptied, she removed it. Then, two hours later she hung a new one, refusing to look at Rapunzel. This continued for quite some time. Rapunzel watched as the thin line of light around the door brightened. The room warmed up. She figured it to be around noon when Vedmak returned.

"Get some rest," he told Gothel. "We'll begin at six."

Gothel smiled, the expression filled with malevolence. She left, and now Vedmak watched over Rapunzel. He didn't seem as content as Gothel to let silence reign.

Sitting next to her, he picked up her braid, which lay on the floor off the side of the narrow cot. He clicked his tongue again, shaking his head. "You shouldn't have done this," he said, lifting her hair and showing her the slice she'd made. Rapunzel's eyes widened. She'd forgotten about that and now feared what he'd do to her because of it.

"Do you know how hard I worked to put the magic into your hair?" he asked, fingering the slice, watching the motion. Rapunzel couldn't speak with the tube down her throat. "It took many, many years of rituals. There were times it nearly drained me of my own power. And now," his cold, hard eyes turned to hers, "one moment of childish temper may have undone all my work." He leaned closer.

"For your sake, I hope enough remains in the unharmed portion."

Rapunzel shuddered at his words.

"I'm very close to becoming all-powerful," he said. "You are my final piece of magic. Learning to harness a specific type of magic and manipulate it at will is the only thing I haven't done. You're going to help me do that, you and that hair that I've invested so many years in. You released some of the magic when you cut it, but hopefully not all. Once I've re-bound the magic to your hair, we will sacrifice you and the magic will become mine. Then I will have everything. I will be everything."

A squawk escaped her throat. She might be naïve of most things of the world, but she was well aware of what "sacrifice" meant. She shook her head wildly, and he smiled at her. The smile was meant to be reassuring, but the intent was lost.

"Don't worry, child, we'll be certain you don't feel anything."

He stood and moved placidly away from her, as if he hadn't just told her he planned to *murder* her. Rapunzel looked around desperately for anything that might help her escape. She glanced down at the straps that held her firmly to the bed. Realizing her panic wasn't helping, Rapunzel forced herself to calm down, breathing deeply. and counted to ten.

Once her frenzy subsided, she manipulated her hands around until she could touch the strap. She moved her hands along the binding until she reached the metal buckle. Her eyes shot to Vedmak. He still faced away from her. She tucked her fingers up as far as she could reach, barely able to touch the edge of the lifting mechanism that would release the buckle.

Suddenly a woman entered the room, someone Rapunzel hadn't seen before. Her eyes barely touched on Rapunzel before lifting to Vedmak.

"I'm here," she announced solemnly.

"Good," Vedmak answered, not turning to acknowledge her in any other way. The woman moved to the side and removed something from a hook. She wrapped the dark cloak around her, pulling the hood over her head, and Rapunzel trembled to the depths of her being. It was one of the hooded figures from her nightmare come to life.

Gothel swept into the room, already wearing a black cloak, fixing Rapunzel with a glare, smirking. "Where are the others?" she demanded of the hooded woman. "It's nearly time."

"They're on their way," the woman said. Rapunzel heard the disdain in the woman's voice as she spoke to Gothel.

"Three others?" Gothel asked.

The woman didn't answer, and Gothel turned to Vedmak. "Three others, right, Vedmak?"

"More or less," he muttered.

"No," Gothel interjected. "No more, no less. Three others, so there are six of us."

Vedmak turned to face her. The look on his face terrified Rapunzel, but Gothel stood her ground.

"Tell me there will be six. You know the importance of the number."

Vedmak sighed as if dealing with a child he had to reveal a harsh truth to. "It's time to stop feeding these fantasies of yours, Gothel."

"Fantasies?" she screeched. "You are the one who confirmed my belief in sixes. All things in sixes to bring my daughter back. The hook, remember?"

Vedmak's voice hardened. "Nothing more than appeasing you. How else was I to get your willing cooperation? Your ideas are ridiculous."

Gothel's shoulders jerked back as if he'd physically assaulted her.

"Sixes are your obsession, Gothel. Not mine. And not necessary to the ritual."

"What are you talking about?" Gothel asked angrily, pushing her shoulders forward aggressively, seeming not to notice the shroud of wrath encompassing Vedmak. Rapunzel glanced at the hooded woman and saw that she watched the two of them raptly. She unhurriedly moved her fingers along the strap again, searching for the buckle's latch.

"The ritual we perform here is not for you, Gothel."

"Of course it's for me! The return of my daughter can be for no one else. You can't back out now."

"Oh, I don't plan to," he murmured ominously.

As if he hadn't spoken, Gothel continued. "Haven't I been working toward this with you for nearly eighteen years? Haven't I done all you've asked? I've continued to build to appease your spirits."

Vedmak burst out laughing, joined by the hooded woman. Rapunzel's fingers froze in their search at the sound. There was not an ounce of humor to be heard in Vedmak's laugh and only contempt in the hooded woman's.

"How else could I get you to stop annoying me?" he demanded, all pretense of humor gone, his face darkening. "Your constant calls wanting your daughter back nearly drove me to the brink. Getting you to spend your time overseeing useless construction was nothing more than a means to an end for me."

Gothel sputtered.

"You're much easier to control when you have a purpose. I admit, when you first came to me I believed you to be a kindred spirit. It wasn't long until I discovered you were nothing more than an insane old bat." Gothel's mouth dropped as did Rapunzel's. How did he dare speak to her that way? Obviously Gothel wasn't as intimidating to Vedmak as she was to Rapunzel. "But we needed your home and your money, both of which were easy enough to get by feeding your illusions."

"You're lying!" Gothel exclaimed, though her eye twitched and her voice quavered.

"No, Gothel," Vedmak said, taking a step toward Gothel. "I'm not."

Gothel moved toward the hooded woman, and Rapunzel slipped a finger beneath the buckle. She couldn't lift the buckle, though. She took a breath, pushed it out, and slid her finger a bit further in.

"You see, Gothel, I doubted you would ever have a child. And I was right, you didn't. But you did the next best thing—you *found* one." Vedmak waved a hand toward Rapunzel just as the buckle lifted. Her heart stopped that she'd been caught, but none of them glanced her way. She held tightly to the two sides of the buckle, keeping it in place until she was sure they weren't going to notice. "Good timing too. I was about to give up on you and find someone else. You brought me the girl I needed for my ritual, and not only found her, but kept her, raised her, fed her. Do you have any idea how much trouble you saved me? How much money? If someone saw her, it would be *you* who took the fall."

Rapunzel would have gasped had the tube not still been down her throat. She blinked a few times at the depth of the underhandedness of Vedmak. And she'd thought Gothel was bad! She quietly lowered the buckles to the bed, careful that they didn't fall and make any noise. Then she moved her hands up to undo the strap across her chest, slowly, carefully so as to not draw any attention.

Gothel took another step toward the hooded woman. "If I didn't need you to bring my daughter back, I'd throw you out right now," she hissed.

"Your daughter isn't coming back." Vedmak's words were cruel, nothing softening the blow. Gothel deflated as if she'd been punched in the chest.

"But, Vedmak," Gothel moaned, her voice pleading. Rapunzel unbuckled the straps across her thighs. "You *promised*. You promised she'd come back to me. Now. Today."

"I lied."

Gothel let out a shriek that would have sent even the bravest of creatures running. The hooded woman covered her ears as Gothel pulled a gun from inside her cloak. She pointed it at Vedmak. Rapunzel screamed—grateful the tube in her throat muffled the noise.

Vedmak lifted a hand toward Gothel. Rapunzel watched in astonishment as a blue light formed against his palm. As if he were throwing a baseball, he thrust his hand forward, the blue light launching at Gothel. Gothel ducked, and the light hit the hooded woman in the center of the chest, flinging her against the stone wall with a sickening crunch.

Gothel immediately stood and pointed the gun again, pulling the trigger. Rapunzel ripped the tube from her throat, choking and gagging as it propelled from her esophagus, the noises covered by the gun's ricochet.

Vedmak roared, the sound terrifying in the enclosed space. The echo swirled around the room, creating a whirlwind. Rapunzel rolled from the bed away from them, ducking as Vedmak threw another blue light at Gothel, slamming her into the wall and pinning her high above the floor. Alarm filled Gothel's face as the force pressed tighter against her, and she turned red with the effort to breathe.

Rapunzel didn't wait. She turned and fled the room. She wasn't exactly sure which way to go to find Fane. She stumbled and found herself at the bottom of a stairway. *Wrong way!* She turned to go the opposite direction when she heard Vedmak's furious yell.

"Rapunzel!"

She bolted up the stairs, knowing her only chance of helping Fane now was to escape. She went up two levels and realized she was on the main level. She dodged around corners, hoping she'd find the entry. Finally she came to an area she was familiar with and knew she was one turn away from the kitchen. She skidded to a halt at the sound of voices.

"What's going on?" she heard a man say.

"Not sure," another male voice answered. "But if there's trouble, I'm not sticking around."

Rapunzel peered around the corner and saw three men and two women gathered in the kitchen. None of them looked her way, so she took a breath and slid around the corner toward the stairs. Once she reached them, she darted to the only safe haven she'd ever known.

chapter

✴ .41 ✴

Rapunzel stood in the center of her rooms, looking around in disbelief. It was gone. Everything was gone. No furniture. Open cabinets revealed their vacant interiors. Her computer and pictures that had hung on the walls were all gone. She rushed into the bedroom. Empty. It was as if she'd never existed.

Realizing she'd trapped herself into the tower, she hurried back into the main room to leave.

"You won't make it," Vedmak said. Rapunzel froze at the sound of his voice from across the room. He stood at the entry to the cove, which housed the window. "Nor will anyone hear you if you scream. Fane is locked up below, and the others have left."

"How do you know his name?" she asked, her mouth gone dry.

"I know all about you, Rapunzel." He stepped toward her.

"What do you want me for?" she asked, backing away from him. "The transformation can't happen without Gothel."

Vedmak scoffed as he continued to slowly stalk her. "Do you really think I have any interest in the delusions of Gothel? There was never any intent to bring her daughter back through you. There was never any chance to bring back her daughter at all. We only needed that story to get her to do our bidding. She was obsessed enough to believe us."

"Why all the construction?" she asked, trying to stall him. She'd heard his excuse below but needed time to form a plan. "What's in it for you?"

"Nothing." Rapunzel was surprised he admitted it to her. "It was nothing more than a way to keep Gothel occupied. Gothel is much easier to control when she's busy. The construction gave her purpose—or so she thought."

"So no spirits live here?"

"I didn't say that," he said, one brow lifted sardonically.

"And the sixes?"

"Gothel's own personal obsession. I'll tell you, I could have accomplished what I needed much sooner had she not been bound by that particular bit of insanity. We were restricted to six in the room each time we met to further the ritual. I'm nothing if not a patient man."

He said it so proudly Rapunzel wondered if he wanted a compliment.

"Why me?" she asked.

"You were pure chance. Gothel wanted a baby to replace her daughter. When it was obvious she wouldn't become pregnant since she lived alone without dating, I planted the seed that she might find you. I didn't care who she found, just an infant girl for me. She wanted details so I told her blonde hair and green eyes. Fortuitously, you fit the bill, all the way down to having hair longer than it should have been on such a young child. Lucky for me too, since I was about to give up on Gothel and move on."

Nausea rose in Rapunzel's throat. *Lucky?* What was lucky about it? She'd been so close to not having been taken, so close to Vedmak giving up. Would Gothel still have taken her if he had? She'd never know.

Rapunzel's panic ratcheted upward. "What do you want with me?" she repeated.

"You're aware of what I want with you. I've already explained it. You must die for me to bring you back. Gothel wasn't completely wrong. Your body is a vessel for someone, just not for her daughter."

"Who?" she whispered, backing to the door as he lurked closer.

"A powerful witch who was taken from the earth far before her time. Another found a way to harness her and trap her in the spirit world. He who can release her and give her a body will possess power you can't imagine. I will be the most powerful warlock in existence. No one and nothing will be able to stop my reign of power. And, with Gothel's death"—Rapunzel gasped—"you'll be sole heir to the fortune the Gothel family amassed. No one will know you're not you—since no one knows you at all."

"Gothel's dead?" she asked, surprised at the grief that choked her. Gothel might have been preparing Rapunzel for her own death, but still, she'd been the only mother she'd ever known.

"Of course she is. That was the plan all along. You've put a bit of a crimp in the plan with your pathetic attempt at escape. No matter. We'll just begin again."

Rapunzel was frantically scanning for something—anything—to use for a weapon as he spoke.

"You're insane," Rapunzel said, inching toward the open door as he continued to circle closer to her. "There is no such thing as magic or witches or warlocks or whatever you think you are."

"No?" he questioned calmly. Rapunzel broke and ran for the door. It slammed shut. She grabbed the handle and twisted. It moved readily beneath her grip, but the door did not budge. She glanced back in panic at Vedmak, who continued to slowly, purposefully stalk her. It was her worst fear, being locked in this tower yet again.

"Stay away from me!" she yelled.

"I don't want to hurt you," he said with a small smile. "But I will if you fight me."

Rapunzel laughed scornfully. "Do you think I'm going to make it easy for you?"

"You don't want to anger me," he said, smile still in place, eyes turning hard. The room began to shake, and Rapunzel looked at the open window. Were they having an earthquake? As she watched, the window slammed shut, and she jumped, a squeak of alarm escaping her.

Rapunzel ran to the kitchen, opening drawer after drawer, looking for a forgotten knife or anything sharp.

"Let me help you," Vedmak said. Every drawer and cabinet door flew open.

Thinking quickly, Rapunzel grasped the closest drawer and pulled it out, flinging it at Vedmak.

He lifted a hand, and it moved harmlessly around him.

"Is that how you want to play?" he asked. Another drawer suddenly launched from its open position and torpedoed toward her. She ducked just in time.

When she stood again, Vedmak had dropped the smile and now looked decidedly cross. "This doesn't have to be so difficult," he said angrily.

"Oh yeah? For who?" she said, dodging to the side as another drawer came at her. The room began shaking even harder, making it hard to keep her balance. And still Vedmak walked toward her, slowly, like a predator.

Pounding sounded on the door. "Rapunzel?" she heard Fane call.

"Fane! Help me."

Vedmak threw a look of fury at the door. "Meddling boy!"

"I can't open the door." She heard what sounded like Fane hitting his shoulder against the door, followed by yells of pain.

"Vedmak is in here," she called.

"*What?*"

"He can't help you," Vedmak said.

She heard Fane grunt in frustration. "Vedmak! You have to let her out now."

The smile was back as Vedmak listened to him. "How touching," he oozed, and Rapunzel shivered at the repeat of Gothel's words. She worked her way back to the door again. She pulled on it as she felt the vibrations of Fane ramming it from the opposite side. It was difficult to tell the difference between his ramming and the house's shaking and splintering.

And then Vedmak was next to her, trapping her between his tall, broad form and the door. She screamed.

"Rapunzel!" Fane cried.

"Enough!" Vedmak commanded. He pulled the tie from her hair, tangling his fingers in the blonde strands. Her braid unraveled beneath his assault, long strands of hair falling to the ground where she'd cut it. Rapunzel tried to twist away but he fisted his hand, pulling and trapping her with pain. He began chanting, eyes closed, and terror seized Rapunzel.

Suddenly, she heard loud chirping. She looked up and saw Angel above them. Sheetrock splintered and pieces of the ceiling fell. She heard the cracking of the rock that surrounded the tower and beyond that Fane's frantic voice.

A calmness came over her as she watched Angel, as if she'd been suspended in time. Angel's blue was shining like the sun glinting off sapphires. For the first time, Rapunzel thought that it wasn't coincidence that Angel had come to her, but rather design. Maybe Rapunzel's naming the little bird Angel was more appropriate than she'd realized. Dipping a wing, Angel looked Rapunzel directly in the eye. It was then that she knew as well as if Angel had spoken. She looked up at Vedmak.

"You can't take the magic unless I give it to you," she said quietly.

His eyes popped open, full of rage. "What did you say?" His fingers tightened painfully.

"You have no power," she said more loudly, "without my hair. It's the final piece and without it, you lose everything."

He laughed scornfully. "This isn't some childish fantasy movie where you can have a happy ending by finding the right words to say."

Fright slithered up her spine. Angel chirped again, drawing Rapunzel's attention. The fear dissipated and she stood straighter, not an easy task with the loudly rupturing, swaying room and Vedmak's painful grip against her skull.

"Maybe not," she said. "But it's true, isn't it? You bet everything on me, on the magic you infused in my hair. But you can't take it without permission. How did you plan to get me to give it to you?" She gasped as the answer came to her. "Fane. You knew about him all along."

"I told you I know everything about you. How do you think the pathetic boy found you in that dungeon?"

Rapunzel glanced at the door. The walls around the frame splintered as she watched. Rapunzel shoved her panic down. She had to play the game. She smiled at Vedmak. "He's safe now. You have nothing."

With a snarl, Vedmak flung a blue ball of light toward the door. Rapunzel unthinkingly jumped in front of it between Vedmak and the door, which wouldn't protect Fane. She closed her eyes, waiting for the pain. When it didn't come, her eyes popped open and she looked down. She wasn't hurt. Vedmak bellowed and threw another. It bounced off of her as if it were nothing more than a cotton ball.

"You only have what power I allow you to have over me, Vedmak," she said more strongly, moving until she stood directly in front of him. "Which means you have *no* power to hurt me. You can't have me, and you can't have my *hair!*"

A low rumble of fury sounded at the base of Vedmak's throat. With a howl, he pushed his hands in her direction, flinging her away from him. She stumbled to the floor, turning quickly to keep her gaze on him.

"You don't know what it is you do!" he screamed.

Rapunzel swallowed. Then she scrambled to her feet. "I'm leaving," she said. "And you can't stop me."

Large chunks of sheetrock rained from the ceiling as Vedmak wailed, fingers twisted in his own hair now. He stumbled his way to the center of the room as if he had no control of his actions. Rapunzel ran back to the door, hands over her head. The door was still stuck.

"Open the door, Vedmak," she commanded.

His eyes opened wide, and he pointed at her. "You don't know what you do!"

"Yes, I do," she said. "I'm taking my life back."

He screamed again as the room began to shake up and down. Rapunzel stumbled, catching hold of the door handle. This time, it opened.

She took one step into the hallway just as the floor dropped from beneath her. She screamed as she fell. Suddenly, she jerked to a halt. Looking up, she saw that Fane had caught her, lying on his stomach, and he struggled to pull her up. And then she was in the hallway with him. She looked back into the tower and saw that

Vedmak still stood in the center of the room—with no floor beneath him. His hands and face began to wither as he writhed in internal pain. Over and over he wailed, "You don't know what you do!"

Suddenly another form appeared next to him, clearly there and yet not quite solid, like a thick mist. Vedmak turned petrified eyes on the creature that was dark, with long, wild black hazy hair and dressed in a vaporous black robe that was shredded and torn. Where eyes should have been were gaping holes into nothingness. Its long black talons were lifted threateningly toward Vedmak. Rapunzel wondered wildly if this were the spirit Vedmak hoped to house within her body.

"What in the—" Fane's shocked voice caught her attention. She saw that he stared with horrified disbelief at the scene before him.

"No!" Vedmak cried, terrified, tremors so violent it seemed to blur his features. "Please, I tried to get her—"

His words choked off as the misty hand moved toward him. She watched in shock as Vedmak seemed to *implode*. It was as if his body collapsed in on itself, aging at lightning speed as bolts of blue light shot from his hands, pinging around the room until finally they converged on him in one glorious, blinding blue ball of light, consuming him and the cloudy form that surrounded him.

A loud reverberation rent the air as a huge portion of the tower's ceiling fell. "Come on, we have to get out of here!" she yelled over the noise of the house cracking apart.

Fane tore his eyes from the tower, focusing on her.

"Right," he said. Together, they turned and made their way downstairs, lurching against the movement and dodging falling items. Finally, they staggered out the front door and ran as quickly as possible away from the swaying house.

Rapunzel looked back and watched as the house crumbled after them.

chapter

✳ ⋆ 42 ⋆ ✳

Rapunzel sat on the edge of the hard hospital bed. Severe dehydration, malnutrition, and exhaustion had required her to stay in the hospital.

She didn't have SCIDs.

That was the first thing they'd tested her for. Apparently it was nothing more than a ruse Gothel had used to keep her compliant with staying locked in the tower.

The police found the papers, read everything Rapunzel had, and now knew that Gothel had been responsible for the deaths of Gothel's parents and husband—and she had kidnapped Rapunzel.

They'd done a DNA test on her to discover who she really was. It was disconcerting, not knowing. Everything she'd ever believed about herself was untrue. She wasn't sick, she wasn't a Gothel, and she wasn't Rapunzel. Even her age and birthday weren't her own. Gothel had given her June sixth as a birthday when in reality her birthday was December third. She was older than she'd thought by six months. In fact, her eighteenth birthday had passed while she was in the dungeon. They told her that her birth

286

name was Sara Rowley. Her biological parents were John and Karen Rowley, who were now divorced.

Strangers.

She had nowhere to go.

Her door opened, and Fane walked in. Her face widened with a smile, faltering a little as her eyes dropped to the white bandage that covered the front of his neck and his arm in a sling. His shoulder was severely sprained from ramming against first the dungeon door to break it down, then the tower door trying to get to her. She cringed when she thought of how badly his battered shoulder must have hurt when he caught her as she fell. He'd been released from the hospital this morning.

"Even in the hospital, you manage to look hot. How do you do that?" he asked, crossing the room to her, placing his free hand alongside her neck, and tipping her chin upward. Rapunzel didn't blush, only grinned as he bent to kiss her. His mouth moved across hers, hungrily, desperately, gratefully. Rapunzel wanted to leap up and press herself more tightly against him but was afraid she'd hurt him or knock him over with her fervor.

"You have no idea how good it feels to do that without having to worry about the harm it might cause you," he said huskily.

"I missed you so much," she said.

Fane laughed. "I was here this morning."

"I know," she said, blushing now. "I mean during the time Gothel had me locked in the dungeon. Every moment of every day, all I wanted to do was talk to you. I wished for you harder than I've ever wished for anything."

"Even chocolate?" he teased.

"You're *so* much better than chocolate."

"I knew I liked you." He laughed.

Fane sat on the bed next to her and threaded his fingers with hers.

"I'm scared," she said.

Fane looked at her, squeezing her hand. "Of what?"

"I don't have anywhere to go now. I don't have a home. Even though she wasn't really my mother, Gothel is the only family I've ever known."

Fane wrapped his arm around her and pulled her close as her tears began to fall.

"Don't worry, Rapunzel. You can stay with us." Rapunzel shuddered against his side. "And that's not just me saying that. That's my parents extending an invitation."

Rapunzel looked up at him. "Really?" Fane nodded. "But . . . do you think *they'll* let me stay with you?" She swept a hand at the doorway.

"Rapunzel, you're eighteen years old. You can do anything you want to."

"Oh."

"Hey, I just realized I'm dating an older woman," Fane said. "I won't be eighteen until February."

Rapunzel glanced down at their intertwined hands, felt the weight of his arm around her shoulder. "You're dating me?" she asked shyly.

"We saved each other. It seems like we *should* be dating after that, right? That is, if . . . if you want to."

Rapunzel pushed her face against his chest. "I know I

shouldn't love you, Fane, but you're everything to me. So, yes, I think we should date."

"Why shouldn't you love me?" he asked.

She shrugged. "I don't know. I guess I just always thought I shouldn't love anyone because it couldn't turn into anything. I never *expected* to be able to love anyone. Plus, you know, my life is mostly just crazy. Who wants anything to do with that?"

"I do," he said with a laugh. "With you, there's never a dull moment." He paused, hugging her closer. "And now you know that you *can* love anyone, because you can do anything with your life that you want to. When I say you can love *anyone,* what I mean is, you should love me."

Rapunzel heard the teasing note in his voice. "I *do* love you," she said.

"Good." He paused. "I love you also. So that works out well for me, doesn't it?"

Rapunzel laughed. "For us both."

They sat quietly, just holding one another. For a few minutes, Rapunzel felt content, even euphoric.

"They're coming in to cut your hair soon?" he asked.

"Yes."

"Worried?"

Rapunzel shuddered. "Terrified."

"I'll be right here," he promised.

"I know it won't be easy for you," he said, "letting them cut it off."

"They said they can use it to make hair for people who have lost theirs. They told me it was a 'generous contribution.'"

"Oh yeah," Fane said. "My mom told me they talked to you about contributing it to Locks of Love. That's a really cool thing to do."

"What if something bad happens?" Rapunzel said with a shiver.

"It won't." Fane squeezed her again.

"How do you know?" she asked.

"I guess I don't. The world could end at any time for any reason, right? But it doesn't. It just keeps going on. When I got up this morning, my neighbor was outside shoveling the driveway, same as he does anytime it snows. I drove past Starbucks and the line was out the door, same as every other day. I had to stop and put gas in my car, and it was as expensive as every time. The world goes on, Rapunzel. And actually, now that you're out of the tower, it's a whole lot better than it was before. With your hair cut or not."

Rapunzel sighed. "I suppose you're right. The world doesn't hinge on me."

"Mine does." Fane laughed.

"Ha, ha," she said, smiling, snuggling against him. She was grateful—not for the first time—for whatever fate had brought Fane into her life.

chapter

* 43 *

The earthquake was the largest to hit northern California in over a hundred years. Damage was extensive everywhere, and yet nowhere had there been as much damage as there was to the Gothel Mansion. Of course, the earthquake had originated near where the manor stood, on an old, inactive fault line that hadn't moved in recorded history, not even as the result of other earthquakes.

Rapunzel knew. She knew why the earthquake had hit and why it had come from the manor. It was Vedmak's fury that had created the disturbance that had shifted the earth itself. She couldn't tell anyone, not even Fane. He believed it was coincidence—or at least he claimed that was his belief. Rapunzel suspected that somewhere deep inside he knew as well. But she wasn't about to force him to admit it. She wished she could convince herself the truth was anything but as well.

Rapunzel was at peace. She knew that no one could hurt her. She'd survived Gothel and Vedmak and had come out a much stronger person.

* * *

"You sure about this?" Fane asked.

She nodded. He shrugged, putting the car in park before opening her door for her. He took her hand and together they walked toward the rubble that had once been Gothel Manor. A construction crew surrounded it, this time clearing away debris rather than building onto the monstrosity.

"How're you doing today, Ms. Rowley?" asked the foreman. He shook Fane's hand.

"Fine, thanks. How's it going?" she asked, indicating the pile of wood and stone with a sweep of her hand.

"It's a mess, but we'll get it done," he assured her. "There's something I think you ought to see."

He gave them both a hardhat, then led the way to the back of the house. As they came in sight of what he wanted to show them, Rapunzel gasped.

"It's the darndest thing," the foreman said, scratching his head beneath his own hardhat. "The logs are old and so should have collapsed beneath the weight of the house. But once we uncovered it, we could see that it stood quite steadily." He shrugged as they looked at the log house standing in the middle of the piles of crumbled wreckage. "Not only does it stand, it's in perfect structural condition. I assumed you'd want it left intact," he said, looking to Rapunzel.

A smile crossed her face. Not only was the "albatross" of a house gone from her, but remaining was the most important part of the home, the original, humble beginnings of what should have been.

"Yes, of course. You say it's okay? Structurally, I mean?"

"Yes, ma'am. It's as perfect as the day it was built. Probably more so, actually." A man nearby called for the foreman. "Excuse me," he said, hurrying toward the man and leaving Rapunzel and Fane alone.

"Well, whaddya know," Fane said with a low whistle.

She turned to Fane, wrapping her arms around his waist. "It's time to let go," she said. "I've held onto this place for so long, I think I was afraid that if I let go, I would lose me." She glanced up at him. "I don't think that anymore. Now the only thing that remains is the most important thing. The beginning."

Rapunzel saw Angel sitting on the only remaining pillar next to where the gate had been. Angel ruffled her feathers and bobbed her head. Then she flew away. Free.

Discussion Questions

1. What was unique about this modern-day version of Rapunzel compared to the traditional fairy tale?

2. Do the characters seem real and believable? Are their predicaments relatable?

3. How do you feel about Gothel? Could you relate to some of her ideas and reasons for the things she did, even if they were extreme?

4. How did Rapunzel change or evolve throughout the story? What do you feel triggered those changes?

5. Rapunzel was doing things she'd been forbidden, such as sneaking out and having Fane over. How do you feel Rapunzel's story would have been different had she complied with all of the rules Gothel set for her?

6. Do you think Fane was key to Rapunzel's evolution, or do you think she would have been able to come to the same conclusions and the same ending without him? How important was he to her story?

7. Do you think Vedmak held too much influence over Gothel? How did you feel about him using Gothel for his own ends?